THE
DREAMERS

THE
DREAMERS

A NOVEL

RYAN ELIZABETH PENSKE

RARE BIRD
LOS ANGELES, CALIF.

RARE BIRD

THIS IS A GENUINE RARE BIRD BOOK

Rare Bird Books
6044 North Figueroa Street
Los Angeles, California 90042
rarebirdbooks.com

For more information, address:
Rare Bird Books Subsidiary Rights Department
6044 North Figueroa Street
Los Angeles, California 90042

Set in Adobe Garamond
Printed in the United States

10 9 8 7 6 5 4 3 2 1

Library of Congress Cataloging-in-Publication Data available upon request

For my mom and dad, who let me dream.

PROLOGUE

The early morning hours are her absolute favorite. The early hours, when the only noises to be heard are deep sleepy breaths, machines humming, and the chirping from birds flying around the garden, basking in the beginning moments of the sunrise as they catch drops of dew and errant bugs.

She enjoys her morning patrols throughout the property, where she makes sure not even a blade of grass is out of line, walks the perimeter of the garden maze, tidies her office for the day to come, and greets early morning faces that try to mask their yawns with nervous and curt head nods.

She treats her office as she does every aspect of her life. Everything—pieces of paper, books, pens, and pencils—is in order, placed perfectly for eventual use. She drags her pointer finger along the edge of her desk and makes her way around its perimeter. She examines the pad of her finger, having collected zero dust because she deep cleaned her office yesterday in an effort to calm her anxious energy.

A satisfied smirk builds on her face, her lips crinkling. She moves toward her desk drawer where she keeps a mirror and supplies. She watches her reflection as she applies red lipstick, careful not to apply outside the natural confines of her lips, not a speck of color out of place. Rubbing her lips together with a pop, she feels empowered and ready for her next tasks of the day.

She looks over her to-do list: a pristine-white, smudgless page of her notebook decorated with her rigid cursive handwriting, which sits at the center of her desk.

Arrange order for lab ingredients
Reach out to top five companies with intel information
Go over the last week's recordings
Compile list of primary intel to sell
Arrange florists and menu for 100th
Schedule C's portrait arrival

The list never seems to end, filled with the important and menial tasks of her everyday work. Today, however, her to-do list and it's never-ending unchecked tasks are not at the top of her priority list, and she leaves them to be a problem for her later self.

With a glance at the grandfather clock ticking quite loudly in the corner of her office, forever reminding her of what's to come, she leaves her office, excited to check on her prized pupils.

On her journey to the dormitory hall, the early morning's silence is pierced by the clicks of her heels, a steady beat that dissipates the silence of the morning. She doesn't have to say anything upon her arrival at the hall, as the rhythm of her walking, the serious gaze of her eyes, and the wicked upturn of her fiery lips says what needs to be said to the men who open doors wide for her. As her legs take long languid steps, her eyes examine each sleeping body, their heads resting blissfully against their pillows as their blankets move up and down with the movement of their breath. She is pleased to see blankets pulled up to chins and restful faces, again accounting for pristine perfectness; not even an inch of bedding is out of place.

She arrives at an empty bed, the bedding tucked tight into the sides of the mattress, the pillow puffed up with no indentation. Her eyes gleam with excitement at the sight as she curls her manicured fingers around the end railing of the bed. Her mind is feverish with possibility and palpable anticipation, so much so that she must compose herself so as not to squeal and awake those dreaming.

Classical music begins to float through the space, making its way like an unseen mist between each bed and over each slumbering body. She removes herself from the hall as the first bodies begin to stir and stutter from the musical alarm. She makes her way downstairs and into the foyer, where the sun that has now fully risen casts beams of light and warmth into the grand space. Gold designs that detail the deep navy walls around her gleam in the light, sparking to life as if they had also just awoken for the day. Stars and moons in the daylight. She moves to stand beside the large mahogany entryway doors, looking out their adjacent windows. Before her sprawls the gardens that are now alight with full sun, a collage of green in her view. Behind her she can hear bodies travelling down the stairs on their way to breakfast.

She smiles to her reflection in the window. Her favorite early morning hours have gone just how she likes—without a hitch and according to plan. And now, as she squints at the sun, full and round in the sky, casting down a glorious brightness, she knows it is going to be a wonderful rest of the day.

The day she has been *most* looking forward to.

Most nights I wake up drenched in sweat. My pillows on the floor, my comforter pushed to the bottom of the mattress. My heart pounds so hard I can practically hear its beat in my ears. This happens around three a.m., as my dream for the night ends. I've tried everything from melatonin to tea to white noise machines, but to no avail. Once my mom even sent me to therapy. Nothing works. Usually I lie in bed until my school alarm goes off, as if I had done my job for the night and was ready to start the day.

Last night was different, though. My pillows were comfortably under my head, my comforter tucked in around my body, shielding me from the AC in my bedroom. I didn't wake up at three a.m., my heart racing desperately, sweat pouring out of me. No, tonight I dreamt of blackness. I was lost, confused. I reached out and felt nothing. My heartbeat quickened as my dream-self scanned the dark void. Right, left, up, down, center—there was nothing, until two blue eyes appeared, piercing through black and overpowering the darkness. They were the guiding light in the pitch blackness that consumed everything. They were not afraid of the dark. They were strong, a shock of color where seemingly no color could exist. My heartbeat began a gradual descent. The eyes stared back at me, never wandered. Then they blinked and the darkness grew before they slowly reopened. Every time the eyes blinked, I feared they would never open again.

They began to move. I followed them around the room. They went left, my feet followed. They looked in a direction, so did my eyes. Slowly, I found the courage to move closer. One foot in front of the other, I ventured toward their glow. The eyes stared back, growing larger with each step. I was close enough now to feel the hum of another body in front of me, the wafting of warm breath.

The blue eyes moved closer and closer. Mere inches from my face, I could make out the fine details of my companion. Now the eyes were not a deep and dark blue, but instead both pupils were encircled and illuminated by gold bands. The color reminded me of the remnants of the day sky just before the sun begins to set. I stood mesmerized, transfixed. My arm lifted, seemingly under its own control, and my fingers stretched toward the eyes. Before I could reach them, though, my trance was broken. I heard a slight dribble at first, and then the rising crescendo of flowing water. The eyes blinked before turning toward the noise, and I turned to follow once more—but there was another noise.

Beep, beep, beep, beep.

My alarm went off.

My phone's weather app says fifty and rain for today, so I opt for blue jeans, a cream sweater, and my favorite canary yellow knee-high rain boots that creak with every step as if a stampede of ducks were closing in. The creaking does not bother me. The boots hold a special place in my heart, and I'll never forget when I first got them. I had come home from school, drenched by the rain my parents hadn't foreseen, my Vans sneakers soaked through and my jeans a darker shade than they were that morning. From the girl's bathroom, I had texted my parents a picture of myself looking like a wet rat. "Don't quit your day jobs and become weather people!" I'd joked, quietly deciding that I would rely on the weather app from here on out.

When I arrived home from school that day, wet footprints trailing behind me, my dad stood in the kitchen, pouring steaming water into three mugs as my mom plopped tea bags into each one.

"Sugar and milk?" My mom asked without looking up.

"Yes, please," I answered, pulling out a stool.

I adored Scottish breakfast tea. Its rich aroma filled the air as my dad walked my Storm Trooper mug over and placed it in front of me. When I was twelve, I'd gone through a *Star Wars* phase—the kind that leaves no blank space on the walls or shelves in your room—and despite getting rid of all the posters, I still drank my daily cup of tea from my Storm Trooper mug.

"You are the best!" I picked up my mug and brought it close to my face, the steam warming my rain-soaked cheeks. "This is just what I needed."

My dad laid his arm across my still-wet shoulders and gave my head a quick kiss. "Sorry about the weather, kiddo. If we had known it was going to be a downpour, I would have offered to drive you."

"Don't worry about it. It's only a bit of water." I shook like a dog would after swimming. "Plus, if being rained on means I get to come home to a fresh cup of tea after school, then it should rain every day!"

My mom laughed. "Well, with what your dad got you, now it can rain every day."

"What did you get me?" I was unable to hold back my excitement. "Is today a holiday? My half birthday?" I began to do the math as my dad walked back into the kitchen with a silly grin on his face and a gift bag in each hand.

"No special occasion," he said.

I lunged for my dad's hands and grabbed each bag. I began with the bigger bag—I'm only human!—pulling tissue paper out left and right. At the bottom, I could see my favorite color blue with specks of white. Folded neatly inside was a shiny navy-blue raincoat with white polka dots.

"I saw this and thought of you," my dad said, helping me hold it up from the bag.

"I love it!" I jumped up and down with excitement, rain drops flying in every direction before I launched myself at my dad for a hug that knocked the other bag out of his hand. The bag spilled to the floor, a rubber squeak announcing the pair of shiny yellow rain boots. I rubbed my hands along the smooth rubbery surface. "I love these, too!"

With a shoe in each hand, I threw my arms back over my dad's shoulders. His chest rumbled as he laughed. Most teenage girls probably wouldn't have been so excited over a raincoat and rain boots, but it has always been the little things in life from the people I love that have made me happiest. Plus, the image of my dad shopping, which he detested, and looking for stuff he thought I would like, made me feel like the luckiest girl ever.

Letting me go, Dad motioned to my gifts. "I can't have my Stella Bella getting caught in the rain, especially not getting stuck in the rain without looking like she's 'runway ready,' as Callie says."

I laughed at my dad's attempt to use the saying Callie, my best friend, and I say to each other when we love each other's outfits.

"Well, runway ready or not, I love them." I still had the shiny yellow boots in my hands. My dad flashed back a smile full of pearly whites and I smiled back brighter. "I hope it rains tomorrow!"

"I love you to the moon," he said.

And I responded, "And back."

For a while after he died, I'd stuffed the boots into the back of my closet and folded the jacket up under my bed. Never mind wear them, I couldn't even look at them, those cruel reminders of happier days and things I no longer had. But then, on the morning of his funeral, I sat on my bed, waiting. From my bedroom door, my mother, dressed head to toe in black, told me it was time to go. I forced myself up. I went to my closet to grab shoes, and that's when I noticed a bit of yellow peeking out from behind a pile of clothes. Thinking back to that gloomy yet happy rainy day, I remembered my dad's vibrant smile. An hour later I stood in front of his grave, surrounded by friends and family, dressed in my black dress, my black tights, and my yellow rain boots.

Now, three months later, fifty degrees and rain on the horizon, I rush down the stairs to the kitchen, already a bit behind thanks to my blue-eyed haze. I spring into the kitchen and find it empty except for a cup of Scottish breakfast tea and a banana lying on the kitchen counter next to a note:

I'll be home by five. Stop at the post office on your way home— your birthday invitations won't send themselves! —Mom

I missed my mom by a few minutes, hearing her car back into the street and the garage door close behind her. I read her scribbled note, throw it in the trash, and grab my raincoat. School isn't too far, only about a twenty-minute walk, which allows me to think as I try to make it on time to my first class. My dad would have spiced that note up with his silly dad jokes that made no sense. He would have started it off with "Good morning, Stella Bella." My mom's was void of anything but her obligatory motherly duties.

I don't even want a birthday party. All of my older classmates' eighteenth birthdays had been worthy of MTV shows, but I couldn't care less about mine. When I was five, I cried hysterically as the other kids and their parents sang "Happy Birthday" to me. I've never been one to want all the attention centered on me, least of all in the form of off-key singing. Anyway, celebrating "my ascent into adulthood" without my dad feels wrong. No amount of cake, obligatory Instagram stories, or "one" and "eight" balloons will change that, and by the end of my walk, I've made up my mind: if the invites never get sent out then no party can be had.

Mr. Clarke, my calculus teacher, doesn't bother turning from the blackboard as I slide through the door on cue with the ringing of the second bell. "Just in the nick of time, Ms. Grey."

I put my head down and rush toward Callie at the back of the room. She gives me a sly smile and pulls out my chair. We sit in the back so we can talk and pretend to be taking notes. More often than not, I am probably looking out the window, daydreaming. Callie is most likely writing Harry Styles's name in her notebook over and over again.

"Hey, what's up?" Callie whispers. "You're never late."

"I slept in and kind of lost track of time."

Callie looks at me puzzled. "You slept in? You're always complaining about how you never sleep. Now you're sleeping in?"

I should have just said my mom was chatty at breakfast.

"Wait a minute," Callie continues. "Did you smoke weed? I hear that will make you sleep for, like, a long time."

"Girls!" Mr. Clarke stands with his arms crossed, facing us with a devilish stare. "Do you mind if we start class?"

We both give him an apologetic look and open our binders. I begin to flip to the last page I had been using when a sheet of paper gets shoved into the way.

It is Callie's perfect handwriting on a piece of paper with hearts and stars from last class doodled on it: *Well, did you?*

I roll my eyes and write back, *It was actually Harry, he came over last night so I didn't get to bed until really late ;)*

In my peripheral, I can see Callie clench her jaw and aggressively scribble her next note before not so gently slamming it on my desk. Mr. Clarke glances back at us momentarily before continuing at the blackboard. I peek down at her note.

In your dreams.

P.S. If Harry Styles was ever in your room for reasons other than to surprise me, I would kill you ☺

We are an hour into Mr. Clarke's lesson on how to find integrals, when I slide into a daydream. The tan, concrete walls of the school fade and give way to a magnificent green. Grass and trees taller than the tallest buildings in our town appear out of nowhere. Beyond the expanse of garden is a towering mansion, grander than anything I've ever seen. There's intricate molding, deep wood accents, large windows with milky glass. I imagine myself walking toward the mansion, searching for a front door. I imagine the prickly grass beneath my feet and the noise of leaves flying across the ground in the wind. I turn a sharp corner that brings me closer to the massive building. There's an odd scent overwhelming my senses, and I am eager to find out what it is. I imagine myself traveling closer in search of answers.

The clearing of a throat breaks my trance.

"Dreaming, Ms. Grey?" Mr. Clarke hovers above my desk, too close for comfort.

"S-s-s-sorry," I stutter, unable to form words after being so abruptly torn from my trance.

Mr. Clarke stares down as if he has just caught me cheating. "Care to share what you were thinking about?"

Heat unfurls along the back of my neck. The rest of the class turns its attention on me, enjoying the diversion from Mr. Clarke's chaotic math equations on the board. I sit up straighter, try to feel less like a helpless animal that's been cornered, but before I can think of what to say the end-of-class bell rings. The back of my neck cools immediately. Mr. Clarke backs away from my desk, yet his stare stays planted on my anxiety-ridden face, his eyes tediously attached to my own.

"All right, everyone," he says, sitting at his desk. "Remember to complete the study packet by next class period for the test this Friday."

Chairs scrape the old classroom floor as the class rises, and like that I'm free from the awkward encounter with Mr. Clarke. I'm up and out of my seat in record time, shoving my way past people as they leave the classroom.

Callie catches up to me outside of the classroom. "Well, that was weird."

A creepy feeling lingers in my stomach, but I brush it off. "I think it's a math teacher thing. I think they all have to take Strange 101 in college before being able to become a teacher."

"I don't think that class is exclusive for math teachers," Callie jokes. "Anyway…I'll meet up with you at lunch." Callie begins to walk away before calling back, "the usual spot!"

I wish I could move on like Callie does, but I can't shake the nausea that settles in the pit of my stomach. Callie and I met on the playground in kindergarten. I wanted to swing on the swings, but none of the other kids would let me have a turn. Callie noticed and marched up to a boy on the swings.

She yelled at him, told him he'd better give me a turn or else she would tell all the other kids that he liked to eat worms. We were fast friends, even if not the most likely friends. As we grew up, Callie became the confident bombshell who stood up for herself and caught the attention of everyone. I was the quiet girl who throughout all of middle school was called "freckles." Next to Callie I must have seemed like one of those fish that follows sharks along hoping for food scraps. The first time I told Callie that she laughed so hard she started crying. And then she said, "I want to be a great white shark, but you're much prettier than a fish."

Callie and I tell each other everything and anything. She's had my back ever since the swings. She was there for me at my dad's funeral, and again when people looked at me weirdly in the hallways for wearing rain boots on desert-dry days. I wouldn't trade her for anything or anyone, even though sometimes I want to wring her neck for being boy crazy and obsessed with every move the Kardashians make. She's brought out a more confident side in me, and sometimes I succeed at bringing her back down to earth. *Sometimes.*

Callie and I meet at our usual lunch spot, twelve o'clock sharp. We sit in the corner of the cafeteria as it gives us the perfect view of the chaos that is lunch period. We go through the lunch line, hunting for anything that doesn't seem to be years past its expiration date. We weave between tables, dodging the wet paper balls being launched between them and avoiding sticky food on the floor. I'll never understand why boys think it's fun to play hot potato with the lunch special.

Callie and I treat lunch period like a spectator sport, and from our perch in the corner, it is hard not to predict what

Callie and I will be watching today as Blake, the new girl, walks into the cafeteria. She has short pixie-cut hair and wears monochrome outfits. Some days it's all green, others it's all pink. I think it's cool and a bold fashion choice, but most of my classmates disagree. A few days ago, Jacob Richards poured his tomato soup down her top to "spice up her outfit."

Today she's dressed in purple overalls with a matching turtleneck underneath. Callie and I watch as she enters the cafeteria and makes a grave mistake. With her head held high, Blake wanders past the boys playing hot potato with a hotdog. That's when one of them notices her and whispers something into another's ear. Suddenly, they've all noticed her and the same wicked smile spreads across each of their faces. Cody Mackey breaks the silence by grabbing a fistful of hot dog from his tray and lobbing it at Blake yelling, "Ten points for hitting her boobs!"

An onslaught of hotdogs launches toward Blake, some hitting her face and body. One makes its way down her overalls and Blake stops frozen in her tracks, her face turning five shades of red. Before she allows the whole high school to see her cry, Blake grabs the hotdog lodged in her overalls, chucks it at evil Cody, and sprints out of the cafeteria.

Callie follows Blake out of the cafeteria with her eyes. "Ugh, that's rough."

"More like disastrous."

"If I were her, I would have begged my parents to home school me."

"That would be allowing the bullies to win." I stare daggers into the back of Cody's head. "I admire her for not letting them beat her down."

"I get that, but she's rushing out of the caf crying, too. And haven't you seen what's written on the bathroom walls or the heard the rumors going on about her?"

I shake my head.

"In the bathroom closest to the library, people have written on the walls that she's a freak lesbian. People are also spreading a rumor around that she changed her name to Blake because she wants to be a boy."

"Jesus," I mutter under my breath. "I think the name Blake is cool for a girl. And what evidence do they have to call her a lesbian?"

"I dunno." Callie's shrugs, nonchalant. "Maybe 'cause she has short hair? People are stupid."

My blood boils slightly. "Her short hair is cool, and people need to grow up!"

"Easy for you to say, you always root for the underdog."

"At least I'm not the one who has a crush on the guy who uses the underdogs as his personal punching bags." I give Callie a scrutinizing look as I motion toward Cody.

"For what it's worth, I don't have a crush on his personality—I have a crush on all six of his abs," she shoots back, wiggling her eyebrows.

I roll my eyes and laugh. Callie could have any guy she wanted, but she's too intimidating for the boys at school. She's tall, thin, and has blonde hair that is always perfectly curled in that beach-wavy way I watch endless YouTube tutorials about. She has big chocolate-brown eyes shaped like almonds and all the boys stopped trying to impress her last summer, once they found out she had a fling with a college guy.

High school boys were training wheels on her bike, and now she was ready for what she called "real men."

"You are boy crazy, Callie," I tell her, "and one day you are going to wonder where all the time went while you were too busy DMing your celebrity crushes on Instagram."

Callie laughs. "Your talk is cheap, Stella. You haven't even kissed a boy yet."

It's exactly one month till my eighteenth birthday, and Callie is not exactly wrong. I slap her arm playfully. "That's mean! And FYI, I kissed Tom Parker at swimming camp in the sixth grade."

Callie mimes waving her white flag. The bell rings before she can comment on my lack of experience with boys, and she gets up from our table, blowing me a sarcastic kiss goodbye as she heads off. I grab my lunch tray, picking up forgotten trash along the way as I head to the doors.

The halls are empty by the time I leave the cafeteria, most everyone already in classrooms by now. Just before I open the door to my English class, I hear a cry down the hallway. I walk toward the sound. The crying grows louder as I approach the girl's bathroom.

I nudge the door to the bathroom open slowly, just an inch, but it's enough for me to see a blob of purple on the floor. Blake is huddled in the corner, her head in her knees, her arms wrapped around her body. Sniffles and muffled cries slip out between her knees and my heart breaks for her.

The bathroom door creaks as I open it slightly wider. Blake looks up, her face painted with pure rage. She stops crying long enough to yell, "Have you come in here to write something on the walls about me? Or did you bring leftovers from lunch?"

Lost for words, I shake my head.

"Leave, just leave. *Please.*"

I stand in the doorway, wishing I had something profound to say. Something so that Blake wouldn't have to feel so crushed and defeated. Not too long ago, I was the girl crying in the bathroom, huddled in a stall, sobbing into my knees on the dirty smelly floor. I would have loved to have someone who cared enough about me to walk into the bathroom, say the right words to me, and pick me up off the floor.

So, why couldn't I do this for Blake?

Nothing but choked-up air comes from my cowardly mouth.

Once more, Blake yells at me to leave before I finally do.

I get home a little past seven. Clear Water High is performing Hamlet this year, and I'd reluctantly auditioned as a part of the extracurricular activities' requirement. Now I spend my afterschool hours fake crying and rehearsing monologues after getting cast in the role of Ophelia. Outside of our Hamlet, junior Jamie Stewart, insisting on spending three hours on our shared scenes, I've come to enjoy the character of Ophelia. More and more, I've found myself entranced in her helplessness and heartache. The buildup of her melancholy and confusion as Hamlet rejects her mirrors my own descent following my father's death.

Now, an hour later than anticipated, the front door slams behind me as I toss my backpack and raincoat to the floor. Faintly, I can hear my mom in the kitchen preparing dinner. She is humming along to music from her phone, and in the living room I can smell cinnamon and clove bud burning, her favorite candle from Anthropologie.

Exhausted, I tiptoe to the staircase, hoping my mom doesn't notice that I have gotten home.

"Stella!" my mom calls from the kitchen. "Come here, dinner is about ready."

Damn it. So close. "Coming!" I call back and walk to the kitchen like a medieval prisoner to the gallows.

"Hey, Sweetie, how was your day?"

I shrug. "Okay I guess."

"Okay, that's all?" My mom's voice is laced with annoyance and suspicion. "Come on, any new drama with Callie, new grades?"

I shake my head, hoping that she notices I'm not really in the chatting mood.

"Any new cute boys?" My mom wiggles her eyebrows in a suggestive way.

"No!" I yell. "No drama, no new grades, and definitely no new boys." Clearly she has no idea that I associate the boys at my school with mustard-covered hot dogs flying around a noisy cafeteria.

She puts her head down and finishes preparing our dinner plates. "Geez, someone definitely woke up on the wrong side of the bed this morning."

I laugh. "No, Mom, it's not that. It's you! You won't leave me alone when I clearly want to be left alone." After a long tiring day, I feel less inclined to filter what I say to her. "You know, ever since Dad died, you won't just let me be. You force me to do things and have conversations I don't want to have, and it's starting to really get on my nerves!"

"What are you talking about?" She looks utterly confused and hurt. "I don't make you do anything you don't want to do."

"Are you kidding me? How about the three therapists you've tricked me into going to see when you said we were just going to the mall or the movies. Or the fact that you are forcing me to throw a birthday party in a month that I want nothing to do with?"

"After what happened with Dad, I thought it was only right to make sure help was available to you if you needed it. I want you to have someone to at least to talk to."

I begin to yell, "What about you? Why couldn't I just have talked to you about everything, not a complete stranger that thinks they know me?" If I were a cartoon, steam would be coming out of my ears.

"Stella, I'm not professionally trained in how to talk to someone grieving the loss of a loved one," she says, as if I'm stupid not to have realized that.

"Yeah, I guess you're right," I say sarcastically. "And you're definitely not professionally trained on how to be a mom, either."

I turn on my heels to go to my room, do the whole angry door slam thing, when I hear her break into sobs from behind me.

Between tears she yells, "Take that back!"

I don't stop walking away from her. "No."

Without another word, she rushes from the kitchen, brushing past me and toward the front door. I hear her yank her keys off the hook and slam the front door behind her. I'm left in the wake of the hurt I had just caused her, the rage still vibrating throughout the house. The longer I stand in the hallway, surrounded by the echo of the slamming door and her sobs, I begin to wish I could take back my words. My mom didn't deserve that. She has been through everything I've been through and more. I need to begin working on my self-control.

My chest twinges as I walk past her empty room, wishing she was in there humming like she always is when I haven't made her cry. I continue toward my own room, where I throw off my clothes and get ready to take a shower.

What problem could a hot shower not fix?

Afterward, all toasty and clean from my probably too-long shower, I stare at myself in the mirror, reflecting on my mom's question about if there were any new cute boys. I haven't allowed myself to crush on boys since my last bad encounter with James Wilson in the eighth grade.

James was in my fifth period pre-algebra class, and he had the most perfect surfer-blond hair and green eyes. I would always catch him staring at me during class, and after a few months of classroom staring, I began to look forward to it. Callie declared right away that James and I would be a perfect couple. I laughed the statement off, but the more I stared at him in class, the more I entertained the idea of us being together. One day during lunch, Callie caught me looking for James in the cafeteria and said it was obvious I was hopelessly in love with him, and that I should bite the bullet and ask him to see a movie with me. I shuddered at the idea of actually talking to him. I was comfortably enjoying flirting through eye contact. Now my stomach was doing somersaults.

Just as I had shut down the idea out of pure fear, James walked through the cafeteria doors and headed to his usual spot in the middle of the room. Before I could so much as blink, Callie had pushed me out of my seat and shoved me toward his table. My feet started to move right then left, and before I knew it, I was face to face with James Wilson. His eyes were even prettier up close.

"Can I help you with something?" He sounded bored.

"Um, I...I..."

James stared blankly.

"I, um, was wondering if you wanted to go to the movies? With me?" I tried masking my nervous shaking and sweating in a smile.

James chuckled, "The movies? With you?"

I nodded like a bobble head caught in an earthquake.

He erupted with laughter and turned to the other boys at the table. "What do you guys think, should I go to the movies here with..." James pointed at me. "What's her face?"

I still remember the sensation of needle pricks along my fingertips.

He continued with, "Of course," and my heart picked up, until he added, "not!" James motioned his arms out as if trying to shoo me away. "Do you mind leaving me alone now?"

Snapping back to reality, I study my features in the bathroom mirror, wondering if it was how I looked that made James laugh at the idea of going out with me. I'm 5' 8", and sure, I could work on my posture, but I've had more important things to worry about, too. I had pimples, but only during that time of the month, usually. Freckles spatter across the bridge of my nose and end just under my mossy green eyes. My mom used to jokingly call me by my dad's name because my eyes are carbon copies of his. She doesn't do that so much anymore. Callie is always saying she wishes she had my "pout," that it's what all the Instagram girls wish they had, but I think I mostly look like I'm having an allergic reaction. Then there's my chest. Callie and the Instagram girls don't have much to envy there.

And topping it all off, I have a mop of thick, heavy brown hair that's always tangled in knots by the end of the day.

The front door opens and slams shut, breaking me from my body-shaming daze. Five seconds later, heavy footsteps stomp up the stairs—my mom's wordless announcement that she is royally pissed off. I hope she will come to my room and talk everything through with me, but then her bedroom door slams shut so hard that the whole house practically shakes.

After two hours, more calculus than I have ever wanted to do, I find myself nodding off into my textbook. Kicking the book and my binder to the end of my bed, I climb beneath the covers, hoping to dream of the blue eyes again and lose the stress of the day in a blue abyss.

My alarm wakes me from a groggy sleep at six thirty the next morning, and I pull an arm out from under my comforter to quickly silence my phone. I roll out of bed and half-heartedly brush my teeth and hair. Without too much thought I pull on a pair of old distressed jeans and a sleep away camp sweatshirt, and then I'm applying a coat of mascara on my lashes and concealer to my face and looking myself over, thinking I look just acceptable enough for public. I grab my calculus book and binder from the floor, but before taking the first step downstairs, I check if my mom is still in her room. The door is open, but the room is empty. Down the stairs and mindlessly through the living room, I walk to the kitchen holding my breath for this morning's interaction with Mom.

I wonder, will she speak to me? Ignore me? Make coffee? Offer eggs?

However, there is no smell of eggs. There is no steaming pot of coffee, not even a shortly worded note. The kitchen is empty. She was mad at me, but everything about this morning feels off. A heavy sense of unease fills my chest. The quiet dread follows me everywhere this morning. Even my footfalls scare me as I walk around in search of my mom.

I run back up to her room only to find disheveled sheets and a creased pillow. I try the garage next, as if I might catch her in the car getting ready to leave for work. I begin through the living room and toward the front door when I am stopped abruptly by what lies in front of me. The living room couch has been knocked over; the pillows are ripped open and a pool of cushion feathers coat the hardwood floor. The glass coffee table sits shattered in the center of the room, a few flowers and some shards of glass creating a hectic collage. The morning news breaks in and out of the battered TV on the wall, the cracked glass in the middle spiderwebbing across the weather girl's face.

Standing in a pool of water mixed with dead sunflowers, my heart rate skyrockets. What in the world happened down here? How had I missed all the ruckus down in the living room and not woken up? The coffee table and television being reduced to mere pieces surely would have woken me.

I run out of the living room, my feet slightly sweaty, my mother's absence setting in now as I see her lying motionless, her blood splashed on the hallway walls and up the front door that hangs off of its hinges, swaying creepily in the morning wind. I fall to my knees and cup my mother's cheek, carefully avoiding touching the monstrous black and blue welt that's begun blooming on her forehead. The carpet squishes as I reposition my knees and try lifting her. A metallic smell hangs in the air, and I almost faint from at the realization.

It's blood! My mom's blood.

I move my right hand from under her neck and it comes away wet. My throat clenches as my crimson hand moves into view. The broken door in front of me begins to move, I open my mouth to scream...

My hands fly to my chest as I try to catch my breath. My heart beats so intensely that my whole body moves up and down with it. I kick my legs out from under the comforter and wipe the sweat from my forehead. It feels like it's a million degrees in my room, so I push my blankets away from my body and go to crack open a window. I tap my phone screen and I catch the time—three a.m. It was another crazy dream.

I get back into bed, praying I'll sleep away the remaining hours before my alarm goes off at six thirty. Instead, I spend the rest of the night on my side, staring out the open window, shuddering as I fail to forget my dream. Scratch that, my nightmare.

I spend time practicing how I will apologize to her this morning. Slowly but surely, the sky outside shifts from an inky navy to cotton candy pink, and standing in front of my mirror, in an old pair of distressed jeans and a faded camp sweatshirt, I shrug at my appearance. Grabbing my calculus book and binder from the ground, I tuck them under my arm and head downstairs. I quickly peek my head in to see if my mom is in her room, but it is empty. She must be downstairs in the kitchen.

I take the stairs down, and it's not until I make the final step that I do a double take at the living room. The smashed-in television, the pillows and feathers and glass shards, the couch on its back, the blonde weather girl with fuchsia lipstick reciting the weather through cracks in the television—I've seen this all before.

The front door, still broken down the middle and hanging off its hinges, creaks in the morning breeze, and as I run toward it, I trip over something and fall hard to the floor. My elbows slam into the carpet and I lay back in pain, my fingers already feeling numb. I roll over, careful to not touch my elbows to the floor, as I come face to face with what I tripped over.

The coppery smell. Blood. The horrible blue-black of her forehead.

"Mom! Mom, wake up!" I shake her shoulders desperate to see her eyes blink open. "Mom, please, I'm—" I cry. Before I can finish, the front door makes a guttural groan as someone pushes it from the outside. I don't dare take my eyes off my mom, afraid I'll miss her eyes opening.

Something swings hard against the back of my head, knocking me to the ground.

"Get her!"

The exclamation is the last thing I hear before tasting metal and feeling the soft wet of the carpet along my face.

The Clorox wakes me up. Mom must be over cleaning again. It's this new habit she picked after my dad died: she fills whatever time she would have spent with him cleaning the house. Washing pillowcases that haven't been used in years, scrubbing scuff marks off the floor, using way too much Windex on perfectly clean windows. One day I even found her in my room under my bed, insisting that the bottom of my bed needed to be dusted.

A mix of chlorine and hand sanitizer wafts around the room as I take deep, heavy breaths, each one accompanied by a full body shudder as pain shoots through my right arm. After a few minutes, I muster up the strength to open my eyes.

The normal off-white ceiling of my bedroom ceiling has been replaced by an alarming, pristine white. The dim fan light no longer shines from the center of my ceiling. This one is much brighter, and I squint against it.

There's mumbling and discreet chatter somewhere in the distance. A deep male voice speaks hushed to a high-pitched woman's voice. I turn toward the noise and open one eye.

To my right is a row of beds, some occupied, some not. A man and woman stand three beds down speaking closely to each other. They wear white scrub pants and matching lab coats. Their clothes are immaculate, no wrinkles or stains in sight. The room to my right seems to go on for another ten beds before it ends with two huge silver steel doors with identical turn dials, each like the vault door at a bank.

A slow, deep panic races through me.

My mom! The last time I saw her, she was bleeding on the floor in front of our broken front door. I look to the beds around me. We must be in a hospital, I think, and my mom must be getting treated somewhere nearby.

"Mom?" I whisper toward the beds to my right.

None of the bodies move or raise their heads to see who is calling out. I turn to the other side, a sharp pain running along my arm and up the side of my head as I lift myself slightly.

I raise my voice a little louder, "Mom?" Nothing. "*Mom!*"

Heads turn toward the direction of my voice now. The woman in the white lab coat notices my nervous body peeking out from under the blankets, and quickly rushes over.

"Oh, look who's awake." A feminine voice says to my left, "I've been taking bets on when you'd wake up. Looks like I'm walking away with extra garden time."

What?

The voice is coming from the bed next to me. A girl sits upright, her legs extended out long and her arms crossed at her chest.

Before I can ask her what she means and to please explain where I am and what is going on, my right arm is yanked out from under the blanket by frigid dry hands. Too fast for my aching body, I whip my head toward the nurse, who grabs my arm and wipes it down with a white cloth, all seemingly in one motion. The smell of rubbing alcohol is unmistakable.

"What are you doing?" My voice shakes in a way I wish it wouldn't. "Am I at Mayfair Hospital? Is my mom here? I think she hit her head really badly. She lost a lot of blood…"

The nurse, unbothered by the urgency in my voice, continues to rub the inside of my elbow before reaching into her coat pocket. Her hand returns a moment later with a syringe filled with orange liquid.

"What is that?"

She brings it toward my arm.

"I don't need medicine, I just need to find my mom."

She positions the needle at my skin. "*Please, answer me!*"

A sharp pinch like a bee's sting courses through my inner arm as she sticks the syringe deep into a vein. I want to yank my arm away, but I'm too afraid of breaking the ungodly long syringe, get it stuck in my arm, or worse.

"Take a deep breath," the girl to my left says.

The nurse gives her an annoyed scowl before pressing the plunger down, the orange liquid quickly disappearing from inside the syringe barrel into my arm.

I've never felt so cold. My teeth chatter in my head, like a knocking in my brain. A chill breaks across my body from head to toe as the shot does its work. I don't notice the nurse pull the syringe from my arm until she's finished and pushes on my shoulder, forcing me to lie back down. I focus on taking deep breaths, trying to keep warm.

There's a newfound weight to my eyelids. As I blink, I feel a stickiness attach to my right temple and then my left before an electrifying jolt passes horizontally from temple to temple. Ouch.

"All set." A voice says from somewhere above me.

The pressure behind my eyes is now too intense for me to open them, static noise rushes into my head beginning at the outer edges before meeting in the middle where the noise swells. "Is the TV broken?" I attempt to ask through numb lips.

The last thing I hear before the static takes over is a muffled underwater voice from somewhere off to my right saying "goodnight." And then I sink into the mattress, like feet in wet sand.

I'm under a tree. Sunlight peaks through the swinging leaves and I squint each time the light crosses my eyes. I clutch the soft strands of grass around me, as my feet echo the movements of the long branches of pale green leaves around me.

I'm humming, the tune rumbling through my body alongside the sense of calm and comfort from beneath the canopy of the tree. I feel giddy and light, like when my dad would take me to the park and push me on the swings until his arms were sore.

I feel someone lie down next to me in the grass. They say something and I laugh. My response is to hum louder creating a rumbling in my chest. In between chorus hums, I erupt into laughter rolling onto my side coming face to face with the person lying down next to me and smiling wider and brighter than I've ever smiled before.

My dad hums along with me as he picks at the long strands of grass tickling the side of my arm. He throws his head back and laughs from his gut. I must have said something funny. His laugh is contagious, and I join in until my stomach starts to hurt. He moves his hands through the branches of leaves that fall around us like a curtain. I watch his mouth move as he talks to me. I stare at his sharp nose, his effervescent green eyes, his dark full eyebrows; I simply take in his figure, the person I love and never thought I would get to see again. Inside our cocoon of leaves and grass, lying next to my dad, I feel safe and protected. Like I've arrived somewhere I'm supposed to be.

In a muffled voice, he says, "I love you to the moon."

It is a voice and phrase I have heard a hundred times before. I hear myself say, "and back."

The tug of baby hairs being pulled from my temples wakes me from my sleep.

I touch my hands to my temples, feeling a sticky residue left behind.

The nurse is back and stands to my right, hanging cords around a now dark screen above my bed. Then she saunters off. If I hadn't been already, I'm now seriously beginning to doubt that I'm in a hospital.

Still tender, I prop myself up into a seated position. The blindingly bright room is now bathed in a milky blue, which lends the hall an air of calm. Through the windows, it is dusk outside and a few stars appear in the sky. I scan the hall for nurses wandering between beds but spot only brown blankets covering the bodies, some of which sit and some of which lie still. The steel doors at the end of the hall are closed, and I wonder if my weak body could open them.

"Welcome back" and a "hey" are muttered from my left. I jump, and a boy with reddish hair at the edge of the bed next to me says, "Oops, didn't mean to scare you." He is tall and lanky, and his feet hang over the edge of the bed and reach the floor. Before him is the girl from before. She sits at the other end, her black hair falling around her shoulders and onto the pillows behind her. Her eyes are a soulful brown, big and round, contrasting the red-haired boy's gray eyes. The complete opposites sit across from each other, him with his milky white skin, and her with her caramel skin and dark features. The only similarity between them is their identical navy-blue cotton pants and tops.

I shake my head, try to chase away thoughts of their dull outfits. "Do you know if my mom is here?" I ask. "She's about the same height as me—brown hair, brown eyes. I think she was wearing a floral blouse and white jeans the last time I saw her..."

"She's definitely not here," answers the girl.

I motion toward the steel doors "Maybe she's in another room?"

"No other rooms for her to go to," she says. "Well, except for..."

Before she can finish her sentence, the red-haired boy cuts her off. "When they brought you in, you were alone. Sorry."

He means this as an answer, but I only feel more confused. "Well, is there a phone I could use to call her or someone, to make sure she's okay?"

The girl laughs. "I'm going to start sounding like a broken machine, but no, definitely not."

"We don't have our phones," the boy adds from the other end of the bed. "And no one here would let you use one if there was."

The awkward part of me that tries to make jokes when I'm uncomfortable asks if I'm in the loony bin or something, and at any rate they both laugh, though when they finally stop the girl answers, "Close enough."

A headache builds at the base of my neck as my confusion crescendos. I throw my hands up, thumping them down hard on the itchy brown blanket. "What is this place then? Why am I here, and where is my mom?"

A few of the others in the room begin to stir, some straining their heads to look at me, others rotating their whole bodies to witness my panic attack. Oddly, there are some people who do not stir in their beds, but instead stay rigidly still.

Before either of them can answer, a loud bang vibrates throughout the room as the steel doors at the end of the hall slam shut.

"Caleb!" The same nurse from earlier who poked me with the huge syringe and creepy orange stuff is stomping toward us. "Get back to your bed!"

The red-haired boy—Caleb, it seems—jumps from the bed next to mine and sprints toward another, three down and across from mine. The girl next to me snickers as the nurse walks past us, ignoring the girl's sarcastic laughter. Caleb is tucked into his bed in no time, and he looks back toward us with a serious face, or perhaps a fearful one.

"What's going on?" I ask the girl.

"It's Caleb's turn to dream."

Dream?

The nurse reaches Caleb and grabs his arm like she did with mine. I want to ask the girl what she meant by "dream," but my mouth freezes mid-word when I see the nurse pull out a familiar syringe full of glowing orange liquid, little drips falling from the tip of the needle. She finishes with the inside of his arm and sticks the needle in, Caleb's face curling into a wince.

"No matter how many times they stick you with that thing, it still hurts like hell." The girl next to me watches Caleb lie down in his bed while the nurse attaches two cords with round ends to his temples.

"She did that to me earlier," I say, watching the nurse turn to the computer screen placed above Caleb's head. She types in a number passcode and multiple graphs show up on the screen. The computer screen above my bed is black. I notice now that everyone has screens above them. Some are off, like mine, and people stir in the beds beneath them. Others are filled with moving charts and graphs. No motion from those beds, though.

The nurse leaves Caleb's side and walks to another bed, taps for a few seconds on the screen above a rigid girl.

"Three, two, one," the girl next to me counts. "And he's out."

"Out? Like asleep?" I ask. "Is that what happened to me, too? The nurse gave me the medicine and then I passed out cold."

The dark-haired girl's expression changes slowly. She rubs her head and says, "I get you're confused and all, but can you please not ask me so many questions? You're giving me a headache." And then she lies back in her bed, rubbing her temples and sighing heavily. She adjusts the white band around her arm, revealing a patch of angry red skin. The lettering on the bracelet reads:

Nora Flynn
#26
D

She notices me staring at her wrist and says, "It's not that special—you have one, too."

Immediately, I glance down at my right wrist, and behold a too tightly applied plastic-wrap-around bracelet.

Stella Grey
#37
D

Nonchalantly, from her bed she says, "Your name, your number, and your classification as a Dreamer. That's the short and sweet of it."

"Number? Dreamer?"

Nora cuts me off with an angry glare. "Sorry, no more questions," she says, but then all the same she moves her body to the edge of her bed that is closest to mine. "Fine, I'll allow you one. Shoot."

Not thinking too hard, I ask, "What does the number thirty-seven mean?"

I hold up my wrist for her to see.

She says, "There were thirty-six people here yesterday. Now *you're* number thirty-seven, and that's how the nurses and people running this place keep track of us. I'm twenty-six." She rolls her eyes. "It's nice, isn't it? Being numbered like cattle at a ranch?"

Her answer only adds more questions, and just as I am about to beg Nora to give me some more answers, she sits up at the sound of a lock clicking. Both steel doors open, held by two tall, muscly men in black outfits. Between the two of them, a woman in a white pressed suit walks effortlessly through.

She has long black hair that cascades down her white suit in waves. She has on a dusty rose lipstick that accents every curve of her lips. She nods at the men holding the doors open, motioning for them to shut them slowly behind her as she fully enters the room. The doors shut, click and lock. The noise loud, but not loud enough to wake anyone around me. Her black heels click and echo as she moves through the room and locks eyes with me. A growing grin crinkles her lipstick. Pretending to be asleep is no longer an option. I am shit out of luck.

Nora whispers beneath her breath, "Uh oh."

The woman stops at the foot of my bed, her shoes making their final two clicks. I see now that her eyes are as black as her hair, and her stare is direct and utterly terrifying. She smiles big, showing off all of her perfectly shaped and clean white teeth, not a hint of lipstick on a canine or incisor.

Too perfect, like a robot come to life, she clasps her hands in front of her stomach and takes a long inhale, blinking once before she says in the most perfect French accent, "Great, you are finally awake! Welcome to the Manor de Rêves."

I stare up at the French lady. "Manor de what?" I hear myself ask.

She chuckles to herself and extends an arm toward the room by way of presentation. "Manor de Rêves. Would you like the welcome tour now?"

"What is going on here, where am I?"

"All of that will be explained on the tour," she replies. And then, with the wave of her hand, beckoning me from my bed, "Come with me."

Slowly but surely, I begin to rise from the hard bed beneath me, my muscles groaning with each movement. Standing proves too much and I sit back down, hoping I don't pass out.

"Easy now, we don't want you getting hurt."

Her accent sounds like a song.

I roll my eyes and push myself up again. Finally balancing, I notice I'm wearing the same dreary navy scrub outfits as the others, a "37" embroidered on my right chest pocket.

The lady folds her arms and taps her heels in rhythm, clearly tired of waiting and making sure I know about it. "My name is Antoinette Aurand. You may refer to me as Lady A."

Like a drill sergeant, she rattles off, "I am third in command here at the Manor. Follow me, do not waver."

I time my steps to the click of her heels, my attempt to "not waver." I turn back and catch Nora staring at me from her bed. She mouths "Good luck," enough of a distraction that I don't notice that the clicks have stopped, that Lady A has stopped at the metal doors, and I walk straight into her back.

She turns and warns, "Watch where you are going," her mouth curving into a mysterious grin. "We don't want another one of those eggs on your head."

Eggs on my head?

I run a hand along my scalp, where I find a bump the size of, well, an egg.

Great, another mysterious injury.

Lady A presses a white button next to the doors and speaks French into the intercom. Through the intercom speaker comes the noise of someone pressing a series of buttons in return. A rush of air comes from the space in between the two stainless-steel doors as they unlock and begin to open, pushed along by the two guards from earlier. There's no mistaking their size and strength at this distance, nor their serious expressions.

"Merci," says Lady A to the guards before turning to me and adding, "Move out of the way."

I jump out of the way before my body is crushed by the men and their doors.

I follow Lady A away from the hall of beds and down a long hallway made bright by sconces and light that trickles through windows. Between each window is a portrait, some of women in gowns and pearls, others with women in blazers, an emblem on each of their chest pockets. The men in the portraits all wear three-piece suits with colorful ties or pocket squares. Regardless of what each figure wears, I can feel their eyes follow me as I move past and half expect them to start talking.

My voice trembles as I ask, "Who…who are these people?"

"These are the portraits of those we look up to and strive to be like."

A simple "Bob" or "Karen" would have sufficed.

Farther down the hall, we stop at two chestnut wooden doors, each with a frame. On the first door hangs a painting: a woman with fiery red hair and icy blue eyes stares out with a straight face, as if afraid her secrets might slip out through the portrait. Her silk red button blouse is perfectly pressed and is accompanied by a necklace hanging loosely around her décolletage. Even in the painting, the diamonds glisten like a disco ball. She looks serious and smart. I assume she smells like an expensive perfume.

The other picture frame sits empty, and before I can ask why, Lady A throws both doors open, revealing a grand square room. The walls are covered in dark brown wood that slowly transitions into an intricate red wallpaper with twirls and swirls along the surface. A crystal chandelier hangs from the center of the room, bathing everything in a magnificent maroon glow. I have never seen something so opulent and rich before. Leaving Lady A in the doorway, I wander forward, my mouth opened in awe at the elegance that oozes from it all. On the opposite side of the landing is a single door, with a single stern warning: "DO NOT ENTER."

Lady A clears her throat and brushes past me onto the landing. I follow her to a grand staircase. The smooth mahogany of the banister passes coolly beneath my fingers as we descend one carpeted step at a time. Halfway down, I look up at the chandelier, feeling both like an heiress striding across her own mansion and Little Red Riding Hood walking into the wolf's trap.

My palms begin to sweat and stick to the railing. The stairs open into another gigantic open room, this one with crisp blue walls. Light from the windows illuminates gold stars and silver moons that are painted on the walls. The room is a starry dream. The grand foyer is filled with smells of fresh wood and a mysterious odor I can't quite place. Something like ripe lemons and dark chocolate, but not.

At the sight of the painted moons, I can hear a distant voice, a familiar one, a comforting one.

"I love you to the moon."

It's my dad's voice.

Under my breath, I respond, "and back."

Lady A waits in front of two huge golden-brown doors at the bottom of the stairs. Because of course. There must have been a sale on huge, intricate doors somewhere. On each side of them there are windows, each giving a hint at acres of green space beyond them. For a second I'm certain I can make out a hedge maze in the distance, and a slight twinge of déjà vu creeps up in me.

"Come here." Lady A waves me over toward the window and away from my thoughts. "Here are the gardens. You may go outside to enjoy them, but only when given permission. I will only say this once before consequences are given out. In here you do not do anything until given orders. At all times, you will be watched," she says, looking up toward a white camera in the corner of the ceiling. "Your time here will go swimmingly if you keep those things in mind."

"What is this place; where am I?" I point outside. "Who are you, and what I am doing here? I need a bit of explanation before you tell me to listen to your orders." The surprise in my voice drags the last few words upward.

She looks me up and down before answering, "You'll get your answers soon enough."

With that she walks away from me, toward the right side of the room. There are two doors on the left side of the foyer. One has a massive cursive "C" painted on the middle, the other an "L." She stops at the door closest to us, the one with the "L."

"This is the library." She opens the door slightly, the smell of dust and paper rushing out. She holds it open just enough for me to peek inside. The room is bigger than my school library, yet it has a cozy feel to it. Thousands of books line the shelves like wallpaper. The walls are a rainbow of spines. "You may take one book at time from the library back with you to the dormitory. The library is at your disposal—unless you are told otherwise."

The library's spine-filled walls remind me of my dad's office and the ever-changing stack of books that covered his desk. Many mornings before school I would stumble half asleep into his office to say goodbye, but his stack of books would block my view of him. I always imagined him as a king sitting in his thrown behind his fortress wall of books, me the errant knight wobbling into his peace. But he never once made me feel like I was disturbing him. One morning, he called me toward the desk and measured how tall I had grown over night in comparison to the tall stack of books toppling overhead.

"I'm too tall!" I whined as my chin met the top of a stack.

"That's not possible." My dad leaned forward and straightened the stack I eyed evilly. "What makes you think that?"

"I'm taller than all the boys in my class and they make fun of me for it. And now look, I'm like five books taller than this stack. I'm never that many books taller."

My dad scanned the stack of books and looked at me with a sympathetic loving gaze, then rumpled the hair on my head and sent me on my way to school.

The next morning, I didn't feel like being measured by books, but my dad called me into his office under the guise of needing to show me something. Instead, when I reached his desk, he gaped at me with wide surprised eyes.

"Oh, no," his voice was sullen. "I think you shrunk, look at this!" His arms encircled a large, crooked stack of books on his desk. He shook his head in disbelief, eyebrows raised. "This stack towers over you."

The stack from the morning before no longer stopped at my chin but reached past my head by at least seven more books. I was doubtful that I had significantly shrunk in height in the span of twenty-four hours, but my dad's enthusiasm allowed me to believe in this triumph over my insecurities.

The positivity and pleasant warmth of my dad's book-filled office is replaced by the Manor's dusty library, one that is neatly organized, void of colorful and ever-growing stacks.

"This," Lady A continues and points toward the other door a few feet down from us, "is the cafeteria…"

"Hence the C," I offer bravely.

She quirks an eyebrow at me, noticing my growing confidence with my words. "Correct. Breakfast is every day from eight to nine a.m., lunch is noon to one p.m., and dinner from six to seven. If you miss those times, you miss the meal. We don't do room service here. Understood?"

I nod, not sensing much else to do that wouldn't irritate her further.

"Great, let's continue on."

Lady A walks back to the staircase. "There is a downstairs level, but anyone without a badge is not permitted, so I will not bother with showing you how to get down there." Lady A keeps her hands clasped in front of her, does not change her expression. "Behind me, on the opposite wall, you will see two doors. The brass one leads to a set of rooms that you will only enter with either a staff member or a head member, such as me, or other authorized personnel." Before I can ask about it, she interrupts. "There is no need to ask questions about what is behind that door, you will find out soon enough." If she means to set me at ease, I can offer some pointers, perhaps. She continues, "The mahogany door is where the head members offices and chambers are. This is a space you may enter, but only if given permission by one of the head members. Let's just say you'd do well to avoid gaining that permission."

"So, it's like being called into the principal's office?" I ask.

"I suppose so." She is silent for a beat, then adds, "but worse. Speaking of those offices, let's go back there."

"What? Go back there? You literally just told me I shouldn't ever want to go back into those offices!" I decide that she likes torturing me slowly. It's the only part of this that makes any sense.

"Now is the exception to the rule. Plus, you will find all the answers to your questions back there."

Too excited by the prospect of answers to argue, I put my head down and follow her toward the mahogany door, where she looks at the keypad above the knob and then back at me, making sure that I cannot see the code she enters. It takes five beeps before the door makes an unlocking sound and opens on its own with a long, slow creak.

Lady A walks through and motions me into the long hallway. A flood of strong perfume makes my nose itch as I step inside. The hall is warm from the sconces lighting the dark gray walls on each side. The first door to our right has a plaque centered on the door. Beneath it is written "Ms. Antoinette Aurand," and this must be her office.

Farther down the hallway sits another door with another empty name plaque. The emptiness is ominous. The door across the way says "Ms. Grace Withers," and Lady A knocks a clean three times. Through the door Lady A and I are met with a husky voice beckoning, "Come in."

I step inside, leaving Lady A at the threshold. The sparkle and shine of a diamond necklace throws disco ball sparkles around the room and I wince at the reflected light. Along with the diamonds, I also recognize the red-haired lady from the portrait, who looks up from her writing and removes her glasses from the bridge of her nose, placing them on the desk.

She looks to me and then at the doorway, where Lady A remains. She nods toward the door and I look back to Lady A, who swiftly shuts the door behind me. The woman's icy eyes bore into my own.

She says, "I hear you have some questions for me."

Her features appear sharper in person than they did in the painting. Her blue eyes colder, icier than I could have imagined, so much so that they physically make me feel chilly. Her lips are plump and cherry stained, matching the fiery red of her billowing hair. She calls to mind the highest point of a flame, where the blue seamlessly transitions into a glowing red. There is not a single smudge of makeup out of place, and each jewel in her necklace must be a least an inch wide in every axis. She exudes wealth and power. My urge to bang on the door, to call out for the relative warmth of Lady A, is not a proud one.

"Please, sit. Make yourself comfortable." Her words float around the room, like a bee waiting to sting.

I remain still, right in front of her desk, unsure of what to do. Before I can make a move for the door or the chair, she stands up from her desk, beckoning me forward. Much like Lady A, her footsteps are punctuated by piercing clicks, these ones courtesy of some five-inch red stiletto heels. She wears black stockings that disappear under a black pencil skirt that has a slit up the right leg. Tucked into her skirt is an ink-colored blouse that looks uncomfortable, buttoned to the very top. On top of the blouse lays her impressive diamond necklace that looks like it was stolen from the Crown Jewels vault.

"My grandmother gave it to me," she says, following my gaze.

"It's, it is…" My brain is void of words.

"I know." She pulls a chair out and moves it parallel to her desk. "Sit."

I take two heavy steps to the chair and sit down. Trying to seem calm and collected, I cross my legs and perch my arms onto my top leg. I hold my head up high, my thoughts gone save the best advice my dad has ever given me: "Fake it till you make it." And you can bet your ass I was going to do that now in order to get what I wanted, needed…the opportunity to help my mom.

The woman returns to her desk. "My name is Grace Withers, but from now on you will call me Ms. Withers. I run the Manor." She looks me dead in the eyes, wants me to feel her position of power, before admitting, "With my colleagues, of course."

I take a deep breath, gather the courage to respond. "That's all good and dandy, but what the hell is this *manor* and why am I here? How did I get here? How do you all know me and where is my mom? The last time I saw her she was lying in a pool of her own blood. Do you know who broke into my house? Was it you?" I barely catch my breath between my hurried questions.

She chuckles at my panic. "Darling, you're going to have to slow down and ask one question at a time. I'm only human."

"Where am I?"

"You are at the Manor de Rêves, which in English translates to the Manor of Dreams."

"Where are we? France? Lady A keeps speaking French to those bodybuilder men." I work hard on slowing my voice down so she can hear my questions clearly.

"I am not at liberty to say where we are."

"I thought you were in charge here?" I say with a slight mocking tone.

She straightens, squinting slightly at my comment. "Next question."

"No, I want to know where I am!"

In a more agitated tone, she answers, "You are not allowed to know that piece of information. She taps her fingers on her desk in impatience. "If I were you, I would ask the right questions before I call Lady A back in here to take you away."

Not wanting to push my luck, I move onto the next question. "Well, what is this Manor de Rêves then?" Despite taking four years of French, my accent is beyond terrible.

"The Manor is home now to thirty-seven young men and women. Seventeen boys and twenty girls live here, each day lending their talents and abilities. In fact, in a few weeks there will be a ball to celebrate the one hundredth anniversary of its opening." She smiles at the mention of the ball.

"What do you mean by talent?" My head feels like I've just stepped off a roller coaster. "Can they sing, dance, act? You should know I wouldn't classify myself as 'talented.'"

"Our girls and boys are not...let's say, normal. They and you are here because you have a rare genetic mutation that only a handful of the world's population has. You and the other thirty-six are Dreamers." She sits back in her chair, as if she hadn't left me on a terrible cliff-hanger.

"And a Dreamer is...?" I barely sit on the edge of my seat.

"A Dreamer in their deepest REM cycle will enter a dream that depicts a true moment from the future. This dream can be a personal scene, one about people you have never met, or set in a country you've never been to. Dreamers dream the future."

I can't control the laughter as the realization hits me. There is no way this is real. There is no way in hell that "Dreamers" and their abilities are real. Through my laughs, I respond, "So you're saying that this place is full of boys and girls who can see the future?"

"No. I am saying that the Manor is a home for boys and girls who have the ability to *dream* the future. That means that, through their dreams, the Manor is able to know what will happen in the future. Your dreams will help us in many ways."

"Me, I'm a Dreamer?" I look at her as if she had just said the sky was green and the grass was blue.

"Exactly, we wouldn't waste our time with someone who wasn't." As if able to read my doubtful thoughts, she responds, "I know you doubt the validity of my words, but why would I lie about any of this?"

I don't have an answer. It would be pleasantly easy for me to just write this off as an elaborate prank that Callie has set up, but my heart clenches in fear that the woman sitting in front of me is telling the truth.

"Do you wake up in the middle of the night after dreaming and never fall back to sleep after that? Are your dreams so vivid and lively, that sometimes your actual day doesn't compare to the clarity of your dreams? How many times of day do you get a sense of déjà vu?" She can sense she is hitting a chord with her words. "Probably too many to count."

I stare blankly at her. My thoughts are a puddle, a complete mess.

"I've hit the nail right on the head, haven't I?"

I swallow the lump forming in my throat. "Okay, so let's say I am a Dreamer. I still don't understand why I am here and not at home. I can dream perfectly well in my bed. I don't need to be in this place and under that itchy blanket to do so."

"You are here so we can utilize your unique ability to its maximum potential and use. Over the course of the next few days, you will learn more about what I mean. But for now, all you need to know is that the Manor specializes in Dreamers and recording their dreams." Her speech sounds rehearsed, and I wonder how many times she's had this conversation. At least thirty-six others, I figure, though who knows how long she's been here. "We have the technology and equipment to utilize your dreams, things that would otherwise become lost fragments of your unconscious."

"Recording our dreams? I doubt that's scientifically, technologically possible." This sounds like an impossible middle school science experiment that the teacher would never approve of. But Ms. Withers seems more mad scientist than hopeful science nerd. "But say it is true, you can't just go inside of our heads! That's definitely an invasion of privacy!"

"So, you believe me now?" She lifts an eyebrow and I shrug back. "We don't go inside your head. We use technology to record the dreams in an efficient, non-invasive way."

I remember the petrifying syringe from earlier, noting how she didn't mention "painless" in her description. "What if I don't want you watching or knowing what my dreams are about?

Plus, it seemed sort of invasive earlier when a lady jammed a needle the size of a steak knife into a boy's arm."

"We have to do what we have to do." Her stare darkens. "And unfortunately, you don't have the option to keep your dreams hidden from us. The moment you stepped foot into this Manor, you gave up your freedom."

Fear and anger spike my heartrate. "I didn't have the great pleasure of stepping into this stupid Manor! Instead, I woke up in it after being bludgeoned on the head and knocked out. And the more I think of it, you guys were the ones who knocked me out and ransacked my house!" My head, our destroyed house... "What did you do with my mom?"

"We figured asking you or your doting mother to allow you to come here wouldn't go our way, so we went with the easiest and quickest option."

"Definitely not the *easiest* option, because I'm NOT staying, and I'm going to call the police and get you put in jail for breaking and entering. And assault!"

A creepy grin slowly forms on her lips, her red lipstick cracking slightly as her lips stretch to a wicked smile. "Darling, you won't be leaving, and you won't be calling the police. You will not have contact with anyone else who isn't in or working at the Manor. As for your mother, forget about her. You are now a part of bigger and more important things."

My cheeks grow hotter and hotter. "Is that supposed to be a threat?"

"No, it's the truth. You came in here with questions, it would have been rude of me to not answer them truthfully." She rolls her eyes. "Would you have rather I told you you're on an all-expenses-paid holiday where you will sleep a lot?

"No!" I'm seeing red. And not just her hair and lip color. "I want you to tell me I have my free will to walk out of this place and go make sure my mom hasn't bled out by my front door!"

"Do not raise your voice at me," she snarls. I recoil back in my chair, a single tear escaping. "In the Manor, your free will consists of what I say you can and cannot do."

"So, I'm basically a prisoner of yours until you suck me dry of all my dreams."

Before I can blink, Ms. Withers scrapes her chair against the floor and rises in one quick motion. Planting her palms on her desk, she stares right through me. "I will not tolerate that level of attitude and slander toward the Manor. You should consider yourself lucky that you are in such a prestigious institution as the Manor."

There are a million things I would like to hurl toward her, but I swallow those words immediately. I try to not to cry, holding my breath and begging myself to hold it together.

"You may leave now," she tells me, making it sound more like a command than an offer.

I snap my head up from my lap. "But I still have more questions."

"And I have no more answers."

I scramble my way out of the chair and hurry toward her office door. Just as I grab onto the door handle, ready to twist it open and get the hell out of there, she calls to me, "I look forward to seeing you again."

I don't turn around or say goodbye, but instead pull the door open and slam it shut behind me. Once outside her office, something damp slips from under my eye and travels down my cheek and hits the side of my mouth. The tear is salty, and as I blink, more fall like pathetic rain drops on a cloudy day. I quickly swipe them away, their wet residue a haunting reminder. I haven't cried since my dad's funeral, and on that day, I made a pact with myself to never cry over little insignificant things in life.

However, I allow myself this moment.

I sink down onto my butt, cradling my knees close to my chest. I attempt to create a cocoon around my body, shielding myself from the unknown. I jam my head into my legs, clenching my eyes shut, creating wet stains of tears on my bleak pants as I try to regain steady breathing.

Click. Click. Click.

I shudder, biting my lips, praying it isn't Ms. Withers walking out to yell at me for shedding tears in her pristine presence.

Click. Click.

I blink my teary eyes open and let out a relieved breath, marveling that I could ever feel a sense of relief in this place, and especially so soon. The determined look on Lady A's face dims the feeling, but only slightly. Nevertheless, her lack of fiery red hair and ice eyes casts her in a more welcomed light.

"I am here to take you back to the dormitory," she says in her heavy accent.

I follow Lady A through the Manor with my head down, too afraid to look up, and before I know it Lady A and I are standing in front of the two huge metal doors that lead into the room where I had woken up. This time she doesn't speak to the guards in French. She prompts the door open with two sharp snaps and nothing more. The dormitory appears the same as when we left it, eerily quiet and still as people lie under their blankets. With each bed we pass, I fight the urge to slip my hand beneath a nose, over a mouth—anything to test for warm breath or not.

When we get to my bed, Lady A pulls from beneath it an old luggage box. Opening it, she pulls out a handful of blue clothes and tosses them on the bed. "These are your clothes, self-explanatory. Also, a toothbrush, paste, hairbrush, body wash. Everything else you will find in the bathroom, at the opposite end of the room. Change and attend to your other needs in there." Her instructions finished, she turns on the tips of her glossy heels and clicks back down the hall.

I grab at the blue clothes inside the chest, and head toward the bathroom. Walking down the row of beds I see that Nora is no longer in her bed. Caleb, the boy who got injected with the orange serum, is still passed out in his bed. I wonder if he is "dreaming" for them right now? One computer screen above his bed shows a line flowing up and down, another has dots appearing in concentrated areas. His breathing hitches, and one of the graphs spikes. Presidential elections? Oscar award results? Natural disasters? I wonder what he's dreaming about.

"Hey, watch it!"

My eyes are still on the screen when she crashes into me. I look up to see Nora staring me straight in the face, a pissed off look already on hers. "S-s-sorry," I stutter.

She mutters "new girl" faintly under hear breath and walks away.

Why she's mad at me when Ms. Withers provides such a worthy target, I do not know.

The bathroom has an obvious divide for the girls' and boys' sides. The whole left side is painted a bright baby blue while the right side is a bubblegum pink. Perhaps the Manor *is* as old as Ms. Withers said after all, according to their dated way of specifying gender.

The bathroom smells like a mix of cotton candy and Crest minty toothpaste. On the wall to the right are ten sinks, all shiny porcelain and, of course, pink. Above the sinks are mirrors that reflect the light from the windows at the top of the farthest wall. The combination of the pink and the light from the moon outside creates an illusion of a pink mist floating around the bathroom. Little specks of dust fly around catching the light, making it look like it's raining pink dust balls.

I feel like I'm inside a bottle of Pepto-Bismol.

Adjacent to the sinks are another ten stalls, each with toilets and a shower. I thought I had seen it all, but when I peer into the shower, I see that each one is accessorized with its own pink fluffy loofa, a pink bottle of shampoo and conditioner, and a glittery pink bar of soap.

Locking myself into a stall, I rush through the motions, feverishly scrubbing away the gross feeling that for the past few hours has inched its way across my skin. I change into a new navy outfit, planning on throwing out the one I had on. I assess myself in the sink mirror, noticing that the shirt sleeves are embroidered with pale gold stars and moons. "Number 37" is written on the right breast pocket of the shirt, and the material scratches at my skin every time I move. It might not be an orange jumpsuit, but it could be.

I look ashy and pale, yellow and gray upside-down half-moons exaggerate the undersides of my eyes. My hair is crunchy, cold, and wet as I run my fingers through the tangles before tying it up with an abandoned tie from the counter, hoping its owner won't be bothered. I take a deep breath and stare back at myself in the mirror.

Stay strong, Stella. You will find a way to get out of here and get to Mom.

The loudspeaker above my head interrupts everything with classical music. Full volume, or loud enough, anyway. The song is fast and full of trumpet bursts, violins playing their highest note. The music is so vivid I can imagine a full live orchestra playing the song outside of the bathroom.

I press my hands over my ears, anything to drown the noise, and rush out of the bathroom. At the end of the hall, Nora and Caleb, among others, are walking through the metal doors being held open by a new set of security guards.

Where is everyone going? The beds no longer have sleeping bodies or people quietly reading on top of them. I am the last one left in the dormitory, and before I can decide to slink back into the bathroom and hide or follow to find out what's going on, a deep voice carries from the far end of the room and yells to me. The security guard's words barely cut through the music: "Come! Dinner!"

And before I can think of how to escape, my feet are already rushing toward the doors, also afraid of getting yelled at again, seemingly. I rush past him, leaving the dormitory in the dust. The loud bang of the doors closing behind me sends a jolt through me, and I fall into step with the people in front of me.

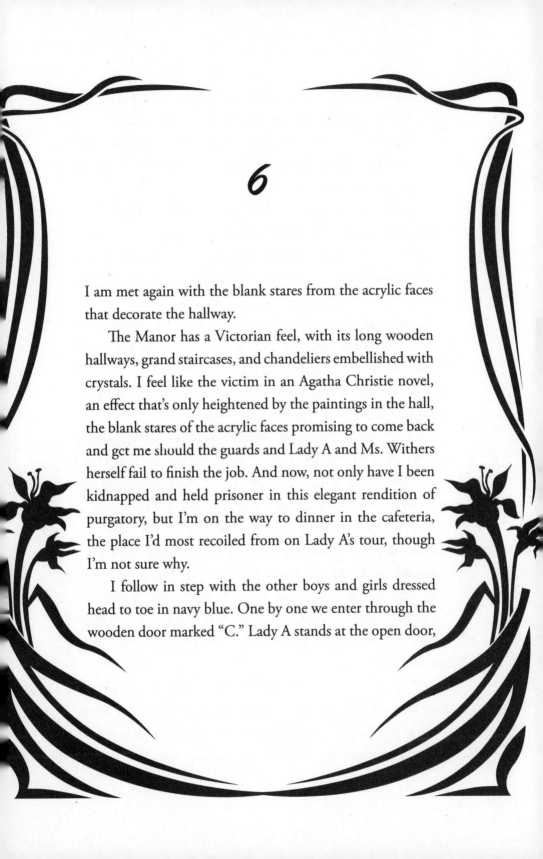

6

I am met again with the blank stares from the acrylic faces that decorate the hallway.

The Manor has a Victorian feel, with its long wooden hallways, grand staircases, and chandeliers embellished with crystals. I feel like the victim in an Agatha Christie novel, an effect that's only heightened by the paintings in the hall, the blank stares of the acrylic faces promising to come back and get me should the guards and Lady A and Ms. Withers herself fail to finish the job. And now, not only have I been kidnapped and held prisoner in this elegant rendition of purgatory, but I'm on the way to dinner in the cafeteria, the place I'd most recoiled from on Lady A's tour, though I'm not sure why.

I follow in step with the other boys and girls dressed head to toe in navy blue. One by one we enter through the wooden door marked "C." Lady A stands at the open door, checking bracelets and mentally cataloging who enters and who does not. I turn back and confirm my suspicion that I am the last one outside of the room, virtually assuring that I will be the fool new girl walking into the cafeteria alone, helplessly looking for a place to sit.

Lady A tugs my right arm and pushes my sleeve up to check the bracelet, as if she doesn't know who I am. She turns my wrist over to see the number and releases my arm so suddenly that it swings down and hits the side of my body. I kind of hope she says something or needs to look at my bracelet longer, but Lady A doesn't read my mind. What she does is put her hand in the center of my back and shove me forward, the surprise of which causes me to fall hard, both my knees smashing into the hard wood floor. My sweaty hands fly forward and squeak along the floor like sneakers on a gymnasium floor.

I wheeze, trying to collect myself. Sucking in tears, I slowly lift my head to find every single head in the cafeteria turned toward me, a sea of upside-down mouths and pitiful eyes and the occasional muffled laugh slipping out from those who couldn't help it or didn't want to. The whole thing makes my temples throb. Not wanting to prolong my sad grand entrance, I quickly rise to my feet and search the room for an open seat. The cafeteria has ten square wooden tables spaced perfectly apart from one another. Each seats four, and I know there should be an empty space somewhere, though that doesn't help me find one.

A sharp whistle rings through the room, and everyone's eyes leaves me for the back-right corner of the space, where Nora is standing on her chair and waving at me. The chair next to her is occupied, but the other two call my name.

A few claps sound as I make my wordless way over to Nora's table. A few whispers, too, but I ignore everyone and everything except for my intended target. Nora jumps from her chair and sits back down. Next to her sits Caleb, with his mop of red hair and pitiful eyes.

I pull out a wooden chair and throw myself down into it with a huff of air.

"Don't take it personally," Nina instructs. "Everyone in here is so bored that a fly on the wall would fascinate them."

"Nora!" Caleb smacks her playfully on the arm. "That's not gonna make her feel better."

"We haven't met formally yet," she says, extending a hand toward me. "My name is Nora."

"I'm—" my voice comes out hoarse, and I clear my throat. "I'm Stella."

"And I'm Caleb." He gives me a calm, sweet smile that I flash back at him, surprised by the slight comfort I feel from the two of them.

Itching from all the earlier focus that has been on me, I try and change subjects and ask, "So, have you guys been here long?"

Nora laughs. "I thought you were about to ask us if we came here often." A single dimple forms on her right cheek when she smiles, the corners of her eyes crinkle. Aside from her snarky attitude, she's gorgeous, straight off the cover of a magazine. "Take a picture it will last longer."

"I'm sorry. I was just—"

"I'm just messing with you. I would be sizing everyone up here, too, if I was new," she admits. "And to answer your question, I've been here for about a month now."

"I came in the day after Nora," Caleb chimes in.

I nod, a mixture of understanding and astonishment settling in. A whole month. How did they survive that long? I've barely handled the few conscious hours I've spent here. How would I handle a month? Or worse, longer?

No. I tell myself. *You are going to get out of here and find Mom.* My worst fear pops into my head. *Alive.*

"How old are you?" Caleb asks.

"Seventeen. What about you?"

"I'm sixteen, Nora is seventeen, too. Most people here are either sixteen or seventeen. There are a few older ones, but they're too cool for school, so we don't bother with them."

"Judging from everyone's reaction to me, I'm definitely *not* too cool for school."

"The people here act a bit cold," Caleb says, "but I think it's how they cope and protect themselves from getting hurt. Or more hurt than they already are, at least."

"Speaking of hurt, how did you get that?" I ask, nodding toward Nora's left cheek, or more specifically the purple-and-blue circle spreading across it like the wrong shade of blush.

"Woke up with it," she says casually.

"Geez." I fall back in my chair. "I feel like I'm in the middle of a *Twilight Zone* episode."

"The lab will do that to you." Nora gives a snicker but winces at her bruise, and my face scrunches in automatic sympathy. Caleb turns and lands a careful arm around her shoulder, his hand finding her arm.

"What's the lab? If you're walking out with mysterious bruises, my guess is that it's a torture chamber," I say, mostly joking but not as much as I would like to be.

"Pretty much," they respond in sync, the same serious expression on each of their faces. Taking up the slack, Nora adds, "However, unlike a normal torture chamber, you're asleep the whole time you're in the lab." Nora points to her cheek, "Didn't even notice this until I looked in the mirror earlier."

Our conversation stops as a swarm of people dressed in gray comes through the doors behind our table, a delicious smell trailing in their wake from the towering plates and trays they carry. My stomach growls at the aromatic circus, and one by one, food is placed in front of us. In front of me sits a chicken breast covered in brown gravy, a blob of mashed potatoes, and a mix of vegetables on the side. The food looks and smells nothing like the food from the cafeteria at school, and no way would I see boys throwing food from these porcelain dishes. They wouldn't waste it, not when it smelled like this.

Nora's fork and knife tear through the chicken before her plate even touches the table. She shoves in a giant mouthful and Caleb chuckles in her direction. He says, "That's why we sit at this table. As the closest to the kitchen, we get our food first."

"And I haven't eaten in a day, so I'm ravenous!" Nora exclaims through a mouth full of food.

"I wasn't expecting to be served. Much less served food that doesn't take my appetite away." I push the mashed potatoes around my plate, the steam wafting upward.

"Ya, this isn't your typical high school cafeteria," Nora says, still chewing. "They serve us five-star food because they want us all healthy and shit. Only the cleanest and healthiest food for their prized Dreamers," Nora says in a mocking voice surprisingly close to Ms. Withers'.

"This place is so confusing." I shake my head. "They kidnap us, they keep us here like prisoners, and then they give us five-star restaurant food and service."

"We *are* their prisoners," Nora says. "Don't ever forget that, even when they're smiling at you or letting you have extra time outside. At the end of the day, they dead bolt us away in the dormitory and hook us up to machines to steal from our heads." Nora's voice gets louder and more agitated as she continues, but she clenches her jaw to contain her rage and keep her meal tact.

Caleb's light blue eyes seem darker here in the cafeteria. He has light brown freckles that dot across his nose and under his eyes. He's tall and lanky and a little awkward, but sweet. His feet seem too big for his body. He reminds me of a puppy, and the thought of anyone here hurting him makes my blood boil. I wonder what he was like outside of this place, what he's missing and who is missing him. It's too early to tell, but I think he has a crush on Nora. He's holding his hands on the table, doing whatever he can to keep them from inching toward hers. When he's not staring at the ground, it's usually at her.

And what was Nora like, I think. When she wasn't waking up with bruises on her face, of course. Would I have been friends with her at school? Her and Callie would clash, probably, only one of them getting to be the dominant friend in the group. I smile toward her. She reminds me of Callie's no-bullshit attitude. I could imagine Nora with her dark stormy eyes and rage-filled fists strutting through the school cafeteria. Callie and I would gape in awe of her, knowing she would brush past the food fight, effortlessly deflecting flying pieces of questionably raw chicken tenders and even intimidating boys like Jacob Richards into using the cafeteria trays the way they were intended.

I really hope they won't mind me sticking around them, begging for scraps of information. No one else seems receptive to me, anyway.

"Stella, Earth to Stella." Nora waves her hands in my face. "You better eat, your food's gonna get cold, and they don't give us much time."

For the next ten minutes the only sound in the cafeteria is the clanking of forks and knives scraping plates clean. The food comforts me, and my nerves ease slightly as my stomach warms. My favorite part of the day has always been coming home, the house smelling like tomatoes, fresh pasta, garlic cloves— whatever my mom was cooking. She wasn't always a great cook. I'll never forget the night I smelled something burning wafting up from the kitchen and into my room. I let the tickle the smell caused in my nose slide for a few minutes before it became so overpowering that all I could think about was burnt popcorn at the movie theatre and no longer pre-algebra. I rushed down to the kitchen, images of disastrous house fires haunting me. Fortunately, there were no flames engulfing the microwave, but there was a neglected, overflowing pot on the stove as she drooled over an open cookbook. I didn't know it was possible, but if you let the pasta sit at the bottom of the pot without stirring for too long, it could burn and stick to the pot. We ate burnt pasta that night in between moments of laughter, and my dad teased her for days because the burnt smell stuck to the cushions. Since then, my mom never lets the pasta burns but instead watches over it like a hawk.

And like that I drop my fork, no longer hungry. I catch my fresh tears with my napkin before they can fall out of my eyes and down my cheeks, and a hand touches my own. "Hey, do you want to go outside to the gardens with us?" Caleb asks. "Nora and I usually hang outside for a little while after meals."

"I'd love that."

Finished eating, the two of them lead me to a weeping willow tree. The long branches and leaves extend out, creating a canopy that covers the ground and trunk of the tree like an umbrella. We pick our way through the veil of leaves and sit by the trunk. Nora lies down, her head on Caleb's legs, and Caleb's cheeks flush pink like the girl's bathroom. I sit with my back against the hard wood of the trunk, taking in the swaying collage of green in front of me.

From the tips of my toes to the roots of my hair, my body breaks out in chills as the wind picks up, kicking the strands of leaves up and toward our bodies. The space under the swaying leaves feels familiar. Memories of happy humming and my dad's white-toothed smile pop into mind.

"I've been under this tree before!" I realize, startling my new friends.

Nora lifts her head from Caleb's legs. "What?"

"This tree! I was here with my dad!" I stand, the emotions too powerful to sit with.

"Stella, that's impossible," Caleb says. "No one's parents are here. Plus, we saw you arrive, and you definitely weren't with your dad."

"I...I saw it." I walk in and out of the falling leaves. "I was lying here right where you guys are and—" My hand flies to my mouth. "Holy shit, that was a dream!"

Caleb and Nora sit up as I storm out from under the willow's branches running fast away from the Manor, unable to sit still with the absurdity of it all. The grass crunches beneath my feet as I sprint farther and farther, no destination in mind. I take random turns left and right until I come face to face with the hulking wall of a bright green hedge. I step through an archway of red roses interlaced between spindly vines and sharp thorns. A labyrinth of mossy hedges, a twisted fairy tale scene rises up around me, the walls as tall as a house and cut into sharp edges and turning at perfect ninety-degree angles. I glide my hands along them, the silky leaves tickling the center of my palm.

Ouch!

I pull my hand back from the hedge. A ball of blood pools from a tiny dot on my pointer finger. I focus on the sweet smell of fresh-cut grass, the clean air, anything to ignore the painful prick. And it must work, because I barely register the heavy footfalls rushing me from behind until a hot, panting breath reaches the back of my neck.

"Why did you run off like that?" Nora questions between breaths.

I shake my head, not knowing where to start.

Caleb's voice is laced with concern. "What happened?"

"Everything Ms. Withers said was true, wasn't it?" I ask, turning to face them. "Everything she said about our dreams was—*is*—the truth!"

Their lack of words, their flushed, guilty faces, confirm everything. I hadn't allowed myself to believe her. It was easier to think this was all some bad joke that I would find my way out of. Caleb and Nora follow my gaze around the garden maze. "This place, the willow tree, they have been in dreams of mine."

"No one believes any of this at first." Nora makes her words gentle. "But then you find yourself paralyzed, suddenly realizing that you've heard this voice and seen that face, that you already know what the next sentence in a conversation is going to be."

Putting his hand on my shoulder, Caleb says, "You have to let go. Let go of the boundaries you have set up around fact versus fiction, allow them to expand."

"I don't think I can do that." Honestly, I don't think I can even contain the tsunami of tears that are about to fall.

"I'm afraid you don't have a choice," Nora says. "Whether you like it or not, the Manor found us, and now we're their puppets to poke and prod as they please."

The walls of the maze begin to feel tight. The cut grass and clean air do nothing anymore, and I march back toward the opening. "I refuse to be that for them. It's illegal and I have places to be, plans, people I need to see. I need to get to my mom and make sure she's okay. Ms. Withers, her diamonds, puppets, and needles don't get to dictate my life!"

Nora claps, smiling brightly. "I knew you had some fire tucked away somewhere."

Caleb chimes in with excitement, like a kid in a candy shop. "So, what's the plan?"

I look up at the bulking hedge that towers above us. "That part, I still need to figure out."

Throwing her arm around my shoulders, Nora jostles me in a playful way. "We'll help," she says, then looks toward Caleb and adds, "we've got nothing else going on."

The three of us walk back to the willow tree.

Caleb admits that at school he was quiet and kept to himself, usually eating his packed lunch either in the library or in the third stall of the boy's bathroom. He loves to read and was bullied for it, he says. At his school if you were a boy and weren't on either the football or basketball team, were you even a boy? "Sometimes I'm thankful for the Manor. For once in my life I'm not eating my PB&Js with the librarian," he admits. "But I need to get home just as much as you do, Stella. It's just me and my little brother. We live with our aunt, but she never wanted kids, so she's always either at the local town bar or on the back of her boyfriend's Harley. My brother is only ten, and I have this terrible feeling he hasn't had anything to eat but stale potato chips and sour milk for the last three weeks."

"Where are your parents?" I regret my question the minute it leaves my mouth.

"My mom died giving birth to my brother." Nora grabs Caleb's hand. "And my dad left shortly after. He couldn't stand to be near to what took her away."

"What is your brother's name?"

"Theo."

"Well, I look forward to meeting Theo," I say.

Caleb's smile is contagious, it leaves the three of us grinning like idiots.

Snapping us out of it, Nora brags, "Unlike dear Caleb, I'm the most popular girl in school." And then, "Well, I guess I *was*."

"I guess the Manor took it all away," I say.

"I was worshipped by almost everyone, even some of the teachers. I never got a grade lower than an A-minus, and I was captain of our soccer team. I had the quarterback, a.k.a. the hottest guy at our school, wrapped around my finger, and I know how cliché it sounds, but we were envied by everyone. Nick and Nora, the power couple. We were on track to being prom king and queen."

Caleb shifts uncomfortably when he hears the name Nick.

"And then one day, when I was waiting outside the boy's locker room for him, I found him making out with his running back. I know, I was just as shocked as you. It felt like a giant punch to the gut. I was in love with him. But honestly, it was easier to see him making out with a guy than one of the girls who pretended to be my friend. He seemed less like a backstabbing cheater for some reason. I decided I was just going to quietly walk away without saying anything, but he heard me accidently run into a gym bag and almost fall over. He majorly freaked out. Of course I told him I was hurt but that I wasn't going to judge him. I swore I wouldn't tell anyone. No matter how many times I said I didn't want to ruin his reputation, he kept threatening that if he ever got word that I told someone, he would reply all in an email to the whole school, with a picture of me attached."

I shudder, knowing exactly what type of picture she is talking about. "He didn't send it right?" I ask, feverish for answers.

"That's the icing on the cake," Nora says. "The minute I left the locker room area, people's phones were buzzing and vibrating. He didn't even give me a chance not to tell a soul. Within the span of an hour, I became the school laughingstock. As much as I hate to admit it, I can't help but agree with Caleb for liking the Manor a tiny bit—for getting me away from those immature, pimply, high school nobodies, anyway."

"That's why Nora likes to play it all tough and suave," Caleb jokes.

"One, never say suave again. And two, I am tough."

The two of them joke some more between themselves while I curse myself for ever thinking my high school situation was cruel. At least I had a best friend I could eat lunch with, and nobody called me names or shared intimate pictures of me.

The air around us grows colder and stings our skin as the wind blows in and through the leaves. The segments of sky that peak through the leaves of the willow have slowly become an indistinguishable blue-black. A chorus of crickets' crescendos, and we take that as our cue to go back inside before werewolves start howling at the moon or something.

Caleb stands and helps up Nora, who says, "Yeah, the guards will come out for us soon, and I prefer to put myself to bed."

Jokingly, I ask, "What? Are the guards going to throw you over their shoulder and tell you it's past your bedtime?"

"While it might seem like we are precious cargo, the people running this place don't mind if the guards instill fear in us. The guards will be aggressive if you don't do what they ask, or fast enough." A scowl marks Nora's face. "A week into my being here, I lost track of time and didn't leave the garden fast enough when they began calling for people to come back inside. The guards found me in the maze and dragged me by my arms all the way back to the dormitory, almost giving me permanent grass stains."

"That's assault. That shouldn't be allowed!"

"Another word of wisdom for you, new girl: Everything and anything is allowed when you make the rules. And here, we don't." Nora cocks her head at the Manor, adding, "*They* do."

7

Nora is the unlucky one. As we walk into the dormitory, a male nurse snapping in the direction of her bed calls her name.

"Ugh!" Nora stomps her feet, balls her hands into fists.

I reach out, try to grab her arm. "Nora, don't go. If you do what they want, you're just confirming their power."

Caleb speaks from behind me, "Stella, she has no choice. If she doesn't go, she'll get a matching bruise on the other side of her face."

Nora breaks free of my grasp and sulks toward the nurse, who has begun prepping the glass syringe. I want to grab the needle and hurl it at the floor, send particles of glass and orange goo everywhere.

When Nora gets back into her bed, she pulls her blanket right up to her chin. I get into my own and hope my proximity can help soothe her.

She closes her eyes tight, crinkling the skin around her face as the nurse pushes the needle into her wrist. After retracting the needle, the nurse turns to focus on the computer screen.

I whisper to Nora, "You okay?"

A silly smile spreads across her face. "Never been better."

I want to ask her what she dreamt of last time, but before I can open my mouth, her head lolls to the side. Her breathing is deep and even, her eyelids shut, but beneath them I can see her eyes rolling frantically from left to right, then up and down, sometimes circling. The orange serum is potent. It takes less than a minute before Nora is sleeping deeply and dreaming.

The nurse does a quick once over of the screen, enlarging some graphs and charts before walking off, as if he'd left a candle burning in the other room.

I stare at Nora for what feels like hours, watching her chest rise and fall with each breath. For a little while, Caleb comes over to my bed and distracts me by telling me about some of his favorite movies, but then I catch him repeating sentences and mostly his attention is on Nora's sleeping figure.

A little while later, Lady A clicks into the dormitory and turns off all the lights. "That's the cue for bed," Caleb says.

Caleb gives me a shy smile before giving Nora one last look as he walks back to his bed. He burrows in, trying to get comfortable. I try and do the same, but instead I spend all night tossing and turning, shuddering at the slightest of noises.

Music drifts in through my right ear and then the left. I peel my eyes open, a light crust of sleep having built up around my eyelashes. Supporting my body weight on my right arm, I reach for my phone to turn off the alarm; however, my phone's not there. Neither is my beside table. Instead, a random boy sits up in his bed, his hair ruffled from sleep and his eyes still puffy.

Oh, right.

The music I hear is not my alarm but the Manor's classical music alarm system.

"Good morning." Caleb stands sheepishly at the front of my bed.

I rub my eye with a fist. "Morning."

"Shall we go to breakfast?" He offers me his arm. He really is a sweetheart.

Yawning, I answer, "Sure, yeah, let me just go and brush my teeth."

I shuffle between a few girls at the pink sinks and scrub my teeth clean. A few girls smile at me in the mirror as toothpaste dribbles out of my mouth, and as I walk out of the bathroom, I pray I don't have any dried toothpaste around my mouth, that none has dripped down my shirt. Caleb stands by Nora's bed, where he pulls up the brown blanket and tucks it around the side of her body.

He spots me. "Good as new?"

"Squeaky clean," I say, and he begins toward the door, following behind some stragglers.

"Hey, shouldn't we get Nora up for breakfast?"

"No," he says, turning toward me. "It's best we let her sleep."

I don't budge from in front of her bed. She looks peaceful, but I can't help but notice the slight grimace her lips form, her eyes still moving rapidly under the lids.

Caleb says, "Trust me, she'll still be there when we get back."

When breakfast ends an hour later, Caleb and I return. All the beds in the dorm hall are pristinely made, erasing our night of sleep. The floors are squeaky clean, damp still in some areas. Nora's bed is not made, however. She is still under the blanket, breathing in sync with the machine above her head.

Only about half of us returned to the dorm hall, the others lingered out in the garden, sulked into the library, or were escorted away by guards and nurses.

I sit gingerly on my bed. "Can't we wake her up or some-thing?" I ask. "She's slept plenty, plus, she missed breakfast."

Caleb perches himself on the end of Nora's bed, very careful not to jostle her. "They don't care. They will keep us asleep for multiple meals—days, even—if they are getting useful information."

His words turn my stomach. "They can't get their precious information if we wake her up."

Caleb shakes his head. "I wish we could, but aside from us getting pummeled by the guards, she would be in hysterics." He catches the way I tilt my head, and continues, "The serum they give us puts us into our deepest REM sleep within a matter of seconds, and we don't leave that REM stage until the serum wears off and leaves our system. It's heavy stuff, too. If you wake the person up before the serum runs out, it wreaks havoc on their conscious mind and all sorts of things can happen. I saw it one time when a girl here woke her friend up. The girl sleeping woke up in hysterics and cried twenty-three hours of the day. I woke up that night to the guards pulling her down from the window." He points toward the window closest to us. "That's why they are all sealed now, nearly impossible to open."

My jaw hits the floor. The horrors here never cease. "So, what happened to her?"

"She stopped eating, stopped talking, and when the guards and nurses would yell at her, she would just stare past them, like she was seeing through them. Ms. Withers warned her that her behavior would not be tolerated, but she just sat in her bed all day, catatonic." His voice grows sadder. "One day we woke up and she was gone, her bed cleaned up and ready for someone new."

"She just disappeared, and no one has any idea what happened to her?"

"Well, I bet some people do," he says, looking toward the doors the guards and staff stand behind. "But anyone who does won't tell us anything, that's for sure. We are in complete and utter darkness."

My blood boils at the thought of being put into sleep because these people want *my* dreams. They are in *my* head for a reason. I promise myself then that I will be strong, that I will not grow cowardly in the face of the Manor.

Nora was like Sleeping Beauty, unwillingly sleeping and without a clue of how to wake from the cloak of slumber. There was no Prince Charming coming to slay the dragon and wake her up.

At least, not yet.

The classical music returns hours later, and so too the grunts and groans of tired people who don't appreciate Beethoven's symphony at this hour, if ever. I extend my legs and arms, stretching like a star fish. This bed makes motels seem luxurious. In fact, the only positive thing about it is that my feet don't hang off the end like they would at home, which suddenly doesn't feel like much of a trade. I would do anything to be back home.

Voices flutter around the room, but not Nora's. Her bed is empty.

She's not in her bed? What? Where could she be?

I scan each bed for her. She is nowhere to be seen. I look over to Caleb to see if she was with him, but Caleb is still in his bed, alone, rubbing his tired eyes back and forth.

I get up to search.

I toss the blankets aside and slide down. The floor is cold to the touch, the wood chilled and hard. When I reach the bathroom, I roll my eyes at the pink glow and amble in. I know Nora is in the bathroom before I get a chance to call out for her. I hear faint cries from the last bathroom stall, and I hesitantly walk toward it, having flashbacks to the time I tried to console Blake at school.

Knock, knock, knock.

"Nora...um, it's Stella."

The cries stop, but there's no response. We've only really known each other for less than forty-eight hours, and she probably doesn't want my help. I contemplate leaving the bathroom, getting Caleb. I could leave the situation alone, too, but Nora was there for me in the cafeteria yesterday, and her and Caleb welcomed me with open arms.

"Nora, are you okay?" As if her cries aren't answer enough. "I mean, what's wrong? Whether you like it or not I consider you a friend in here, and my best friend from home would kill me if I left her alone when she was crying…"

Callie is an open book. Her thoughts and emotions are one in the same as mine, that's how tuned-in I am to her. Whether her brother had said something mean to her or she'd been nervous for a test or crushing on someone new, I always knew.

"Stella, you have to let me be a bit mysterious every now and then," Callie once said on the phone after school. She had spent the whole day with her eyes downcast, hardly getting excited over the football team's homecoming announcement.

I called her the minute I got home because I couldn't shake the feeling that something bigger was wrong than just a broken nail or a bad quiz grade. "You don't need to act tough and mysterious with me." A thought occurred to me. "Is it Trooper? Is he alright?" Trooper was her family dog.

There was a sharp intake of breath on the other line, and Callie's voice got wobbly, "How'd you know?"

"Just a feeling. I'm really sorry Callie, I'll come over right now." I didn't know it then, but I knew from a dream. A few weeks before, I had dreamt of Trooper giving Callie slobbery kisses while she wheezed and coughed in between tears. My inclination to ask about Trooper wasn't just a hunch, and it gives me chills.

But I haven't had dreams of Nora and she's much harder to read. So seconds pass with awkward silence. Before I can beg her to talk to me, the lock starts sliding. The door creaks open and I spot Nora's blue pajamas. I ease the door open the rest of the way and find Nora sitting in the corner on the floor with her knees hugged tight to her chest. Her face is buried deep in her crossed arms, her shoulders shaking.

I lean against the wall and slide myself slowly to her level. I sigh, realizing I have no idea how to console her. Do I hug her? Touch her hand? I place my hand on her arm and we sit in the silence of the bathroom stall for a few minutes, both of us trying to regain our sanity.

When Nora finally speaks, her words are weak and laced with hurt. "I don't think I can do this much longer."

"What happened?" I panic, remembering Caleb's story. "Did someone wake you up from your dream?"

Nora shakes her head and lifts it to look at me. "I wish someone had woken me up from my dream."

"What was it about? If you don't mind me asking."

"It was a nightmare, and usually I wouldn't have thought twice about a bizarre dream like this one, but now that I know that my dreams actually mean something, it scared the hell out of me." A single tear rushes down her cheek.

I wish I knew the right words to say to her, but I honestly have no idea what would help her. I'm the new girl, and I'm still grappling and trying to wrap my head around this place and what I'm here for.

"It was my sister," Nora says. "She was in a hospital bed, and my mom and dad were standing next to her. My mom was crying and sniffling into a tissue. My dad hung his head low, his shoulders uncontrollably shaking. Stella, I've never seen my dad cry before, so that can't be good news." The tears come quicker now.

"Oh, Nora, I'm so sorry." Without thinking I push myself onto my knees so I can give her a hug. She is warm in my arms, and I hold her tight as she shakes with each sob.

To my surprise she unhooks her arms and tightens them around my torso, squeezing back hard. The two of us sit there embracing on the surprisingly clean bathroom floor. This feels like I am home, with Callie, sitting on her bed holding her hand as she tells me about how Trooper hasn't been doing well lately, while she scratches him behind the ears with her other. I sense Nora loosening, and I unlatch my arms and sit back.

"I thought I was tough enough to be here and allow them to play with me like a puppet on strings for a little while. But after that dream, I feel like I'm being slowly tortured, unable to call home, warn my family, or even give my sister a hug." I wipe away an escaped tear from Nora's cheek. "You want to know the worst part? The day before I came here, I told my sister I wouldn't care if she was no longer my sister because of a stupid argument we had over clothes. Clothes!" With a loud bang, she slams her head back into the wall. "I'm going to go batshit crazy soon if I don't regain some sense of control."

I nod at her words. It's barely been a full day now and it's already eating at me. Nora's been here for a month, and I can't imagine how that must feel.

"You know," Nora says, "at home, I was a control freak. I had my room in complete order, and I was on top of assignments weeks in advance. My sister was always telling me I needed to loosen up before I popped like a balloon from too much inside pressure. After the Nick incident, my sense of control was shaken, especially the control I had over my image at school. Fast forward, and I'm here living under the fingers and needles of Ms. Withers and her minions. Stella, I don't think I can hold on for much longer, especially if the last words I might have ever spoken to my sister were cruel enough to make her cry."

I shake my head. "We need to get out of here."

Nora's eyes snap to mine, and she laughs. "And how do you suppose we do that?"

"I don't know yet," I say. And then, never having felt more certain of anything in my life, I continue, "But not even Ms. Withers and her minions can keep us from the people that need us the most."

"I appreciate your optimism, but it won't last long."

The pink floor of the bathroom irritates my eyes, but I shake off the dull throb the Manor gives me and look Nora dead straight in the eyes. "We'll watch the nurses and guards, work out where the Manor's weak spots are, and we'll disappear in the night, not a crumb left behind."

At first, she looks at me like I've grown a third eye, but she slowly digests my words and grabs my outstretched hand with her own, squeezing hard, like her hug. "Deal."

I rest back, and we sit for a little while longer before returning to the dormitory, where we find Caleb frantically searching the room for us. His face is redder than his hair, his eyes nearly bursting out of their sockets. Nora chuckles as she follows his desperate steps down the hall, before sneaking over to his bed and throwing herself under his blanket. Turning around he spots her mop of dark brown hair against his white pillow.

"Not funny, you guys. You gave me a heart attack." Caleb swipes the back of his hand across his forehead, wiping away sweat.

"Don't worry," Nora reassures him, flashing a knowing smile. "When we go somewhere important, we'll drag you with us."

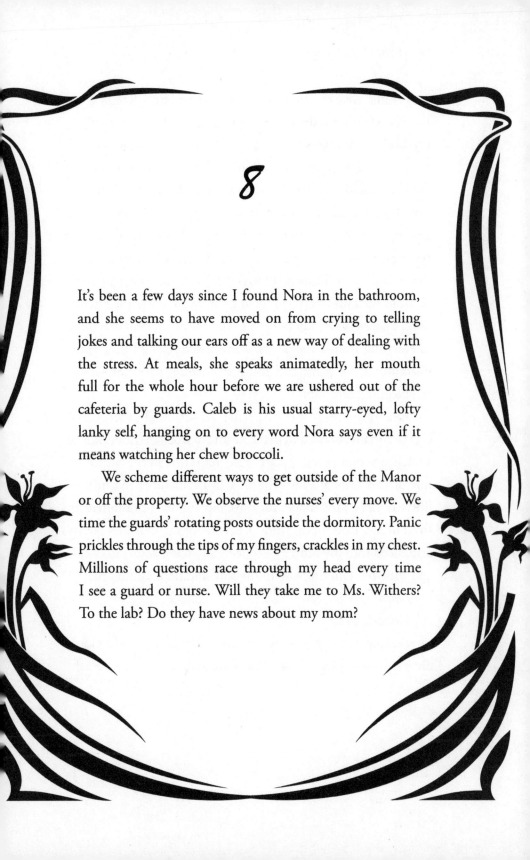

8

It's been a few days since I found Nora in the bathroom, and she seems to have moved on from crying to telling jokes and talking our ears off as a new way of dealing with the stress. At meals, she speaks animatedly, her mouth full for the whole hour before we are ushered out of the cafeteria by guards. Caleb is his usual starry-eyed, lofty lanky self, hanging on to every word Nora says even if it means watching her chew broccoli.

We scheme different ways to get outside of the Manor or off the property. We observe the nurses' every move. We time the guards' rotating posts outside the dormitory. Panic prickles through the tips of my fingers, crackles in my chest. Millions of questions race through my head every time I see a guard or nurse. Will they take me to Ms. Withers? To the lab? Do they have news about my mom?

It is ironic that the only time I get to be stress free is when I sleep, when I am dreaming—when the Manor is controlling my body and brain. I have dreamt twice since I arrived: the first day and yesterday afternoon. Otherwise I have been wide awake, watching other boys and girls, including Nora and Caleb, get called away by guards, disappear for hours on end. During yesterday's breakfast, there was only me and two other people eating. I have no one to sit under the willow tree with or share reading recommendations with in the library. I sit alone at meals, vibrant smells still floating in from under the kitchen door. I lie awake at night, listen to the chorus of even breathing as everyone around me sleeps. The only company I keep is the portraits in the halls, and my flushed pink reflection in the bubblegum bathroom.

One minute I was worrying about ACT scores and eighteenth birthdays, and in the next I am stuck in the middle of a science fiction movie. I stare at my reflection in the bathroom mirror and tears fall into the sink as I remember my normal life. My right arm shoots forward and splinters the mirror in front of me. Pain shoots from the center of my knuckles up my arm, deep into my muscle. I squeeze my hand across my heart and little red rain drops stain the sink and floor around me.

Ouch!

Nobody hears.

Peeking through one eye, I assess the damage. My vision blurs and everything vibrates. The pink bathroom turns to black.

Two warm arms cradle my neck and knees, apply pressure as my body lifts upward. My head lulls toward the mirror, or what's left of it. Pink wall shows from behind the chunks of missing glass, the vanity reduced to some abstract art piece. The light has faded. The night sky finds its way in through the windows and turns the pink walls to a muted magenta. I'm floating through a candy river, the current rushing me along.

Pieces of our bodies show up in the shattered mirror, mine limp and horizontal, the person carrying me hulking and strong. A guard, I think. Are they going to dispose of me like the girl from Caleb's story? All because I broke the mirror? I kick my legs out, trying to break free. The attempt fails, and I knock my head into a pile of bricks posing as a chest. I rotate my head up to inspect my captor's face, or at least I try.

A grumbly voice barrels into the bathroom. "Hey! What are you doing up?"

I make weak eye contact with a stern looking guard. Little miss sunshine makes his way over after spotting my bloodied hand and yanks me into his arms. His arms are less warm than the last. They are painfully taut against my back , and if I was now in the arms of a guard, then who was holding me before?

"Go back to bed," the guard bellows behind him. "Now!"

The guard charges out of the bathroom and down the dormitory. If I weigh anything at all to him, he doesn't let on.

A sarcastic "you're welcome" follows from the person behind us, the voice deep yet youthful, laced with a twinge of playfulness.

"Bed! Now!" Yells the guard, not bothering to look back.

But I do. I crane my neck, hope to place a face with the cryptic voice, but in the shadows of the bathroom entrance, all I can make out is a masculine outline. And then a burst in my chest. The last thing I see in the dark is two blue eyes staring back from the blackness.

Everyone in the dorm remains sound asleep, not bothered by the guard man handling me toward the doors. Everyone expect for the mystery guy in the bathroom.

"Where are you taking me?" I ask the guard, whose response is a barked order to the guards manning the doors, after which he carries me down to the first-floor foyer and toward a door adjacent to the office hallway.

Lady A mentioned this door on her tour.

I shove my non-bleeding hand into his chest, as if that might slow him down. "I want to go back to bed." He doesn't stop walking toward the door. "Please, come on, please! I really don't need to go in there." My voice cracks. I feel tears pooling behind my eyes.

He looks down at me. His voice is stern and unforgiving. "Too late. Maybe you shouldn't have picked a fight with a mirror and stayed in bed." He steps up to the door and lifts his right wrist to the electronic lock pad. He positions his wrist bottom-side up against the lock screen as a red line scans his special security bracelet. The scanner turns bright green, there's a ding. The door opens slowly on its own and once we're through, it closes on itself with a satisfying thud. We enter a long silver empty hallway and he sets me down on the icy floor. I swear I've just stepped into an alien spaceship. The chrome floors and ceilings shine back my reflection. Single light bulbs hang from the ceiling. I squint, readjusting as best I can.

The guard's strong hand shoves between my shoulder blades. "Go," he says, his voice bellowing through the hall.

I turn back to him, my hands held up in confusion. "What is this place? And where do you expect me to go? I have no idea where this alien hallway goes."

His huge hand grabs my right shoulder and pain radiates down my arm, into my mirror-punching hand. I clench my teeth against the pain as he moves me away from the exit.

"I. Said. Go." He bites every word before turning toward the door and rescanning his bracelet.

The door slams shut behind him. I'm alone.

I flip him off with my left hand, hoping my anger burns down the back of his neck. I blow my hair out of my face and turn back to the hallway, count to three, and try to find the courage that will carry me down this hallway. I take a few steps and my bare feet make waddle noises on the chilled chrome floor. My reflection echoes back up at me from the ground. I'm pale, except for the tired circles under my eyes.

A door opens at the end of the hall and I snap my head toward the noise. A man in all white scrubs pulls a gurney out of a room. A woman in a matching dress pushes from the opposite side. Blond hair peeks out from under the white sheet. The shape doesn't move.

Does the Manor have a morgue?

"Hey, what are you doing?" The man calls to me.

The female nurse motions for him to continue with the gurney and makes her way toward me. She looks old and tired, with peppery gray hair and vines of wrinkles, the two deepest lines appearing between her eyes as she squints at me.

"Who brought you here?" Her voice sounds like my grandmother's, but there's no accompanying oatmeal cookie smell.

I wait a few beats. "A guard."

"And what happened to your hand?" She raises her eyebrows in suspicion.

I want to say, "Hey, lady, if anyone here should be suspicious, it's me." I bite my tongue and land on, "I had an accident," which only makes her look grow more suspicious, followed by, "…in the, um, bathroom."

I sound like a toddler. I cringe inwardly at myself.

She waves her hand at my story, either unsure what to make of it or deciding it doesn't matter. "Come with me," she says. "I don't have all day, and you're bleeding all over the floor."

I keep my eyes glued to the floor, watching blood drip from my hand onto the reflective surface like raindrops, reminding me of my yellow rainboots. I follow the nurse down the hallway, where eventually the chrome walls end and windows appear that allow for a look into what seem like desolate hospital rooms. The first room is empty aside from a basic white bed and medical equipment next to it. The one across from it is the same.

Farther down, the rooms are no longer empty. One has a boy with buzzed hair lying on a bed. Carter, I remember. Wires run from his temples, forehead, and scalp to the equipment next to him, which features three television screens, a black box, and a massive glass cylinder filled halfway with a murky purple substance. The gigantic overhead lights bathe the room in a navy glow that spills into the hall.

In the next room, a blonde girl named Katie sits up in the bed with a solemn look on her face. She's crying or has been, and the male nurse from before plays with the screen and instruments next to the bed before detaching a sharp syringe from the glass cylinder and puncturing her arm. The purple liquid moves slowly, appearing almost black through the cord as it moves into her arm. In mere seconds, the veins in her arms turn purple beneath her skin.

He returns the syringe to the cylinder before grabbing cords and sticking them randomly to her chest all the way up to her scalp. He places a see-through mask over her mouth and nose, and in the blink of an eye, her room flushes bright green. The glow is suffocating, it envelopes everything.

I catch up to the nurse if for no other reason than to avoid looking in more windows, light bursting out from each of them—pink, red, purple, orange, more blue and green. I turn my head down to the chrome floor, too afraid to see more.

The nurse holds open a door for an empty room. This one does not glow. Rather than run in the opposite direction, I enter hesitantly, my fingers crossed.

The door slams behind me. I hear the lock move.

"No, no, no!" I yell, rushing over to the door's window.

Instead of the hall, I come face to face with myself. A goddamn mirror, like the ones on detective shows. One side a mirror, the other a window.

I stare at my hopeless reflection.

Time stands still. I keep staring for seconds, minutes, hours—longer, maybe. Veins decorate the undersides of my eyes, the corners of my pale lips. Freckles spatter across the top of my nose and sporadically make their way across the tops of my cheeks. To distract myself I count them, but it gets too hard to remember which ones I've counted. I stop at fifteen. I notice a small, jagged fleck in my right eye—dark brown, almost matching my pupil. Call it sixteen, I guess. My eyes have gold circles enclosing each pupil, making them appear more yellow than green. The usual stack of tears crowds the bottom of my eyes. I have never really looked at myself before. Like, really looked. I've never examined every inch, discovering new lines, colors, freckles, and features, and aside from my eyes, I realize I look a lot like my mom. But there is no life peering back at me, only hopelessness. I've never felt so emotionally and physically exhausted. And at a place designed for people to sleep their lives away, no less.

I wonder if this will be the last time I see my reflection.

The door bursts open and causes me to stumble back, nearly knocking me off my feet. The floor is icy and slick beneath my sweaty, nervous palms. My heart feels like it is going to escape through my chest, try for its own getaway. I struggle to push myself up.

"Did I scare you?" I recognize the voice immediately.

Ms. Withers stands above me in all of her red-lipstick, pressed-clothes-wearing, high-heeled glory. "I, um, was in here for so long by myself that the noise frightened me," I quickly regret admitting.

"I can see that." Her voice is condescending and impatient.

I turn back toward the mirror and push myself up before realizing something. "Were you watching me?"

She laughs. "You caught on quicker than I thought you would. You are very pretty—I don't blame you for staring."

"So, I'm a hamster in a cage for you to just observe, poke, and prod when it suits you best?"

"That's putting it harshly." She shakes her head and takes a few more steps into the room. Pointing at the mirrored window she says, "These are actually for your protection. With these windows, we can monitor patients more properly when nurses and staff are moving throughout the hallway."

"Well, why can't it be both ways then?" I cross my arms and lift my eyebrow, feeling smart with my retort.

"Ignorance is bliss, my dear Stella."

"Okay, well what can I know? Because right now I feel like I've woken up in an alternate universe. A terrifying, sci-fi version of life."

"You are hungry for answers. This is natural: most are agitated when they come to the lab." She gives me a knowing look. "I will give you the answers you seek. Only because our bathroom mirrors are very expensive and the materials hard to source." She looks to my hand and adds, "We'll have a nurse see to that shortly."

Ms. Withers makes me feel like I just stepped off the spinning ride at the summer carnival. She is sharp yet soft. Her words are venom, yet there are hints of affection, and dare I say motherly love. None of the soft parts matter, though. She's the one calling the shots here.

"Let's sit down." Ms. Wither walks over to the bed and pats the other side. She offers, "We'll talk, I'll explain more about what is going on—especially here in the lab."

I sit on the bed across from her and Ms. Withers crosses her legs and places her folded hands on her lap, looking around the room, a proud look on her face that I'd like to slap back into the hallway.

"What would you like to know?" she asks.

I would like to know how to get out of here!

Counting down from ten, I regroup and ask her, "What is this place?" I motion with my good hand around the room and point toward the mirror.

"This is the laboratory of the Manor," she states without elaboration.

"Well, what happens in the laboratory? What are these little rooms for, and why does it look like we're inside a disco ball?"

"Don't get ahead of yourself. One question at a time." She laughs. "You have noticed by now what happens in the dormitory."

I nod.

"In the laboratory, we go a few steps further than just keeping people deep in REM sleep."

"So, what? You guys put people in, like, a coma to sleep?" What starts as a joke ends with me praying she doesn't nod her head.

She nods her head...slightly. "For lack of a better word, yes, that's exactly what we do here. Except the patients are awake when we induce them, because we have found it is too risky to have someone fully asleep when they reach such a deep level of catatonia."

I bunch up my eyebrows, none of her words making sense to me. "What does that mean: catatonia?"

She looks annoyed at having to explain everything. "Catatonia means to be in a state where you are unable to move. Just like when doctors induce a coma to allow for better patient recovery."

Now I laugh. "You can't be saying you guys are like doctors here!"

"You would be surprised how many people working here have graduated from medical school."

"Does that include you?" My voice oozes sass.

"I am being very generous by taking the time to sit here with you and answer your trivial questions. It is within your best interest to not get on my bad side." She adds, "More than you already have."

"I'm sorry," I say. I'm really not, but I can play her game. "This is just a lot for me to process." She stays silent for a minute. "Can we get back to the catatonic stuff, please?"

"Over the years, the Manor has concocted a special serum, an anesthetic of sorts that immediately induces a type of sleep paralysis. While in normal sleep paralysis, you are in-between sleeping and waking—this puts the patient into a state beyond REM. We call it REM Five, as it is the fifth level of sleep we have discovered here in the laboratory."

"And what is so special about REM Five? We all seem to dream perfectly fine in the dorm hall without being in REM Five."

"That is true, but those dreams are like the rest of the world's." Her fiery red nails tap along the pale part of the inside of her arm. "They are slightly fuzzy, short. Lacking in fine details. Nonetheless, those dreams are useful, but we wouldn't be such an esteemed facility if we didn't strive for quality. Have you ever noticed that the better the night's sleep, the more intense your dreams? The nights where you can't tell where your body and the mattress meet, and you wake with dreams you carry for the rest of the day, unable to shake how real they felt—those are the nights when you've entered the body's deepest natural

REM state. That's why we induce you into REM Five here in the laboratory. We want your clearest, most vivid dreams."

The blue eyes leading me through the darkness.

"But it's not natural! It sounds to me like you are risking our health and well-being for clearer colors in our dreams."

Ms. Withers' expression goes slack and bored, as if she's heard this before. "We are not a group of high schoolers half-haphazardly dissecting a frog. We are trained professionals versed in the science of dreaming. Liken the laboratory to being the NASA of dreams. We take any necessary precautions to ensure the safety of the Dreamers and the precise extraction and collection of their dreams."

Extraction. The words makes me want to hurl all over her outfit. "Is that why the rooms are flushed in certain colors? Is that a safety precaution?"

"Exactly." Ms. Withers perks up. "We employ color-controlled rooms to ensure that each dreaming experience is best suited to their individual qualities. We study your behavior outside of the laboratory while monitoring your brain activity during your dreams in the dormitory. We note how you act once you enter the laboratory, and then we assign a color to each Dreamer depending on what would be most beneficial. Blue is the calmest color and immediately soothes a troubled mind." She looks me straight in the eyes, as if to say, "like yours."

"What about the others? I saw pink and purple and green and…"

"The other colors are for other needs. Pink wakes up your cerebrum. Purple calms whilst soothing anxiety, same with green, which also relaxes muscles. If we know a Dreamer is fidgety, we use green. Red is my favorite color."

"I can see," I say directly to her cherry lipstick.

"Red targets the temporal lobe, which controls facial recognition. We have discovered it plays an important role in the creation of dreams. When your temporal lobe is active, your dreams appear clearer and more precise. The littlest details— eye color, street signs, nose hair, you name it—we can see it all when your brain is swathed with red."

"And you say this is for our safety?" The words sound silly coming from my mouth.

She smiles at this. "You're getting the hang of it!"

"Wait a minute, how long do these people…?" I don't know what to call what they do in here. I imagine being laid out here, fully conscious yet helpless, like I've been buried alive.

"See. We call it seeing because the patients' eyes are open. Usually your dreams are in your head, merely figments of your imagination; however, here, with your eyes open, they are visualized in front of you. You are quite literally seeing in a whole new way." Motioning around the room, she continues, "This space was specifically designed to bounce the colored light off of every surface while also acting as a projector for your dreams, reflecting the colors while also playing the dreams along their chrome mirrored surfaces." That proud look spreads across her face again. "We've really mastered it all here."

"Yay for the Manor," I quip, the world's least enthused cheerleader. I stand up from the bed, needing to create some distance between us. "How long do people see for?"

"I didn't answer the first time you asked because there is no set time, just like in the dormitory." My heart sinks. "We keep you in the state for as long as we need. A few minutes, an hour, a day—" her expression darkens, "or longer."

I clench my fists tight, suddenly reminded of my injury but not backing off. "This is—"

"I need you to get this in your head: you are not in charge here, I am. I will decide what you do, when you do it, and for how long—no matter how cruel and wrong you think it is."

She rises from the bed and begins pacing, fun house copies of her pop up around the room, a Ms. Withers to my right, a Ms. Withers to my left, a Ms. Withers above, below, and in front of me. And then all of them stop, fix themselves on one common point of interest: me. "Don't worry, Stella. Your time will come. Sooner rather than later, in fact, and you'll yearn for the days you had the library all to yourself."

She stomps toward the door, stopping once her hand touches the handle. "Oh, and Stella," she says, making eye contact with me through the mirror and then with my bleeding hand. "Don't forget, we're always watching."

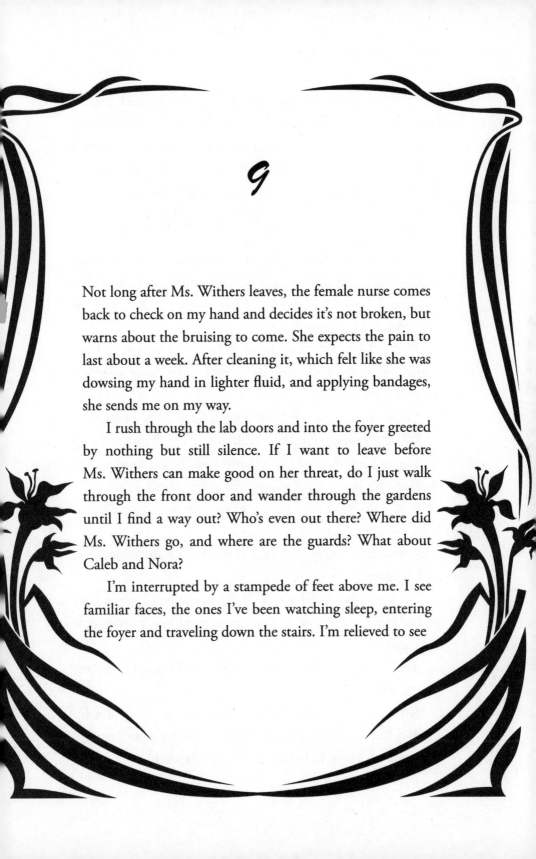

9

Not long after Ms. Withers leaves, the female nurse comes back to check on my hand and decides it's not broken, but warns about the bruising to come. She expects the pain to last about a week. After cleaning it, which felt like she was dowsing my hand in lighter fluid, and applying bandages, she sends me on my way.

I rush through the lab doors and into the foyer greeted by nothing but still silence. If I want to leave before Ms. Withers can make good on her threat, do I just walk through the front door and wander through the gardens until I find a way out? Who's even out there? Where did Ms. Withers go, and where are the guards? What about Caleb and Nora?

I'm interrupted by a stampede of feet above me. I see familiar faces, the ones I've been watching sleep, entering the foyer and traveling down the stairs. I'm relieved to see everyone awake and no longer dead asleep. I study each passing face, note the ways their eyes dance from the floor to the banister to the ceiling and to the other faces around them. Everyone looks happy to see each other, as if they are kids on the first day of school. A twinge in my chest: Katie and Carter are nowhere amongst the group. They're trapped in the laboratory.

"Stella!"

Caleb waves frantically from the top of the stairs. Nora tries to shove his hands down out of embarrassment, and I'm glad to see them as they fall in line and follow everyone else down the stairs and into the main foyer.

I meet them at the bottom of the stairs. "Hey, guys," I say, trying to keep my cool when all I want to do is throw myself at them and never let go.

What was I thinking? I could never leave without them.

"Where have you been?" Caleb asks. "We all just woke up in time for breakfast and you weren't there. Nora panicked and thought they had taken you to the lab or something."

Breakfast already? Strips of sunshine slip through the cracks of the wooden doors.

I must have really lost track of time since my incident in the bathroom.

Nora punches Caleb's arm. "I did not panic. I might have freaked out, but it's never a good sign around here when people disappear."

The cafeteria smells of greasy bacon and fresh eggs, and my mouth waters.

Sitting down, fork and knife in hand, ready to dig in, Caleb finally notices my hand. "Jesus! What happened there?" he mumbles, a fork full of egg in his open mouth.

Before I can answer, Nora does. "She had a date with the bathroom mirror," she says, giving me a knowing smile that only confuses Caleb more.

I say, "I punched a mirror then proceeded to throw up and pass out from the ensuing pain." Now I turn to Nora. "How did you know?"

Before gulping down a mouthful of orange juice, she says, "I had to brush my teeth, didn't I?"

I flex my hand, barely extending my fingers fully. Caleb continues to eat while Nora shadowboxes next to him.

In record time, our forks are scraping empty plates.

Caleb sits back, rubbing his stomach. "Funnily enough, I wouldn't mind taking a nap after that delicious breakfast."

The irony has us all laughing into our plates and loosening the drawstrings on our pants.

Bang!

Our laughter is interrupted by the cafeteria door flying open and hitting the wall followed by hushed angry voices. Three massive bodies tumble in, two of them guards dressed in their spy-black outfits and the third, a struggling figure between them, is a boy dressed in blue. The guards grunt and shove him into the cafeteria. Everyone in the room watches the mid-morning entertainment from the edges of their seats, eager to see who is joining us for breakfast. The boy rises from his crouched position at the front of the cafeteria. *Boy* seems unfitting as he seems to go on forever. He's easily over six feet tall, and he shakes his legs and cracks his knuckles, following the guards with his eyes as they hastily leave the cafeteria. Once the door slams shut, he lifts both hands and gives the door a glorious double-bird salute. My kind of guy. Most the room's, too, judging by the eruption of laughter, a few going so far as to clap even.

Finally, he turns around, and I'm shoved back in my chair.

His eyes are the first thing I notice.

A vivid blue cuts through the room like a beam wherever he looks, and then his eyes settle on me. My face goes red, a heat rises in me. He notices the empty chair beside me. My heart rate skyrockets. A small smile plays at the corner of his lips, and he begins this way. My fork slips from my hand, clattering onto the table. The noise startles me out of the blue-eyed trance and he is called over to another table by some boys to my right.

"Stella…hello?" Nora waves her hands back and forth in front of my face, forcing me to focus on her.

I shake my head, clearing off the fog. "Sorry, sorry, I, um, just got a bit distracted."

Caleb and Nora laugh.

"You could say that again," Nora says.

"How come you don't look at me like that when I walk in the room, Nora?" Caleb asks jokingly, which is followed by another punch to his arm, my turn this time.

The boy has settled a few tables diagonal from ours, he is sitting at my ten o'clock. I feel stuck, glued to my chair. I take three deep breaths, attempting to calm my heart. Once I no longer feel like I've just raced a marathon, I glance his way.

He's already staring back at me. Our eye contact feels like a tidal wave building out of nowhere on a calm sea. Never the best swimmer, I avert my gaze. It's safer than his eyes, anyway.

"We find you with a nearly broken hand outside of the laboratory, and now you are acting like you've seen a ghost." Nora won't let anything slide. "What's up with you?"

"I kind of do feel like I've seen a ghost," I admit.

Caleb and Nora look each other before Caleb says, "Sorry to disappoint, but there are no ghosts here. This place may be old but no midnight walkers here."

"Don't ever say midnight walkers again," Nora says, more threatening than joking.

From my left ankle to my left ear, I feel a fire from the inside. It's how I used to feel in class when Mr. Clarke would stand, arms crossed, feet tapping, at the front of the classroom as he waited for me to answer his question. I never knew the answer, though, because he usually had caught me daydreaming out the window. Waiting for him to move on to the next student was a torturous handful of seconds. Now all I can do is look back down at my folded hands in my lap.

"Don't look now, but he's staring at you," Nora says.

I snap my head up. "Who is he?" I ask.

Caleb says, "That's Charlie."

"You guys know him?"

"Yeah, of course. He's been here longer than us."

I rack my head. "But I've never seen him before. And trust me, while everyone was dreaming, I got very well aquatinted with people's sleeping faces."

"I'm the best-looking person here, right?" Nora asks.

Caleb answers before I can. "Nora! Stay on track, we are telling Stella about the love of her life."

"Caleb!" My face flushes. "He is not!" I cross my arms. "It's just that I feel like I know him, or at least I've seen him before today."

A puzzled look crosses Nora's face. "Well, you definitely haven't seen him before now. He was taken to the lab the morning you arrived."

I shudder, the very thought of the lab making me want to throw up my eggs and bacon. "But I was there this morning, and I didn't see him there."

"You were in the lab this morning?!" Both Caleb and Nora yell at the same time, earning some questionable glances from our neighboring tables.

"I was, but that's not important right now." I dismiss their curious faces and continue with my inquiry into Charlie. "Charlie has been in the lab for multiple days now without coming out?"

"Yep, that's how it works," Caleb answers, just as Nora says, "If they decide to keep you dreaming for longer than twenty-four hours, they attach an IV to you so you don't die of dehydration. Kind, right? They take Charlie to the lab a lot."

I'm floored by how casually they answer, as if what they are talking about is not a big deal. "So, I'm guessing his dreams are important then."

Caleb shrugs. "No one knows. Charlie doesn't really talk much to anyone, and if he does it usually consists of 'move' or 'watch it.'"

"Oh, so he's a jerk?" Why do I suddenly feel let down?

"That's not what Caleb is saying," Nora answers. "What he means is that Charlie keeps to himself, and like most of us, he keeps his head down, avoiding eye contact with anyone who could keep him imprisoned in his sleep for days on end."

Before I can inquire any more, the staff pushes carts toppled with cleaning supplies into the room, the smell of dishwasher soap announcing the end of breakfast. I kick my chair back, standing with Nora and Caleb and getting ready to leave. But before I do, I glance over to where Charlie is sitting.

He's gone.

Some people are forced back up to the dormitory while others are greeted by nurses outside of the cafeteria. I now understand where certain people would disappear to. They weren't hiding in the bathroom or lost in the garden maze. No. They were comatose, bathed in color, forced to see until their eyes dried out.

The glow of the laboratory hallway peeks through the open door as nurses drag people in. Ms. Withers is a terrible person and wrong about a lot of things, but there is one thing about which she was correct: Ignorance *is* bliss.

Caleb and Nora want to go outside while the sunny day lasts. They say their best moments in this "hell hole" are when they're blissfully alone under the willow tree, the warmth of the sun creeping through the falling leaves, a chance to pretend they're elsewhere. When they ask if I want to go outside with them, the matchmaker inside of me says "no thanks," giving them time to themselves. Anyway, after the morning's onslaught, I need some time to myself, to let the words in my head slow down. I opt to take a breather in the library, where the tips of my fingers glide across the crackled old spines in a comfortable quiet. It's not so eerie as other parts of the Manor, and it has quickly become one of my favorite places here. The books cushion the room, keep it from feeling like a stiff, frigid space. My favorite feature of the library is the wooden ladder tall enough to reach the top stack that leans against the bookcase. It was stuck at first, hard to move due to lack of use. Most of the books are covered in a light layer of dust, the top ones especially dusty, making me sneeze every time I climbed the ladder.

My last visit in the library had been interrupted by the dinner bell. Scrambling down the ladder, I'd left a book I was interested in behind. Now, the ladder sits where I left it, only my fingerprints having disturbed the dust.

I stand on the fifth rung, scanning titles and reading synopses until my knees feel stiff from the ladder. I climb a few more rungs, stretching my legs. The top shelf is by far the dustiest and least familiar with human contact. Pulling the first book that sparks my interest, I pray that my disturbance doesn't unearth a spider or anything with more than two eyes. Instead, a wave of dust kicks up and twirls toward me like a tornado. Immediately I feel the tell-tale tingles in my nose and sneeze.

"Bless you."

The book I am holding jumps from my hands as I stumble on the ladder from the fright caused by the voice behind me. If Nora hadn't been vehement that there were no ghosts here— "midnight walkers," as Caleb calls them—I would have had my suspicions, but I've heard this voice before. Attempting not to fall off the ladder and add broken leg to my injuries, I shift my body slowly around on the ladder.

Charlie.

His smile is mischievous, and he says something I can't make out before chuckling, "Are you all right?"

I shake my head, cover up my nerves as best I can. "I'm fine, why?"

"I didn't mean to scare you."

"I didn't hear you come in. Your voice…"

"My voice what?" His voice is dead serious.

"It startled me." He doesn't look satisfied with my answer. "I wasn't expecting anyone else to be in here, that's all." He knows that my surprise wasn't just from thinking a ghost was blessing my sneeze. "I also feel like I've heard your voice before," I sheepishly admit.

The upturned side of his mouth goes down and he grows serious. "Come down from up there."

I raise my eyebrow, not liking being told what to do.

"Please," he adds.

I carefully climb down the ladder, and when I reach the last two rungs, he holds my sides, warming me. I freeze in motion. They are huge, his palms resting on the sides of my stomach while the ends of his fingers curl around to lay on my back. I clumsily jump forward from the ladder, forcing his arms to detach from my sides, which suddenly feel cold without him.

He must notice the awkwardness seeping from my every pore, because he tries to fill the uncomfortable air with conversation. "Do you like to read?"

"Love to," I say, walking over to another stack of books, attempting to act casual and not freaked out by the emotions running through me. "What about you?"

He walks over to some books, picks one up, and flips the pages mindlessly. "I indulge every once in a while."

I can't help but let a laugh escape.

"What's so funny?" he asks.

"It's just the way you said 'indulge,' as if reading were some vice you give into at your weakest moments."

"Well, what would like me to say then?"

His sounds slightly pissed off, and I panic. "Everything. I need to place your voice, I've heard it before. I just know I have."

Oh my God. I said that out loud and not in my head.

I stop dead in my tracks, no longer casually perusing the shelves. He stops too and turns to face me.

I really wish he hadn't done that, because now as he looks at me head on, I find myself distracted by his appearance. He seems taller up close than he did in the cafeteria. The parts of his body that come out from under his blue uniform are slightly tanned. Veins bulge in his arms and travel down to his wrist. His long lean fingertips hang at mid-thigh. His jawline comes to a perfect point at his chin, which has a slight bit of stubble. His nose comes to a blunt point and points upward, toward his dark, defined eyebrows. His chocolate brown hair swings mindlessly around his face, sometimes covering his eyes. Peeking out from his hair, are two little round ears that stick out the slightest bit.

And then there are his eyes. I feel lost at sea.

"Paint me like one of your French girls while you're at it," he says, his voice deep yet boyish.

Cool is the furthest thing from my middle name.

"While you're *devouring* every inch of my face and body, I mean." He laughs and walks over to the long couch at the back of the library.

Devouring.

He throws himself down on the couch. "You know, it's usually common courtesy to at least get to know someone before you shamelessly check them out."

"I was not shamelessly checking you out." I try my best to imitate his voice.

"Then what were you doing?"

Shit.

There was a fly, food in your teeth, leftover egg on your cheek. All of my excuses sound like exactly that, and so I shoot for honesty. "I have this strong sense that I've met you before, known you my whole life or something. I guess I was just looking at you to try and figure out where I could place you from."

While also drooling at your face.

Something ticks in his eyes. His cool demeanor is slipping away slowly, as his body seems to curl in on itself from head to toe. His looks at the floor, as if no longer able to look at me. With his head hanging low, lengths of brown hair hide his eyes, prompting his hands to anxiously yank away the obtrusive strands.

I say, "Your eyes, they—"

"Stop!" He shoots up from the couch and takes a quick look at me and then back to the ground. "I need to go."

His shoulder brushes mine lightly, leaving me in his electric wake, and I throw myself down on his spot in the couch, surrounded by his smell and lingering presence.

10

The three of us gather on Caleb's bed, like three girls at a sleepover, Caleb and Nora badgering me about why I was in the lab earlier that morning until I tell them everything, tiny details and all. Nora's been to the lab, though Caleb has heard plenty of whispers about the chrome section of the Manor.

"Let's just say the popular opinion is not great," Nora remarks about the lab. "It was really crazy in there, not at all like the rest of the Manor."

Caleb hangs on every word like a kid listening to a ghost story. All I'm missing is the flashlight shining in my face. "Everything was shiny chrome and bright—sterile feeling, too. I felt like I had been abducted by aliens and was on their spaceship."

Nora adds, "I feel like that every day."

"From what we know so far, Ms. Withers and the like aren't aliens," Caleb says.

"I wouldn't be so sure." I lower my voice. "She is too perfect, her lipstick is never off, always perfectly applied. Red lipstick is impossible to apply!"

"Plus, how the hell does she walk around in those sky-high heels?" Nora looks perplexed by the idea.

"I got it!" I say, my voice a little too loud. "She has to be a robot, you know, like *Ex Machina*."

We switch topics, exchange our most embarrassing moments, memories from our lives, and Instagram—anything to pass the time. The others stare as our laughter builds to an annoying crescendo, Nora sometimes snorting when she laughs too hard. High on our giddy happiness, the three of us float up from Caleb's bed, soar away from the Manor, leaving everything dark behind.

Sleepless nights with Callie, discussing anything and everything, come to mind. Whether at my house or hers, we would strip our beds, grabbing all the pillows we could find, and build a fortress in the living room. Within the electric glow of a flashlight covered in a sequined top Callie owned, the two of us would lie under the clean white sheet that looked like an early morning sky that still had a few stars lingering. We would watch movies from dusk until dawn, never sure of the time until we could hear parents in the kitchen firing up the coffee machine. Or we'd gossip, talk about which celebrity couple we couldn't believe was breaking up and who we wished would get together. Those moments under sheets propped up between armchairs and pillows were blissful, and Caleb, Nora, and I reached moments of happiness like them that only last like blinks of an eye before the inevitable nurse or guard ruins the moment.

I wonder what Callie is doing right now. Is she worried about me, wondering where I am? Has she put up posters with my face around town? I imagine my mom in a hospital bed recovering from her wounds, while Callie sits biting her nails in the chair adjacent to the bed.

"Hey, what's up?" Nora asks.

I shove my worries aside. "Nothing, I'm fine."

"Are you sure?" Caleb asks. "One minute you're holding your stomach from laughing so hard, and now you are staring blankly into the ceiling."

Nora's hard to fool. They both are.

"Geez, you guys are really observant." I laugh to lighten the mood I've soured, or try to anyway. "I was just thinking about my best friend from home, wondering if she was worried about me. My mom, too. I was thinking about her."

Nora scoots toward me and gives me a hug. "I'm sure everyone at home is worried about you, sounds like you had—" she corrects herself, "—*have* a lot of people who care about you."

Caleb joins in on our hug. "Including us!"

Before Nora can shove us off, someone asks, "What's wrong?"

We separate and find at the foot of Caleb's bed none other than Charlie, who has the nerve to look concerned.

"What do you want?" I ask sternly.

"Are you sad?"

"Why do you care? With the way you stormed off earlier, you seem like you could care less about talking to me." My voice gets louder and angrier with every word, surprising everyone, myself included. "Where were you even going off to?"

Caleb and Nora move back on the bed and out of the cross fire.

Charlie shakes his head. "I had somewhere to be."

"Ha! Pathetic. Spare me the lies; where would you possibly have to go? The lab, to beg to be put into a dream coma so you don't have to spend another minute talking to me?"

"No, you're wrong." Charlie grabs at my arm. "That's not how I feel."

"Then how to do you feel? Why did you act that way? I was just trying to talk to you. Everyone here is already mean enough—you don't have to be."

His gaze is almost scarier than Ms. Withers'. I don't like the way his eyes roam back and forth between mine, the way it feels like he's reading my mind. I hold my breath, hoping, pleading, praying he will say something to ease the knot in my chest.

He says nothing.

"That's what I thought." I pull my arm from his grasp. "Leave me alone."

I rush to the bathroom, needing a minute to cool off. I hear chuckles from behind me and Nora saying, "Damn, she showed you!"

Why did he make me so angry? I don't even know him, and the only person I ever really get angry with is my mom, because I feel comfortable enough with her to speak my truth. There is something about him, his presence, something that affects me like no one else does. I don't like it. I feel out of control, like I'm running and can't slow down.

A girl emerges from a bathroom stall, but I hardly notice. After what feels like the one hundredth time walking the length of the bathroom, I freeze.

The bathroom.

It's spotless, clean, and pink as ever. All the mirrors above the sinks are too perfect to touch, not a single smudge mars them, not a single piece of glass out of place.

A headache forms between my eyes, pounds harder as I breathe in huge gulps of the ammonia-soaked air. I would kill for some Advil, but in my search of the cabinets I find nothing of the sort. Instead, I find a flashing red light. Tucked away behind a deodorant bottle, a camera peers through, with the perfect view of the bathroom.

"We're always watching."

Ms. Withers' warning raises goosebumps across my body.

Nora comes into the bathroom, walks over to me. "Hey, are you all right? That was quite the show you and Charlie put on."

I pull her close the second she's close enough.

"Whoa, hey," she exclaims as I pull her into a hug. She tries to push me away from her, but I hold her tight. "What are you doing?"

I whisper, "Stop, I don't know if they are listening to what we say."

"Listening? What do you mean, we're in the bathroom?"

"The cabinet, behind the deodorant—I found a camera." She tries to move to look but I don't let her. "Don't, if you look, then they'll know I found it."

"A camera!" Nora shakes with anger. "Oh my God. This place is even more insane than I originally thought. Now *I* want to punch a mirror."

"Now we know for sure that they are watching us, probably always. And they could be listening, too."

"Ms. Withers and her minions are going to seriously regret the day they did this to all of us."

"You can say that again."

Nora clears her throat. "I know you are trying to have us act natural right now, but I'm pretty sure this minute-long hug we're having probably seems less than natural."

"Oh, yeah, right." We break apart, both casually standing at the sinks.

We look at each other through our reflections, mischievous expressions spreading across our faces.

Nora tips her head toward the door. She's right—we should go tell Caleb.

Lady A meets us outside of the bathroom. Unlike the guard from earlier, she waits patiently outside the pink glow.

Does she know we found the camera?

"Stella." Lady A's voice is serious, ready for business.

"Yes…"

"It is time for you to dream." Lady A turns around, wasting no time at all. "Come with me."

I turn to Nora, who stands near the door with a pitying look. I mouth to her, "Oh my God, what do I do?"

"You have to go," Nora whispers. "Now that we know there are cameras around, I don't think running is an option." She adds, "At least not yet."

I follow Lady A to my bed like a prisoner to the gallows, no one seeming bothered by my panic-stricken aura. None of this is out of the ordinary to anyone here. Two guards join us, one on either side of my bed.

"Get in," a guard barks.

I crawl under the covers, attempting to get as comfortable as possible.

"How long will I sleep?" I ask, holding back tears that Lady A can hear in my voice all the same. I'm sure of it.

"At least for the rest of the day, possibly the whole night." This makes me feel slightly better. "Maybe more."

My heart drops.

Lady A types something into the machines next to my bed and the guard next to me prepares by strapping a rubber band tightly around my forearm. He pinches the soft skin at the crease of my arm looking for a vein. A few weird beeping sounds come from the machines next to me, and Lady A clasps her hands.

"All right, all set and ready." She looks down at me. "Do you have an issue with needles, Stella?"

"No, not usually."

I definitely have an issue with what you guys are doing with these needles, however.

"No need to strap you down then," Lady A makes sure the guards hear this. They walk away after handing her the syringe.

Her manicured nails clink against the syringe, orange liquid sloshing around the tube. I look down the hall, feverishly searching for any distraction from the needle. I catch eyes with Charlie, who sits up a few beds down from mine, his fists balled at his sides and his eyebrows furrowed as he watches Lady A insert the needle into my arm. Unbothered by her, my focus is glued to the piercing eyes down the hall. I find them soothing, appearing like a faraway oasis to a lonely desert traveler.

What begins as a heaviness in my toes slivers upward like a snake into every corner of my body, finding its way to the tips of my fingers, to the top of my scalp. The coldness settles deep into my bones. My teeth chatter painfully. Charlie's stare is the only thing rooting me in consciousness, while on the inside I play tug-o-war with a beckoning force.

I blink. Once, twice, a third time before his blue eyes fade black, and I can hold on no longer.

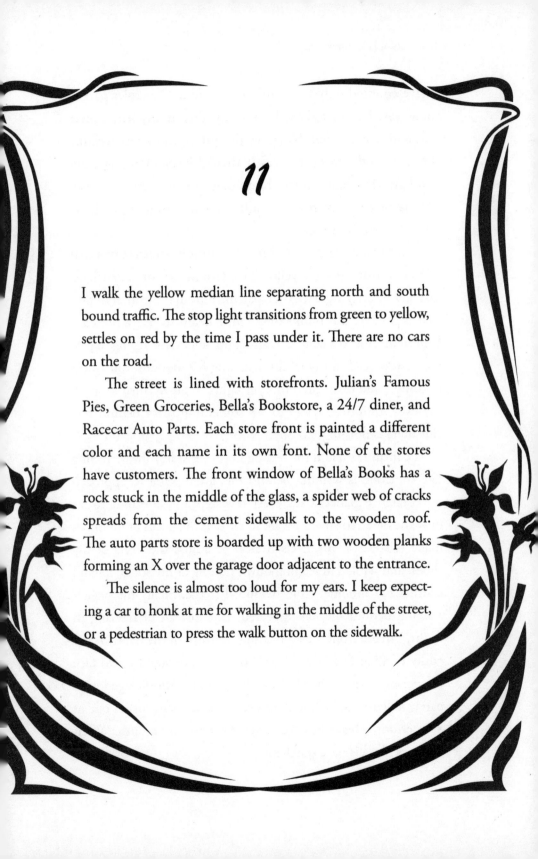

11

I walk the yellow median line separating north and south bound traffic. The stop light transitions from green to yellow, settles on red by the time I pass under it. There are no cars on the road.

The street is lined with storefronts. Julian's Famous Pies, Green Groceries, Bella's Bookstore, a 24/7 diner, and Racecar Auto Parts. Each store front is painted a different color and each name in its own font. None of the stores have customers. The front window of Bella's Books has a rock stuck in the middle of the glass, a spider web of cracks spreads from the cement sidewalk to the wooden roof. The auto parts store is boarded up with two wooden planks forming an X over the garage door adjacent to the entrance.

The silence is almost too loud for my ears. I keep expecting a car to honk at me for walking in the middle of the street, or a pedestrian to press the walk button on the sidewalk.

I have counted only four cars so far: a blue Chevrolet parked some ways back, a red truck parallel parked to my left; a silver one and a black one blocking the intersection I'm walking through, both sitting here as if their drivers simply got out and left. The engine is still humming as I near the black car. The navigation screen is on and the air conditioning is set on high. No one is inside.

I keep walking. I walk through multiple intersections that transition from green to yellow to red for no cars or pedestrians, just my ghostly figure. After passing through an intersection that is broken and blinks only red, I begin to feel a presence behind me, like someone is rushing up behind me trying to pass me. I stop dead in my tracks, listening for footfalls, but I hear nothing aside from the blinking lights. I slowly turn around, my eyes squinting, ready to see something scary behind me. But there is nothing, no one.

I continue on and the feeling never subsides, always feeling like someone is walking behind me, attempting to approach me. I chance glances back every few steps but continue to see only the deserted street. I walk so far that the backs of my shoes make blisters on my heels. I stop to adjust the heels of my shoes, and while I'm leaning down pulling at my socks, a hand brushes my shoulder from behind. I freeze, finally the person stalking behind me has appeared. But instead of freezing in fright, I freeze from the comforting warmth of the hand, at the oddly familiar feel of the hand. Before I can stand up to face the person, a door ahead of me dings, and a middle-aged man barely able to hold a bunch of brown paper bags rushes out of a storefront, a black face mask over his nose and mouth. When he spots me, his pace quickens.

"Excuse me!" I call, sliding back into my shoes, ignoring the confusing presence at my back, and I follow him. "Where is everyone?"

He doesn't stop to answer. Instead he throws his bags into the black car that is still running in the road before climbing into the driver's seat.

I pound on the window, trying to grab his attention. "Hey!"

He shifts into drive without acknowledging me. The car launches forward and almost knocks me over, narrowly missing my feet. I can see into the shop he ran out of, its door hanging sideways, barely swinging from the top hinge. The glass covering the sidewalk is the only evidence that a window once existed there. Inside, the shelves are knocked over, some leaning onto others. I lift my leg up and over the windowsill, mindful of the shards still stuck in the frame. The floor is covered in ransacked products, and I wander down what used to be the candy aisle, Sweet Tarts and lollipops crunching under my feet. At the back of the store, the clerk desk stands empty, the cash register open and empty. A bottle of hand sanitizer lies on its side, the gooey liquid dripping off the counter.

I move toward another destroyed aisle, this one covered in cosmetics and empty medicine bottles. I walk carefully, trying not to stain my shoes with all the pink nail polish that's seeped into the carpeted ground. I'm almost to the open window when I hear glass crack behind me, and then footsteps drawing closer. The smell of apples and spices hits my nose. I throw my arms up, my eyes instinctively scrunch shut. But the person never crashes into me. Instead I'm hit with a salty wave that lulls me back and forth, carrying me farther out to sea. A new wave comes, pushes me back, closer into shore. I float atop the water; it is comfortably warm, and the sky above is cloudy, not a speck of blue. Gray and white clouds fill my sight. I am no longer in the destroyed store but floating on the ocean, the transition between places happening heartbeat quick.

Another wave builds and I smell the salt as it crashes down on my body, pushing me under the surface. Sea water rushes up my nose, burning the back of my throat. I extend my legs and sink my feet into the sand before I push up, bursting through the water. My eyes sting now covered in a light layer of salty residue and I blink a few times before my vision clears.

As I barely stay afloat amid the monstrous waves that crash upon me like the angry jaw of a sea monster, I feel hopeless, scared, and lost. Ocean water burning the insides of my nose as I inhale bunches of it. I wish to be at home, in the comforting warmth of my house, where my mom unknowingly sings her favorite songs as she cooks dinner. I wish to be with my dad, enveloped in his tall, long arms, his sweet and spicy cologne tickling my nose. I wish my dad was here with me now, pulling me from the ocean like he did when I was eight, when the waves at the beach hit my feet and swept me away. My dad pulled me from the choppy shoreline as I gurgled and spit spicy sea water from the surface of my lungs. I held onto him for the rest of that beach day, his sun-warmed chest comforting to my trembling salt-covered body.

The shore seems like a single speck of sand floating farther and farther away from me. I watch a wave as it crashes onto shore, upheaving a muddy mix of whitewash and sand. When the water clears, I notice a figure on the beach. Their arms flail, as if calling me to shore. I see only the outline of the moving body, hearing only the faint outline of a deep male voice above the sloshing waves around me. The figure is hypnotizing, pulling me toward them and acting as a life vest as an energy kicks in and surges my legs to keep kicking, holding me above the waterline.

I open my mouth to yell in response to them, but before I can make a sound, a wave rushes over my head, making me swallow an uncomfortable amount of water. The pressure is too strong for my sore legs to keep treading, and I begin a slow descent to the bottom of the sea.

As I descend, I think of home and what home means and has meant to me. And before my feet hit sand again, I think of blue eyes.

Like a movie, my next dream starts.

12

Light filters in through my eyelids, and I begin to hear more and more voices. A nurse's face comes into view. She stands above me, her long dark hair tickling me as it brushes the bridge of my nose. She straps something around my arm and it begins to squeeze tighter until she unlatches it. The screen beeps a few times as she aggressively punches something in.

A few minutes later she walks away.

Only a handful of people are in the hall—some sleep, others chat. Nora and Caleb's faces are nowhere to be seen, and I can't help but look for Charlie. He's not here either. The lack of natural light here keeps me from figuring out what time of day it is. I have no idea how long I have been asleep for. All I do know is that my bladder feels like it weighs twenty pounds, and I rush to the bathroom.

After taking care of business, I stand in the flush of pink, the soft tap of water droplets in the sink acting like a metronome, hypnotically transporting me back to my dreams, the memories of which course through my body, the accompanying emotions of each dream visceral and clear in my fingertips; however, the lack of clear meaning in them makes my head spin. What did they mean, and why did I have them? My legs feel weak and heavy, as if imaginary weights bind me to the glossy pink floor.

I yearn to breathe fresh air. I hurry past the guards and into the hall of creepy old portraits, noticing that the one next to Ms. Withers' is still empty. Carefully avoiding eye contact with the fake Ms. Withers, I descend the stairs and head for the doors leading to the garden.

I would like nothing more than to walk outside and find a car waiting for me, the engine revving and hot, the driver willing to go wherever I commanded. Instead, there is only the expanse of lush green that is the Manor's gardens, no smoky exhaust in the air. There is no sign of Caleb and Nora outside, only the soft chatter of bugs and the sway of the grass in the wind.

I begin to run, wishing I might escape my dreams, leaving the horrors of the Manor in my wake. I run past the weeping willow, under the rose entryway, and into the maze. The towering magnificent green hedges surround me. My feet move quickly, as if on their own, turning this way and that.

Left or right?

I can barely catch my breath. The maze is ongoing, a never-ending mind trick. Where I could once decipher between spots of dirt and mud amidst the grass and leaves, everything now is a blend of green, the ground tilting upward creating the walls around me. The sky disappears as I travel deeper and deeper.

Hidden and protected by the towering hedges, the unease and stress slowly fade with each stride. I burst through a final stretch of maze and make it to an opening, lit up by the descending sun and its accompanying orange and pinks.

At the center of the open space is a fountain. Giant and bronze, a moon and star intertwine as if in an embrace, with water cascading around them and trickling into the base.

On the tip of the light breeze, and moving water, I can hear the familiar, "I love you to the moon."

Stepping into the open space, I close my eyes and respond back, "and back." But before I can refocus my attention, I slam into something solid and the wind is knocked out of me.

I throw my hands out to break my fall, but my body is swung up and falls on a warm surface, not the damp grass I was expecting. The smell of a fresh burning fire fills the air and I open my eyes. All I see is skin, my face buried in the neck of whomever broke my fall.

Charlie.

I lift my head from his neck and immediately miss his smell. And like that I'm deep in his blue gaze again.

"Sorry." I put one hand on the ground beside us to lift myself up, but Charlie keeps his arms tight against my back.

"Don't apologize. There are worse positions I could be in."

I wrench myself out of his hold. I'm afraid what I might do if I stay tucked into his warm embrace too long.

"Did you just wake up?" he asks.

I walk over to the fountain. "Yes. I needed some air. I needed to move, do something, feel something other than… that," I flick my hand toward the Manor.

"I get it, you were out for a while."

I turn back to him, "How long?"

"It's been about a day," he says regretfully.

He takes a few steps forward and I take a few back, an awkward dance. My shortness of breath returns, and everything blurs momentarily.

"So many times I wanted to wake you up," he says, shaking his head and laughing to himself. "You're gonna cause trouble for me in here."

"Me? What do you mean?"

"Well, for starters I almost beat up every guard and nurse I saw because I was thinking about you being stuck in a dream experiencing God knows what." His face saddens. "Helpless."

I want to dunk my head in the fountain, clear it of all this fog. "You're so confusing, you're giving me whiplash!" I begin to walk around the fountain clockwise. There are too many things coursing through my mind, I can't stand still.

Charlie's eyes grow worried. He looks at me like he's afraid I might run, and he follows my movement. "Everything was bad, no disastrous, before I went to the lab. Confusing, frustrating, upsetting," he says. "But now I'm even more confused after walking into the cafeteria and seeing you here."

"That's not a good enough excuse for acting like an asshole. We're all confused, frustrated, and upset." I pick up my pace, not wanting him to catch me around the fountain. "I woke up one morning, found my mom bleeding out on the hallway floor, and ended up here. And *I* don't walk around treating people badly."

"I'm sorry."

"Why did you act like that then? You're the one who found me and started talking to me." We continue our walk around the fountain. Him on one side, me on the other, our movements echoing each other as if mirror reflections through the water.

"Seeing you...it scared the hell out of me." The words are hard for him to get out. "I knew I was seeing you in person for the first time, but it wasn't my first time *seeing* you." I stop dead in my tracks; he doesn't stop walking toward me. "I have seen you so many times before in my dreams that I know the outlines and contours of your face better than I know my own. The dreams that you're in are my most vivid, the ones that feel the most real. Hell, I get mad when I wake up from them." He is only a few steps away from me now. A fluttering begins in my stomach. "In the library, you said you felt like you've known me, or at least seen me before. That meant that I wasn't just dreaming of you, but you were also dreaming of me." The blue of his eyes grows more intense. "All of that has been hard for me to process."

We are toe to toe, face to face. I suck in what feels like the last breath I'll ever take. "I dream of your eyes. I have these recurring dreams where I'm lost in total blackness. It is so dark I can't even see my hand in front of my face. Your eyes are the only thing I can see. Your eyes are like the first few stars to appear at night."

"You only see my eyes?"

I answer breathlessly, "Yes."

"Don't you think it's a bit unfair that I've seen all of you, while you only got to see my eyes?" A slight smile builds on his face, his eyes lifting by his temples.

As if on autopilot, I admit, "Your eyes are enough."

He brushes a strand of loose hair behind my ears, inches closer. "And the rest of me?"

He brings his face closer and closer to mine. His eyes focus solely on my lips. I'm no longer stuck in his gaze but caught off guard by something to our right. Breaking the moment, I step away, toward what catches my attention. I walk over to the hedge that's encircling the back wall of the maze and move aside some leaves and vines.

I uncover the one thing in the world that could break my gaze from Charlie.

A door.

A big, dark brown, glossy wooden door, leading who knows where, peeks through the hedges. The metal handle is cold to the touch, but it doesn't budge. Under the handle is a keyhole. Like everything else in the Manor, this door is locked. Keeping secrets in, or out?

From behind me, Charlie calls, "What is it?"

"Hurry! Come look." I move out of the way when he gets close.

After a minute of studying the handle and trying to jiggle it open, he turns to me, an incredulous expression on his face. "What does this mean?"

"I think this means what we want it to mean." I take his hands in mine, grasping his full attention. "They don't come out here when giving the grand tour. They don't mention a single thing about this locked door. This door," I look back toward it, "this door is hidden from plain sight, tucked away on the outer edges of the maze." I pause in utter disbelief. "This door means we've found our way out."

Charlie gapes at me, then the door, then back at me. Before he can utter a word, I'm already on the move, yanking his arm along with me, "Come on! We have to tell Caleb and Nora!"

By the time Charlie and I reach the Manor, we are breathless and sweaty. I would rather die than appear out of shape in front of a cute boy, but like most things lately, I have no choice in the matter, so I decide not to care. We quietly open the front door and creep through the entryway so as not to alert anyone. We spot a few lingering people as they enter the cafeteria.

Charlie guesses it must be dinner time, and my stomach growls at the mention.

Now *that* is embarrassing.

"Ha ha, come on, let's go. We'll get you some food and find Nora and Caleb. I bet they're in there." Charlie takes my hand and leads me toward the cafeteria. Unlike when I held his hand through the maze, our fingers are intertwined now, like how couples hold hands in movies, their fingers a pretzel of skin. I'm unsure how to process this gesture. All I know is that I don't want it to end.

I immediately spot Caleb and Nora at our back table. "Hey! You're awake!" Caleb exclaims.

"And you're holding hands with Charlie…" Nora points out.

Immediately we drop our intertwined fingers. We must look like shop lifters that have just been busted. "Good to see you too, Nora," I say.

I go to my usual chair and sit down. Charlie stands awkwardly at the side of our table, unsure of his next move, and I make it obvious for him by pulling out the empty chair next to me, raising my eyebrows. Before I can say a word to Caleb and Nora about our exciting news, the kitchen staff brings out our food. A hot plate of spaghetti and meatballs is placed in front of me and I dig in. I devour the too-hot-to-eat pieces of pasta and meatballs, hardly taking breaks to breathe. The table watches me with a look of slight terror in their eyes over how fast I am consuming my food. I clear three quarters of the plate before stopping to drink some water.

"You might want to slow down there before you make yourself sick," Caleb says.

"Yeah, or slow down before you make any of us sick from your freakishly fast ability to chew and swallow food," Nora adds. "Did you happen to have a secret life in hot dog eating contests you haven't told us about?"

"Yes, actually, and that's what I'm so desperate to get home to. Big competition coming up soon." I gulp down all of my water. "I didn't realize how starving I was."

"Dreaming for an unnatural number of hours will do that to you. It's like a marathon for your brain," Charlie says, and I flush, knowing I must look like a chipmunk with my cheeks stuffed full.

Nora taps on her glass with her fork, like she is about to make a speech. "Stella, while we have you between bites, do you mind telling us about what's going on..." she wags her finger back and forth between Charlie and I, "...*here.*"

"Oh, right, yes. Well, I woke up and went out into the gardens, needing some fresh air. I started running into the maze and came upon this clearing with a fountain, which is where I ran into Charlie." I decide to rip the Band-Aid off instead of avoiding the truth. "We both came to the realization that we dream about each other. Also, we discovered a hidden locked door at the back of the maze."

Caleb and Nora stare at me, their mouths agape.

At the same time, Caleb gasps, "You and Charlie dream about each other," while Nora tries, "You found a hidden door!?"

I respond to Nora first. "Yes! Charlie and I were…"

What were we doing?

I look over and Charlie flashes me a knowing smile before jumping in. "We were talking, and Stella noticed something out of the corner of her eye. And there it was. Hidden in the back hedge of the maze behind this huge—and honestly distracting—fountain."

"I tried opening it, but it wouldn't budge." The words tumble out of my mouth, partly from excitement and partly fueled by the food. "It has a lock, so we need to find a key that looks look it could fit into a two-inch sized keyhole!"

"Holy shit!" Nora practically shouts, unable to mask her excitement. "Do you guys know what this means?"

The four of us cannot hide our smiles. We grin sillily at each other, reveling in what has to be our happiest moment at the Manor, a light at the end of the tunnel. We promise each other that no matter what happens, we will not tell another soul. There might not be a better chance for us to escape, and we cannot risk someone jumping the gun or tattling. We continue eating dinner and try to decide what the next step in our plan to get the hell out of here should be. Nora is telling Charlie and Caleb how we discovered a camera in the girls' bathroom when her voice grows quieter, hushed by an approaching figure. Behind me I feel a looming presence.

A guard's gravelly voice states, "Stella Grey, I need you to come with me. Ms. Withers expects your company."

And just when I thought my day was looking up…

"Glad to see you are awake." Ms. Withers stands at the back of her office, her back to me.

I take a seat in front of her pristine desk. "Are you? It seems to me like you would have me under for three hundred and sixty-five days straight if it meant more dreams for you."

Her laugh is too controlled to be genuine, but it certainly manages to be unsettling just fine. "That wouldn't be valuable for us. Your body would weaken after a while." She readjusts some books that are already perfectly placed. "Three hundred and sixty-five days are unnecessary, as your dreams from just twenty-four hours were perfect."

"How so?"

She takes the seat across from me, finally back in her throne. "Your dreams were very, what's the word…enlightening." She looks completely and utterly pleased with herself. "Oh, and plentiful. That was the most exciting part."

"All I did was get put to sleep and dream. Nothing different than what you guys do to the rest of the people here."

"Well, that's where you are wrong, my dear Stella." She stands up, crosses over to my side of the desk. "You did not do what everyone else does when they dream under our control. In the history of the Manor, we've only ever gotten one dream or two dreams max under REM 4. And in that second dream, typically everything gets fuzzier, less detailed. The dreams become increasingly harder for us to comprehend."

"How many did I dream?"

Do I really want to know the answer to this?

"Four."

"Four!" My voice climbs an octave or two higher than normal. "Did you guys give me too much of the serum?"

"Of course not—we're not trying to kill you. We monitored every single dream, and they were all the same clarity and intensity. You brainwave lengths also increased the more you dreamed. Usually, it is the opposite the longer the Dreamer spends resting."

How in the world did I dream four dreams?

I only remember two: in the first I was walking alone along a deserted street, and in the other one I was floating in the ocean. I wouldn't be surprised if she was telling me lies right now, after I just found a hidden door that Lady A failed to mention during my introduction tour.

Does she know?

"I only remember having two dreams, not four," I say.

"I don't doubt that. The first one you remember was most likely from when you were first put under the serum, and the second from just before you woke up. When you are under for long enough, your body takes over and actually begins to sleep, thus rendering you unconscious. Our serum however has an element to it that prompts your brain to continue imagining dreams even though the rest of your body is technically sleeping. Therefore, it would be typical for you to remember your first and last dreams from when you are falling asleep and waking up, which is when you are not fully unconscious." In eighth grade algebra, I would sit in the back of the class and understand nothing—a talent I find myself indulging again now. "It is unfortunate you do not remember all of your dreams, they certainly were all very interesting," she notes. "Especially your third dream."

If it is true that I had four dreams, I am upset with myself for giving them so much information for whatever plans they have.

"Why my fourth one?" I question. "The ones I remember were all weird."

I can sense Ms. Withers walking behind my chair, pacing back and forth like a lion stalking its prey. And then her heels stop clicking. "Your fourth dream took a turn compared to the other ones. Your first was of you in a deserted town. Your second, you were observing a conversation between two men dressed in military uniforms. The fourth dream was of you in the ocean, and someone on the shore was beckoning you in." Her eyes close tighter when she explains my third dream. "In your third, you were running through the Manor's garden." Her voice gets closer and closer to my ear, and before she finishes her last sentence, I can feel her hot breath wafting in my hair. "Do you know why I found your third dream so interesting?"

I don't have to think before answering, the answer already clear in my heart and mind. My voice barely rises to a whisper. "Charlie," I say.

"Bingo. The boy with the blue eyes."

She moves away, returning to her chair, knowing she got her point across.

"Why do you care? You got four dreams from me that seem to be worth your while." I can't hide the anxiety in my voice.

"I care because you are dreaming about another Dreamer here. And it isn't just a dream about your two little friends, but of someone who is also having the same dream about you."

I'm floored by her declaration. "Charlie had the same dream as me? That seems impossible."

"I also never knew that to be possible—that is until a few hours ago."

The fluttering in my stomach begins again. This time it is in my chest, near my heart.

"Maybe our dreams are broken then, like records that just play the same song over and over again." I hope she will see sense in my silly explanation. "Our dreams are obviously not useful, you should send us home."

She laughs through her nose. It's genuine this time, but still unsettling. "Wouldn't you like that to be the case? Unfortunately for you, you just became number one on our priority list."

"I wasn't already? That hurts." I feign disappointment, do my best to look wounded by this information.

"Your spot was pending."

I cross my arms and legs. I'm tired of her dancing around the truth. "What does this mean for me then?"

"It seems that you can dream coherently no matter how many times your brain begins a new dream." Her words sink deeply into the pit of my stomach. "Think of all the things you can dream about, at double, triple the rate the rest of the Dreamers are dreaming them at." She has never smiled so big in her entire life, I'm willing to bet. "You are our greatest wish come true."

My heart plummets to the floor. Ms. Withers' veiled compliments about my ability to dream feel like punches to the throat that I can't defend. "Can I go?"

"One more question."

I wait in the painful silence that so comfortably sits in.

"In many of your dreams we noted a presence within them. Another person. Not just people you were dreaming about, observing, but a presence that felt like they were actively experiencing your dreams alongside you. You wouldn't happen to know who that is, would you?"

I answer her with complete honestly, "I have no idea."

"Interesting." The tone of her voice sounds like she doesn't believe me. "We noted a drop in your serotonin production during your fourth dream. You became quite sad. And then, this figure appears on the beach. I'll ask again, does this mean anything to you."

"No."

She looks me dead in the eyes, as if searching for the answer within them. But I'm not lying, so no matter how hard she looks she won't find the answer she's hoping for.

"Can I go *now*."

She doesn't answer.

"Please?"

"Be my guest," she says. "We'll see each other soon."

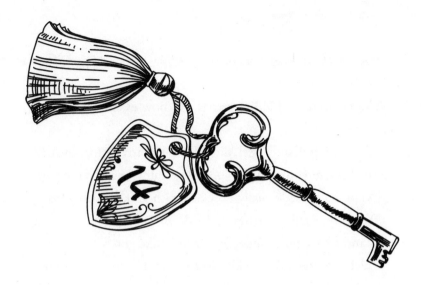

It takes roughly thirty seconds to make my way from Ms. Withers' office to the dorm hall. This time I make it back in half of that, my hatred for Ms. Withers acting as a rush of adrenaline, pushing my feet as fast as they can move up the stairs.

I find Nora and Caleb huddled together whispering on Nora's bed. I sit on mine, and they beg for a total recap of my meeting with Ms. Withers. I tell them everything, reliving everything and hating it just as much the second time. They both listen to my story without interruption. Afterward, Caleb says that he can't believe I stood up to Ms. Withers the way I did. All Nora can bring herself to do is nod. "Girls are definitely stronger than boys," she says.

Meanwhile, Charlie is sitting on his bed reading an old copy of *The Catcher in the Rye* he must have grabbed from the library. I couldn't stop myself from staring at him as I walked past his bed on the way to my own, but he didn't look up from the pages.

Was he about to kiss me in the garden? How do I feel about that if the answer is yes?

There's no sense kidding myself. I know exactly how I feel about that.

"You can probably feel the hole currently being burned into the back of your head," Nora says, "but Charlie is staring."

"Man, he must be really obsessed with you," Caleb adds.

"Yeah, it's really starting to freak me out." Nora looks at Caleb and sticks her tongue out. "Kinda like you."

Caleb's response is to tickle Nora under the arms, apparently his version of playing it cool. Nora squeals and tries to pry his arms away. The two are so obviously into each other, and it kills me that they don't just admit to it.

While the two of them fiddle with each other, I take the opportunity to crane my neck back to Charlie and see what he's doing. He has resumed his position of sitting cross-legged reading. He flips the pages mindlessly, like he already knows the story by heart. I'm taken back to my high school English class, where I was swept up in Holden's view of the world.

I'm still lost in thought when Charlie finally notices me looking at him, smiles, and waves me over. I make a "Me?" gesture, which he responds immediately to with a mouthed, "Yes, you."

I pick myself up and make my way over to him, sitting down on the slim portion of the bed that he hasn't stretched himself across.

"You again," I say.

He laughs, "Yep, me again. And get used to it, because I don't think I'll be slipping away on a vacation any time soon."

He gives me his shy, boyish smile. "Unless you'd like to take me out on a date, that is."

"A date?" I guess we are on good ground. "Well, I could take you to my favorite local spot. Really popular, though. And it might be hard to get a reservation."

"Oh, yeah? I wonder if I've heard of this place…what's it called?"

"Le Cafeteria." My fake French accent is horrendous.

We both laugh together, and it feels like opening presents on Christmas morning. Although his laugh is deep, he laughs like a kid, unable to control it.

"You're funnier than expected," he tells me when he catches his breath.

"What do you mean?"

"I just feel like I already know everything about you, because of the dreams and everything. I guess it feels weird to be discovering things about you now."

His honesty is refreshing. Mostly I'm glad he isn't storming out of the room anymore. "I bet there is a lot you don't know about me—and me about you."

"Hit me with an exclusive Stella Grey fact."

"Hmmm, let's see." I tap my chin, making it seem like I'm thinking really hard and long about something important. "My first ever pet was a squirrel I rescued from outside our house when I was four. He had fallen out of tree, so I took him in as my own."

This has him laughing again. "What did you name him?"

"I named him after my dad, actually." The mention of my dad darkens my mood. "He told me he was honored, but the more I think about it, he probably didn't love me giving his name to a random squirrel."

"Stella! Put that thing back outside!" My mom had yelped as I trudged mud inside the house, a squirming squirrel in my tiny hands.

"Mom, he felt out of a tree, he needs my help." I ignored her flabbergasted stare and continued into the kitchen.

I held tight to the squirrel with one hand while grabbing for a Tupperware big enough to fit his trembling body. The one we usually put our stir fry leftovers in fit him perfectly, and for the rest of the day I bathed him, gave him milk, and force fed him peanuts until he bit my pointer finger. Later, when my dad came home from work, he stopped dead in his tracks outside my bedroom when he caught me singing a lullaby to the squirrel.

"Who's that you got there?"

"I haven't named him yet, but I found him today under our tree and I thought he was dead. Look at him, though—he's okay!" I smiled up at my dad, half of my mouth empty of baby teeth that I had been pulling out left and right. "I'm going to keep him and make sure he is happy!"

My dad looked between me and my newfound squirrel friend, weighing which way to politely break my little heart by telling me that I couldn't let a wild rodent live in our house.

"I think that is a great idea." He leaned down and ran a finger along the squirrel's side. "I don't think you should keep him too long though. He probably has a family he needs to get back to. Keep him for another day to make sure he is recovering okay and then we'll reunite him back outside." My dad patted my shoulder. "How's that sound?"

I hated the idea. I had really begun to love the feeling of his fur along my hand and his weirdly adorably beady black eyes. But my dad was right, and if it were me, I wouldn't want to be taken from my family.

"Okay, but will you help me tomorrow?"

"Of course I will. I wouldn't miss the little guy getting back home safely."

After my dad left my room, I finished my rendition of rock-a-by baby, before saying to the squirrel. "My dad seemed to really like you, I think I should name you after him!"

Picking up on the sad tone of my voice, Charlie chimes in, "Well, if you ever find a squirrel you feel like saving, I give you my permission to name it after me."

I can feel myself start blushing immediately. Our connection is unexplainable but nice, even though we met under terrible circumstances. It's all so weird, yet it feels like the most natural thing in my life at the moment.

"I'm sure your dad felt the same way. My guess is that he loved you so much, he wouldn't have cared if you named a leaf after him." At first this comforts me, then I realize what he's said.

"Wait, you said *loved*. As in *no longer loves*—past tense." I search his face for the truth. "Why did you say loved?"

He looks like he's been caught. Letting out a breath of air, he finally answers my desperate question. "I know he died. I saw it in a dream. It was you at his funeral. You gave a speech in my dream about how his cologne still lingered in your house and that sometimes you thought you could hear his voice in the other room. How much your heart hurt to have him gone from your life for forever. That dream wrecked me and made me feel so connected to you at the same time. Hell, I even woke up to a wet pillow because I cried so much in that dream."

I reach out and place my hand on his. I squeeze it tightly, letting him know I understand the intensity of his dreams, like how mine were…are. A weight also lifts off my chest, my heart no longer feeling the hurt of going through my dad's death alone.

I had Charlie alongside me the whole time.

"Your turn to tell me something juicy."

"I would hardly classify saving squirrels as 'juicy.'"

I place my hand over my heart, pretending to be offended. "Well then, tell me something…scary."

"Scary?" He laughs.

"Yeah, something that scared you once, like going to your first haunted house, or something that is scary to think about, like your crush finding their name scribbled in your notebook." I giggle at these thoughts, but his eyes grow more serious.

He's contemplative for a moment. "The first day of a new school year has always been scary. Or really any time I go somewhere new and meet new people, it's scary. I always dread the moment someone inevitably brings up the topic of parents, asking what they do for a living, their names, if they're strict." The corners of his lips turn downward. "It's only my dad and me. I never knew my mom."

I'm struck by this confession, shocked to find out that he is harboring a similar pain to mine. But his seems worse, heavier, to never have known one of your parents. For me, the memories that I have of my dad are a life preserver in the rocky waves of life, he has nothing to help him float.

He continues, "She left shortly after I was born, so I don't remember anything of her, or what it is even like to have a mom. I thought it was normal to just have a dad, and for the longest time it didn't register that it is the norm to have two parents. I remember feeling perfectly fine with it just being my dad and I huddled together on the couch, him reading me picture books, trying but failing miserably to capture a different voice per character, or when we'd sit nose to the screen watching sports games, his voice explaining the rules hardly noticeable over the announcers. The bliss my dad and I lived in only lasted until the kids at school would brag about what they got their moms for Mother's Day, or until parent teacher conference week, when the class would be assigned to draw a picture for their parents. The reality that I only had one parent, and not a loving mom who would cry when I gifted her a macaroni necklace on Mother's Day, slowly sank in over time, eventually hitting like a truck and souring my time with just my dad."

"Why, Charlie? You and your dad sound like a great pair."

He looks down, his head hypnotically moving left to right. "Thinking of kids getting walked to school with both their parents holding their hands, or moms staying to volunteer for lunch duty, it made me slowly begin to resent my dad for not being able to do what everyone else's moms were doing for them. I look back now and hate that I ever had ill will toward my dad. He couldn't help that he was a single parent who also needed to work. At the time, I wanted him to split himself in half, one half staying to assistant coach my soccer team while the other half went to work. I grew out of that though and I think now—"

"It's okay, Charlie," I interrupt him before he can finish. "I know how scary it is to feel the gaping hole of where one parent should be. I understand you."

"No, not having a mom was never scary—it was confusing, and it made me angry that I couldn't be like everyone, experience things like everyone else. The scary thing is now I don't want a mom, and truthfully, I never want to know her."

My heart plummets in a downward spiral. Charlie's truth is finally sinking in.

"That's scary to me, knowing that there is someone out there so closely connected to me, but if I ever walked by them on the street, I would have no idea who they are, and I also wouldn't care to get to know them. I probably won't ever know who she is, and truth be told I don't want to." He shakes his head around as if shaking an icky feeling from his mind. "Well, geez, I really darkened the mood—you asked me about going to a haunted house."

"No, you didn't. I'm really happy you told me." I give him a half smile. "It gave me a glimpse into how those cogs and machines in that mysterious head of yours work." This moment is fragile, his words floating in the air like snowflakes before they hit the ground and dissolve into nothing. He is giving away secrets to me that I know he would only ever whisper into the darkness at night. So, I don't linger, but collect the snowflakes, allowing for the significance of their beauty, his admissions to me, to sink into my chest. I change the subject. "Also, I hate spooky stuff—like, pee-my-pants hate scary stuff—so a haunted house story would have been much worse for me."

He chuckles, a relieved look crossing his face. I know he appreciates that I didn't drag the conversation out longer—that further talk about parents that aren't around can be like torture.

"How does a ghost unlock a door?" He redirects the conversation.

"What?"

"It's a joke. Let me tell it, it feels oddly perfect. How does a ghost unlock a door?"

"I don't know…it doesn't need to, it can just walk straight through."

"No, it uses a spoo-key!"

I burst out in laughter, not at the joke but at how cheesy he is. "Oh my God, you just told me a dad joke, arguably the cheesiest dad joke ever!"

He shrugs his shoulders as if saying, "Yeah, and what's wrong with that?"

"But you're right, it is oddly perfect."

The blue effervescence of his eyes spark with joy, transitioning from the earlier troubled darkness. We talk back and forth, sharing silly jokes and unknown truths about ourselves and our lives. His truths make me laugh, are serious, and sometimes make me want to cry for him. After clutching my stomach from laughing to the point of crying, I transition into yawning, until eventually my yawns become infectious, as Charlie joins in.

"I think I have to go to bed. Surprisingly you wouldn't think I'd be tired after sleeping for at least twenty-four hours."

"You can sleep for as long as you want in here, but the stress of being in the Manor will never cease to exhaust." His words validate how I feel, and it makes me feel weak. "Here," he says, and gets up and gives me his hand. "I'll walk you to your bed."

I can feel the creases of his palm as the two of us walk the short distance to my bed hand in hand.

It's weird to think we'll be in the same room sleeping, possibly dreaming about each other.

"Thank you." I climb under the covers. "Chivalry is not dead."

Charlie looks at me intensely for a few beats, as if deciding what his next move should be. Do you kiss the girl when you drop her off at her house/prison bed, or just leave? Making up his mind, he leans down, inching down in impossible slow motion. Everything around us disappears—the dreaming, Ms. Withers, the Manor. Even Caleb and Nora. For a moment, the only thing that exists are his lips on my cheek.

One, two, three seconds and then he stands back up.

He gives me one last look before he goes back to his bed.

High from what has just happened, like a balloon that's been released and drifts off into the sky, I fall asleep.

I am awakened in the middle of the night by a pinch on my arm. My eyes shoot open to find a nurse and guard standing over me. The nurse is tightening a rubber band around my arm, preparing it for another shot, and before I'm fully awake, she pokes me with the needle and pushes the plunger down into the syringe, orange liquid quickly disappearing into my arm. Like before, the serum spreads like icicles throughout my body. To my right and left everyone is asleep, some by choice, some not. Straining to hold my head up, I spot Charlie fast asleep in his bed, the equipment next to him off, so I know he is sleeping from his own volition.

There isn't much I can do to save myself from the impending sleep that is barreling toward me like a train. Remembering Ms. Withers parting words to me earlier, it seems like the days when I was the only one not dreaming have come to a dead halt.

My daily routine for the next few weeks goes as follows: wake up from dreaming, shower, go to the bathroom, find Caleb and Nora or Charlie, eat, interact socially for what feels like mere minutes, then run into a guard or nurse who takes me to the dorm hall to get injected with the serum. Eighteen, nineteen, twenty hours pass at a time. I miss some days entirely and wake up days later, dazed and confused, my stomach and throat aching from a lack of water and food. The bags under my eyes have permanently turned a dark gray color, my blue veins a stark contrast to my pale skin. Despite getting record hours of sleep, I look as tired as ever.

When I can, I hang out with Nora and Caleb, shaded and protected under the leaves of the willow tree. They do their best to reassure me, wash me of the icky feeling the serum leaves.

"Stella, I have been dying to tell you this." Nora stated one day, while the two of us took in the last few hours of daylight under the willow tree.

"The other day during lunch, a bunch of food got spilled all over a table of people, and it was a soup lunch, so I bet you can only imagine how bad it was. It made me think of you because I remember you telling me all about the crazy antics people would get up to at your school's cafeteria."

"Did a food fight break out?" I asked.

"No, Lady A stepped in right away to make sure lunch resumed like normal. A lot of people laughed, though, and it made me wish you were there to roll your eyes with me. But it also reminded me of something that had happened to me, and I really wanted to tell the story to Caleb and Charlie, but to be honest I just wanted to tell it to you. I felt like you'd understand it more than the boys."

Her confession of only wanting to confide in me warmed me. "Tell me!"

"Do you remember that series of books, I can't remember the name, but the one about the girl who hit her head and then started to see this really dreamy boy all over her town, and it turned out he was a fallen angel looking after her, blah blah blah."

"Kinda, maybe. They made it into a movie, right?"

"Yes!"

"Ya, I remember, Callie begged me to read all the books before the movie premiere, but I just never got around to it."

"Well, me and my group of friends did go to see the movie. We went to see it the night it was premiering at our town's theater. The *midnight* premiere."

"Oh, my gosh! Me and Callie did that for midnight movie premieres!"

"See!" Nora exclaimed. "This is why I knew I had to tell *you*. I cannot picture Charlie waiting in line to see a movie at midnight."

We both laughed at the image.

"Well, anyway, I had to sneak out of my house to go to this midnight premiere. My curfew at the time was a strict ten p.m., and my parents are like the strictest most by the book parents there ever were. 10:01 p.m., grounded. 10:02 p.m. kiss your car privileges away. Like ridiculously strict. But I had to go to this movie, because Nick, remember Nick, my disaster of a boyfriend."

"Yes."

"He was going and had asked if I was going, and that we could sit together. Now that I think back at it, it was totally cringe that I was drooling over the opportunity to sit next to a boy at a movie. But hey, we live and we learn."

Nora shrugged and I laughed.

"For all this trouble, please tell me you at least got to sit next to Nick."

"Of course I did, nothing was stopping me from getting what I wanted. I sat next to him, he did that whole pretend to stretch but really put your arm around the girl spiel, and we shared a popcorn, knuckles brushing and all."

I pointed a finger in my mouth, feigning being grossed out by her date description.

"Same. But at the time, I felt like the coolest girl in the world. I was sitting and watching a movie about a girl and the guy of her dreams, and there I was with the guy of *my* current dreams. That is until about an hour into the movie, and I felt a tap on my shoulder. I turned to see who it was, and lost my mind, Nick and my's shared popcorn went flying all over us. It was my parents, dressed in their pajamas, arm crossed glaring at me from the aisle. I was so dead, grounded for a month."

I had so many questions for Nora, but I could hardly sneak breaths in between my laughter.

"I just had to tell you, because the food spilling the other day took me right back to the popcorn falling all over me. My hair smelled like fake butter for days and felt like it, too!"

"Oh, my," I laughed. "Nora," more laughter. "That has to be one of the worst first date stories."

"Trust me, I know. To this day I don't think I've mentioned going to the movies to my parents."

"If it's any consolation, you and Nick did date after all."

She squirmed at the mention. "I'm beginning to think the first date was a warning sign I should have listened to."

I motioned her closer to me, grabbing at a piece of her hair, and sniffed it. "Mhmm, yummy. I do love movie theater buttered popcorn, though."

She swatted my hand away and said, "If we ever eat popcorn here, I'm definitely dumping it on you."

Other than tell each other secrets, cringey stories, and distract ourselves from the scary inevitable of the day-to-day at the Manor, Caleb and Nora have been keeping up with our escape plan. They've been doing their jobs of scoping out cameras and learning the guard/nurse rotations. So far, they've made notice of two cameras in the cafeteria, one in each corner of the main foyer, another that monitors the hall outside the dorm hall, and three more spread out in the dorm hall. Caleb investigated the boys' bathroom and found one in the same place we'd described to him in the girls' room. They left the search for cameras in the library up to Charlie, who reported one by the door, watching who enters and leaves the room. Every room in the Manor has at least one camera, sometimes more.

The guard schedule has proven more elusive. None of us has been able to come up with a distinct pattern to their movements. All we know for certain is that they rotate groups throughout the day, a new group of guards replacing the previous group at four-hour intervals.

Some days when I wake up from dreaming, Charlie is there by my side, already close by, waiting for me to wake up, a book in his lap and his hair canopying his eyes as he sits perched at the end of my bed. Or I will find him already staring at me, the blue of his eyes the first thing my eyes adjust to after being closed for a long while.

The worst days are when I wake up and he is dreaming, the serum still coursing through his system, stranding him beyond my reach. Since the day we met he's only gone to the lab once. I slept through most of his time there, but the day he returned I awoke to a dejected and angry version of Charlie. His normal talkative demeanor was gone. He refused to spend time with any of us. His avoidant gaze and self-induced isolation lasted a few days before he finally shook off the eerie effects of the lab and returned to his normal self.

When he is feeling good, he reminds me of a kid entering a sugar high. His brain thinks too fast for his mouth, and every detail of his life comes spilling out at the same exact time, from his first memory, the time he pushed his sister into the pool when she was wearing her school uniform and was grounded for a whole month, to his most awkward moment, when he asked a girl to the sixth grade dance, to what he was doing the day before he came here.

"That day we were buying new brakes for the truck. The original ones almost got us killed going down a hill in town when the truck wouldn't stop even though we were pushing down on the pedal. Ha, we pulled over, checked under the truck, and found brake fluid leaking all over the place. It stunk. None was left in the cylinder, and things could have gone much worse, but luckily my dad had the wherewithal to pull over into the side of the hill. Every day here I wonder if he is still working on restoring the truck or if he's holding out hope I'll be back to finish the job with him."

For the past few years, Charlie and his dad had been slowly restoring a 1955 Ford F100 truck. While on a road trip, they spotted it rusting away on the side of the highway, bought it off the farmer who thought it was nothing but an eye sore, and ever since had been enjoying the dirty but fulfilling process of bringing it back to life.

"What color is it?"

"We haven't painted it yet, we were saving that step for last."

"Well, when you *do* paint it, I think you should paint it cherry red. That'll really make it pop!"

"Hmm, I'm not sure about red. Red has kind of been ruined for me now."

He doesn't need to explain why.

"Ha-ha, that's fair. Let me think…" I place my hand on my chin, picturing the rainbow.

"I'm thinking green, like your eyes."

Chills erupt throughout my body. My cheeks must flush ten different shades of pink.

"I…I like…green's good."

He laughs at my stuttering, a smug look on his face, proud of his smooth words and ability to trip me up like a schoolgirl.

When I regain my cool, we continue talking and I return the favor and tell him stories of my own. I tell him all about Callie, my mom, how I was asked to Winter Formal once and was in such shock that all I could do was stare back at the poor boy, not saying anything. We share our favorite books and movies and even hate each other for a little while when he

learns that, because of my father, I'm a diehard Eagles fan—the rival of his beloved Giants.

Despite our everlasting sleep schedules, we find time to continue our marathon of talking and getting to know each other. It's safe to say that I feel more than a butterfly in my stomach when I wake up, excited to see him. Or more than the pins and needles in my limbs when I catch him staring at me. Instead, my body feels like a honey hive full of bees that have just returned from a new patch of flowers in the spring.

Waking up today, however, is a completely different story.

The nurse waking me up from my dream is startled when Lady A bursts through the doors, her pristine white outfit blindingly bright and her heels ringing out like an alarm clock and breaking me from my sleepy daze. Two guards struggling to hold up a flailing body follow behind her. The girl they are holding has her head hung low as she kicks her legs and pulls her arms back and forth, trying to break free. If Lady A is aware of the chaos following in her wake, she does a remarkable job of not letting it show.

A fight between Lady A and Ms. Withers would end badly, I think. I imagine high heels wielded like weapons, their perfectly manicured nails like claws.

I have no idea who would win.

The girl makes her last few useless attempts at breaking loose of the Hulk-like guards.

Finally, she flings her head up grunting and knocking foreheads with the guards holding her upper body.

"Ouch!" Her voice is ragged, probably sore from all the screaming she has done.

Lady A's stomping stops once she reaches the girl's bed. She nods and points toward the bed, where the guards throw her body down onto the brown blanket.

Bang!

The sudden weight of her body on the mattress causes her bed post to smack into the wall, making a dent in the plaster.

Lady A stands above the girl's weeping body. "Think about this the next time you try to run." Lady A twists her body, facing the greater part of the dorm hall and addresses us all, "Let this be a warning for all of you. You can run, but you cannot hide."

She makes sure to scan each and every bed, making eye contact with all of us, scaring us into submission.

I hear Nora whisper from the bed next to me, the word "bitch" carrying under her breath.

"Guards," Lady A snaps in her French accent.

The guards look whimp-ish when Lady A yells at them. They jump into action, pulling the wrist and ankle restraints from under the girl's bed and restraining her flat on top of her blankets.

I wince at how tight the guards have tied her restraints.

As Lady A struts out of the dorm hall, with the guards following behind her like obedient puppies, the girl erupts in feverish cries. The surrounding boys and girls jump from their beds trying to calm her panic, but her desperate wails are like nails on a chalkboard.

"God," Nora scoffs. "That woman is worse than the bullies at my school. And that says a lot."

Impassioned by my absolute hatred for the Manor, I add, "Sooner rather than later, we need to get out of here."

We spend the next day twiddling our thumbs lazily in the dorm hall. Needing to stretch my legs, I leave the dorm hall and stop in the grand foyer, where I spot Charlie standing next to the window, staring outside. He doesn't notice me at first. His gaze is longing and serious, like a sailor in search of land. Charlie really feels like something special in this terrible place. I have no idea how to explain this instant connection I feel toward his presence, aside from our dreams. I can't find a word in all of the English language to describe how I feel.

Maybe Lady A can tell me one in French.

He notices me staring and says, "Take a picture, it will last longer."

"I would, but they didn't let me bring my phone here."

"Bummer, I wonder why?"

"Did you see how Lady A treated that girl yesterday?"

"Yeah, to Anna," he says, his expression turning grave. "I saw them carry her in, but I couldn't watch them throw her around as if she weren't a living, breathing human being."

I've known his eyes for a while now, and I can read them pretty well. He may be able to put on a brave smile here and there, but his eyes can't hide his true feelings. I move closer to him, hoping my presence will help him feel better.

I pray he doesn't move away.

"Is everything okay? I noticed you weren't around when I woke up, and that's a first for you."

Please don't storm past me like last time, I chant inwardly.

He leans gingerly against the windowpane. "To be honest, no. I feel…hell, I don't even know how I feel." He shakes his head, his voice low. "On top of all this craziness going on around us, I had a bizarre dream that put me into a funk."

"What was it?" I don't even bother to think that he might not want to tell me.

"It was all black, like someone had put a blanket or something over my eyes. I knew I was dreaming because I was consciously thinking about what was going on. I just kept waiting for something to happen, a noise, a smell, someone to appear or start talking, anything. But no, nothing happened, I was just stuck in this black abyss for what felt like hours. The darkness became suffocating and eventually, when I woke up, I was panting and covered in sweat." His eyebrows pinch together. "The worst part was when I laid in bed after trying to figure out what the hell that dream could have meant, the only thought I could come up with was that it felt like what death must be like. Me shrouded in darkness. No one around. It scared me. It's still scaring the shit out of me." He turns his gaze toward the ground and the walls around us. He stares absolutely everywhere except at me. "That's why I left. I had to get out of there, out of that bed. I couldn't watch you sleep for any longer or I'd put a hole in a wall."

I take his hands in mine. "First of all, that was a nightmare, not a dream. So don't beat yourself up for feeling spooked. Secondly, I don't think that was about you dying—it could mean a lot of things. Maybe the serum didn't work. Maybe it put you to sleep but it didn't prompt a dream, so all you had to see was nothing."

My words hang in the foyer for multiple heartbeats.

"Thank you." He finally looks at me and says, "What would I do without you here?" It is more of a statement than a question, and it sets the butterflies racing around my chest again.

"You did it before. You've been here longer than me."

"Those days were just meaningless minutes, hours." It takes everything in me to not visibly swoon at his words. "It's the craziest juxtaposition being here at the Manor with you. I hate this place with every fiber of my body, yet with you I feel like I could be anywhere and grin and bear it."

I smile at him. "Anywhere?"

"Anywhere."

His blue irises fill with intent, and they reel closer and closer to me before his lips are on mine. The feeling is foreign, bizarre at first. But then our lips move in sync and the electric buzz that forms in the space between them turns into a warm hum. I peek my eyes open to make sure this is not in fact a cruel dream. His black eyelashes touch the tops of his cheeks, creating little shadows under each lash. I want to count his lashes and trace lines between each of the little barely there freckles that lay atop his nose.

He pulls me closer, and I close my eyes again as he wraps his arms around my waist. Unconsciously I wrap mine around his neck, doing whatever feels right. The ends of his hair tickle my arms and we smile into each other's mouths. Not liking the chill that replaces his lips, I dive toward his again, finding delicious comfort in our embrace. Everything around us slips away. The chandelier twinkling light down on us is gone. The cafeteria tables fly away, and the books from the library fold in on themselves. The walls of the Manor fall to the ground, leaving only the maze directing us toward the door. The colors surrounding us bleed together, only one blur of magnificent blinding light, and everything except the two of us ceases to exist.

The library becomes our sanctuary. We stay there for a long while, not caring about anyone looking for us or what's going on outside of the book-covered walls. I lie with my head in Charlie's lap as he combs his hands through my hair. I doze off at one point, happy to sleep without fear of dreaming. I awaken to the sound of his voice calmly reading a book, but he stops once he notices I've woken up, embarrassed.

"Am I really that boring?" He closes the book he was reading aloud and places it by his leg.

I yawn. "It's less you and more the content of what you were reading." I squint my eyes to read the side cover of the book.

"I'm reading *1984*?" Charlie asks in mock astonishment. "This is a classic, and I'm afraid I may have to rethink how I feel about you if you think Mr. Orwell's words are yawn worthy."

Giggling through another yawn, I snatch the book and leaf through it. "I didn't mean to insult your reading preferences." He gives me a dubious look. "What I mean is that the content of the book is just too real right now for me. It was either doze off or have a panic attack."

Charlie brushes a stray hair from my heated cheek, furrows his brows.

"The whole being watched thing...the Manor feels too much like Big Brother. With Ms. Withers and her obsessive watching and monitoring of us when we are conscious and unconscious. Despite its literary power, the last thing I need right now is a book that's going to add to my..." I wrack my brain for the right words to voice the feelings that have settled into me since I arrived here.

"To your what?"

I shake my head, my hair scraping against Charlie's pant leg. "My paranoia, my suspicion of every creak and crack I hear, my fear of falling asleep and then of waking up, the pain I feel every time I wake up in that uncomfortable bed and remember where I am and where I should be. All of it, it makes me feel so helpless."

I drop the book onto my stomach and look up at Charlie, who runs his fingers through his hair with a frustrated huff. "The general lack of free will is what really drives me crazy. At home I wasn't good with taking direction from my dad. *Clean your room, leave early so you can run an errand for me, tell me about this and that*—it drove me crazy. I acted like I couldn't be bothered to lift a finger, so you can only imagine how I feel now when one of those ogre-like guards barks at me to get into bed."

I chuckle at his response, the mixture of seriousness and comedy is refreshing. Charlie is never too severe, never makes me feel like I'm in a courtroom somewhere where one foot out of line means jail.

He adds, "I would like nothing more than to be told to do something by my dad right now, though."

"I can give you an order."

"I bet you can," Charlie plunges his fingers into the sides of my waist, tickling me into oblivion.

In the process of my body attempting to squirm out of his attack, the book falls off my stomach and onto the floor near his feet. Charlie grabs the book from below us and flings it across the room, kicking up a pile of dust in the corner of the room. "For now, we will avoid depressingly real dystopic novels and stick to…" With a finger tapping on his chin, he scans the shelves of books to our right and left. "*Moby Dick, Pride and Prejudice, On the Origin of Species, Dra…*"

Before he can finish making fun of the eclectic selection the Manor's library has, classical music gusts through the space: mealtime. Before Charlie, I was acutely aware of time's slow crawl. But now, as I become more and more comfortable in my skin around him, that painful crawl of time dulls from a migraine to a minor ache.

He stands up and takes my hand, pulling me up into his body. He bends down and plants one kiss, then another, on my lips, before draping a heavy protective arm over my shoulder, an arm he does not move from my shoulder as we exit the library, not caring who sees our embrace.

I guess we've past the point of friendship…

We are some of the first to arrive at the cafeteria, so he opens the door motioning me forward. He dusts off some old-school twentieth century etiquette and offers, "After you, my lady."

I curtsey in response and begin to walk in.

"Not so fast, Ms. Grey." Her voice cuts through me like fingernails on a chalkboard.

Charlie steps protectively in-between Ms. Withers and me. One second, I'm chilled from her words, the next I'm warmed by his show of affection.

"We are just on our way to eat," I say, peeking from behind Charlie's broad chest.

"Very well, Charlie, you may go." Her red nails flick at Charlie, laced with poison.

"And Stella, she's coming with me, too," Charlie asserts.

"Charlie." I hate to hear the way she says his name with such malice. "Stella will do as I say, and she is coming with me." She smiles at me, wickedly, "She has a date with destiny in the lab."

I almost crumble to the floor. I run up to Charlie, clutching the backs of his shoulders, wishing it was still just the two of us cozied up in the library. He snakes his hands around me, clinging to me.

"Don't make me count to three before calling the guards like a patronizing mother. I'm not opposed to doing what I have to in order to get what I want." Each of her words hits like a punch to the nose.

Even though I would like to jump into Charlie's arms and tell him to hide us away, I don't want him getting in trouble, so I step between him and Ms. Withers.

"What are you doing?!" Charlie's pearly blue eyes are frantic.

"I have to go. I have no choice but to do what she tells me to do."

"No, that's not true." He sneers.

"Yes, it is." I turn to him, whispering carefully, "You can say no and then get beaten up by the guards. We can run and then get restrained to our beds like animals. That behavior will only set us back and alert them to our willingness to defy. The more compliant we seem, the less they will be suspicious of us in the long run." I lower my voice even more. "And then the easier it is for us to slip from under their noses and disappear completely."

He lets out a defiant huff of air and says, "I'll see you soon." He gives me a quick kiss, but it all sounds more like goodbye than see you later, and my heart plunges as he drops his hand from my arm, turns, and walks into the cafeteria, his head hung low.

Ms. Withers looks genuinely surprised that we didn't put up much of a fight, but her stone-cold facade is back within seconds. She turns to walk toward the lab. I follow, and she takes me to the second room down the hallway. It's empty except for a nurse and a guard by the door.

Why is there a guard here? I came willingly, didn't I?

"Just in case you felt like fighting my orders," Ms. Withers replies to my unasked questions.

"Is this something I should be putting up a fight for?"

"You can put up a fight for anything in life, my dear. Some of them you just won't win." I hate when she calls me "my dear," the feigned sweetness reminding me of the evil stepmother from a fairy tale.

I get under the covers and rest my head on the surprisingly comfortable pillow. The nurse quickly does her job by readying the equipment and applying sticky cords to my head and chest. I must look like a crazy science experiment. Let's just hope this one doesn't go wrong, like my failed fake volcano in the seventh grade. At the medical station set up on the side of the room, the nurse mixes different substances and readies a syringe twice the size of the ones used in the dorm hall. I watch her tamper with her tools. The hope I'd had before, whatever rope had kept me tethered to it is fraying fast, my connection nearly severed.

"What are you thinking about?" Ms. Withers asks.

"Nothing."

"Nothing? How meditative of you."

"I wanted nothing more than to run when you told me I had to go to the lab. I've wanted to do nothing but run since I've come to the Manor." There is no gusto left in my voice. "I'm tired of feeling on edge all the time, wondering what punch in the gut will come my way next. I've just concluded that I'm going to stop swimming against the current. You can stick as many needles as you want in me, but the only thing I will feel will be the physical pain—nothing else." All the terrible feelings I talked to Charlie about spin like a tornado around my chest before dissipating. "You have made me numb."

Half of what I said was true, the other half was to tear her sick satisfaction away. I might as well suck the fun out of all of this for her, like she's done to me and my life. I want my words to be like chips in her manicured claws.

"How interesting," she looks down at me as if I'm some weird new species of bug she has stumbled upon, ready to squash it with the point of her shoe. She moves out of the way, allowing the nurse to finish her work. "I guess I will see you in…" she begins, letting the words hang between us. She pauses, and then to really drive the dagger home, she finishes with, "…a few days, maybe."

And then the only sound left is her heels clicking down the hallway.

I take three deep breaths, defending against the sour air that follows her wherever she goes.

"All right-y then, let's get started," the nurse says, carrying over the syringe full of purple liquid. She sprays something cold on my arm, burning the skin the spray touches. A few seconds later, the area is numb; however, I can still feel the puncture of the giant needle breaking my skin, and I make a note that the next time I see her, I should tell Ms. Withers to invest in better numbing products.

The serum used in the dorm hall cools. This one burns hot, a fire alight throughout my veins. I clench my fists, piercing my palms with my own fingernails in an attempt to feel anything other than the burning serum coursing through my body.

One finger and then the next, my bones become stiff. My fingers uncurl themselves from their grip. I want to move my arms, stretch my legs out from the burning, but my motor skills are completely lost. All I can move are my eyes, back and forth across the chrome ceiling. I try to get a glimpse of what the nurse is doing next, but red erupts throughout the room, setting it ablaze. Each inch of the room is bathed in color, and I feel like I am stuck in the core of a volcano. Suffocating and hot.

Soon, I can't move at all.

I try to take a deep breath and find myself coughing instead. A scalding feeling races through my chest every time I inhale. My eyes sting as I open them, like when you have them open for too long in the swimming pool. I push myself up from the ground, gravel shaking loose and sounding like rain as it sprinkles around me. It takes a few minutes to lose the sensation of swaying on a boat amongst waves, to feel confident again in my legs' ability to move.

Everything is gray. The sky and surrounding land are different shades of gray, some black dusted with brown. Hazy, foggy June morning clouds hover lower, but the air contains no hint of ocean cool. It swelters and sizzles, practically vibrating and sticky on my skin. It is smoky and thick with tiny pieces of something stuck in it—something falling from the sky.

Red flashes from under my shorts as I move my legs. Lifting the bottom hem, I find a deep gash on my right thigh, blood pooling at the top of the cut. The blood drips from the wound, slowly and then faster and then racing down my leg.

The pain from my leg never registers.

I feel nothing but confusion.

Standing in one place won't lead me anywhere, so I decide to move on and explore. With each step I'm aware of a heaviness in my right leg, a pronounced limp asserting itself with each step. I see the blood, the dark red almost brown of my cut, and I can feel the limp, but there's still no pain.

Without any way of marking time, I stumble around the gray, sometimes yelling out "hello" or a desperate "help me!"

The only response is the echo of my own voice.

In the ground is a body-shaped hole marked red from my bleeding leg.

"No!" I've been walking in circles.

I fall back into the burrow, utterly defeated in my attempts to find answers. All I've done is exhaust myself on my way to ending up where I started. I lie in the ground, reaching the point of complete and total surrender. But then I'm struck by a thought.

I'm dreaming!

The gut-wrenching feeling of aloneness lifts.

I've never felt so happy.

This is a dream. I'm not actually living this, I'm only experiencing it. The realization has me back on my feet, remembering that no matter what I will eventually be lifted from this place and awaken back in reality.

Reality is not exactly what I would choose, but it beats this post-apocalyptic dream, hands down.

Not that anyone is offering a choice.

I set out in the opposite direction this time, carefully placing one foot in front of the other and feeling more confident in my search for answers. After all, whatever I come upon can't hurt me. I'm not actually here. Which must be why I can't feel the pain from my leg; I can only see it.

I begin to count my steps.

54, 55, 56, 57, 58…

My voice is cut off by the sound of rushing water cutting through the boiling fog.

59, 60, 61, 62, 63…

And now mucky water races below my legs. Hundreds of pieces of metal and chunks of branches zoom past me in the growing current. Despite the blistering air around me, I can feel the cool temperatures rise from the water as I lean down. I can't see across the length of it through the fog, but I take my chances and reach down to feel the enveloping coolness on my hands. The water is freezing, like the creeks on mountains that carry snow melt. The cold is shocking and feels unnatural on my scorched hot hands. I lift my hands temporarily out of the water, half of them now clean from the dirt and the other half a gray-brown mix.

I reach to submerge them again but pull back just in time. A huge floating object moves quickly toward me. Flung back by my own momentum, I land on my butt in the dirt by the water's edge.

What the hell was that?

I scramble to my knees and crawl over to inspect what nearly tore my hands from my arms as it propelled through the water. I catch only a glimpse of the green bronzy object as it bobs up and down on its way past before it disappears into the fog. I keep my distance from the water, not wanting to get pulled in by any of the many chunks of stuff that are floating by, until the urge to clean the remaining dirt off my hands and arms grows too strong and sends me crawling back to the waterline. Before I can resubmerge my aching hands, more items catch my eye. This time the objects bobbing in the water almost blend in with the muddy blue. As they break the surface, I see flashes of sharp green edges and letters on the objects. I can make out a "J" on one and "U" scripted on another green object before it goes back under the water and swims past me.

It takes another few minutes before the water carries the next piece over. The object bobs under the water and only resurfaces for a few short seconds. I squint tight, hoping to catch more details. This one is circular, with spikes reaching out on one end. Another similar piece caught in the current goes by, and another, but this one seems to be the side of a sculpted nose. However, it becomes harder to make out details of the broken-up objects as they are the covered by slimy leaves and clumps of wet dirt and debris.

The next object leaves me breathless, at a loss for words. It floats by me slower and closer than the others, so I am able to quickly reach down and tug it with great effort from the water. It is immensely heavy, and with water pouring off it, it almost slips out of my hands. I stare at it, wide eyed and in awe. Droplets of water coat a piece of a single gold flame. I drop the gold flame to the ground as if it is hot to the touch, and yank another piece of debris from the water, this one just as heavy. This piece is a faded scratched chunk of green. I turn it over and see a bronze internal structure. I drop this piece next to the other with a thump, racking my brain for where or what these pieces could have come from.

A loud ominous noise snaps my head upward, and there it is, jagged and broken, hints of the once glorious statue peeking through the cloud of ash. The shocking reality of what I've just held has me wanting to scream out in terror, horrified. Through a break in the smokey fog, the Statue of Liberty stands broken, her top half completely gone. Only the remains of the bottom of her billowing dress remain on top of her brick pedestal. Chunks of brick are missing, and holes that look like craters decorate the statue's once perfect facade. A shrill cry escapes my lips, laced with terror and sadness. I know in the back of my mind I'm only experiencing this in a dream, not in real time.

A loud scream from somewhere breaks the silence. Then another, followed by many more from somewhere in the distant fog. It takes one more scream before I fall back and I'm lying down. One minute I'm staring up into the hot haze, seeing glances of the destroyed Statue of Liberty through the smokey fog floating around me, and then next I can see a figure walking toward me. The fog is thick, but as the figure nears, I notice it has a familiar gait. I rub feverishly at my eyes, the sting of the hot air painful as I squint toward the figure. A slight smell breaks through the smoke-filled air, and I sniffle it in. Hints of sweetness reach my nose, confusing me greatly.

Vanilla and what? Apples? Where is that coming from?

I finish rubbing my eyes clean and go to rub at my prickling nose, but before I can do so, I catch my own reflection screaming down at me from the chrome ceiling of the lab.

I wake up crying, the dream having torn a hole through my heart and soul. I can do nothing with this dream aside from tell my friends and scare them. The only people who have the power to share this information are Ms. Withers and her evil minions. They hold all the vital information and can do with it whatever they please.

They can use it for money, fame, leverage—anything.

All I can do is try not to throw up about it.

The harsh outside light that greets me when I step out of the lab and into the foyer is too much for me to face, and I choose to go back to the dormitory. Feeling sick to my stomach, each step feels heavier than the one before, the energy having completely drained from my body and brain. Solemnly, I make my way up the stairs, passing a few other people, some with smiles on their faces and others with blank stares looking off into the sun-laced windows.

The hall of portraits still haunts me, and it takes everything in my power not to tear down the smug painted faces. I could rip at the canvases, the sweet sound of the fabric breaking, the paint holding together their fake smiles and mocking gazes flaking to the floor. But I don't, I don't have the energy. The guards open the doors quickly as I approach, and I all but crawl through into the dorm hall with my arms crossed and eyes cast down, striding toward my bed without bothering to check if Charlie, Caleb, and Nora are in their beds.

A few tears escape my eyes. I do nothing to brush them away.

"Stella."

I hear my name but don't bother to look up in acknowledgement.

I take a final shallow breath before throwing myself onto my bed. I crawl into a fetal position, pulling my blanket up trying to protect myself from all the craziness that floats around in the air. I have my eyes clenched shut. For once, it feels marvelous to see nothing but darkness, no dreams, no ill-fated futures, no ladies with red lipstick dressed in suits, no nurses with syringes, no guards.

Just plain, simple blackness.

A hand slides up my back to my shoulder, resting calmly. It is a big hand, its warmth heating my shoulder through the blanket. I don't need to be shielded from Charlie. I roll onto my back and find his eyes. I knew there was a reason why I loved blue. His hand travels from my shoulder to my cheek, where he brushes away the wetness from my tears with his thumb.

"Not a fun first experience in the lab, huh?" His comment is playful, but his voice is laced with sorrow.

His question needs no response on my part, my tear-streaked cheeks already answering clearly enough.

He wipes away a few more tears and says, "Well, on the bright side, you were only in there for five hours."

"*Only.*"

"Five hours is a record for least amount of time, trust me."

"It felt like days."

"Nora made fun of me." He looks down at his hands, now in his lap.

I push myself up to a sitting position. "For what?"

"I couldn't sit still. I paced up and down the stairs, and I couldn't eat dinner."

He can't meet my eyes, embarrassed by his reaction to my being gone. "She said, and I quote, 'Calm down, you're even starting to stress the guards out.'"

I laugh, and the smile it produces feels good, like the sun after several days of storms.

"Hey!" Charlie playfully pushes me. "It's not funny, I practically bit off all my fingernails. I did, however, get a good workout walking up and down the stairs a million times."

"You'll have the best-looking calves in this place."

His gaze grows serious, and he catches my eyes again. "I counted the minutes."

I can't help but blush. "Well, I'm happy it was only five hours then. Any longer and your head would have started to hurt from all the counting."

He takes my hand and begins to lean in closer, his eyes still glued to mine. "I would've counted no matter how long." He eyes begins to drift ever so slightly south, toward my lips.

"Happy to see lonely boy over here is not so lonely anymore." Nora plops down on the end of my bed, shaking it. "Caleb and I were seriously worried for his health."

Charlie glares back at Nora and I can't tell whether it's her words that piss him off or the fact that she just ruined our almost romantic moment.

"It's nice of you guys to be so concerned for him," I tell Nora, "and not for me!"

"We didn't need to be worried for you, Stella," she says. "We know you could beat Ms…"

"Guys! I have something I need to tell you!" Caleb interrupts Nora mid-sentence as he run-bounces toward my bed.

"Caleb, what are you on about?" Nora flashes him a disturbed look, not knowing how to handle his frenetic energy.

His excited energy is a shot to my drowsy system, like bright light after first opening your eyes in the morning. It's a refreshing twist to how I feel on the inside.

"You guys!" He flings himself hard between Charlie and Nora, the bed legs scratching against the ground like nails on a chalkboard.

Those awake in the room look toward my bed with worried glances, but I avoid them and instead huddle closer to Charlie as he scoots away from Caleb.

Nora reflexively shoves Caleb's shoulder away after it hits hers. "Caleb, seriously, what the he—"

"Shhh!" Caleb holds his finger up to Nora's lips, and her eyes quadruple in size.

Caleb is telling *her* what to do.

Charlie and I both laugh at her look of befuddled astonishment.

Caleb turns his attention to me. "Hi, Stella, I'm really happy to see that you're back from the lab. And I hope you're okay and all, and I don't mean to take away from your return."

"But you are." Nora points out.

Caleb threatens with his silencing finger again, but Nora ducks her head out of the way.

"But...there is something really important I need to tell you guys, and it just can't wait." He looks to me again. "I hope that's okay?"

Charlie clears his throat to disagree with Caleb, moving in defense of me and my emotions, but I don't let him.

"Yeah, of course, Caleb." My hand clenches around Charlie's bicep, holding him back to me. "Honestly, whatever it is, it will be a welcome distraction. Anything to distract me from the Manor's menacing power is fine with me."

Caleb clears his throat. "They won't have that power for long."

"Don't tease us with your glass-half-full ideas," Nora says.

"I have a plan. To get us out."

In unison we all say, "What?"

"Last night, I couldn't sleep. So instead I wandered around the bathroom and dorm hall for hours, and then I heard the hall doors opening so I quickly jumped into my bed and pretended to be asleep. Two guards came in and inspected each of the beds. They left after a few minutes, so I ran to the door and listened in on their conversation. One said everyone was accounted for sleeping and the other said they were clear to go to the 'meeting.'" Caleb does air quotes. "Next thing, I heard them walking down the hallway before I heard nothing at all behind the door."

Caleb looks at us intently, makes sure we're all still listening before he continues. "I opened the door. It was unlocked. There was no one in the hallway with all those old wrinkly portraits, so I went down it. I kept going until I made it all the way down the stairs and into the foyer. There wasn't a soul in sight. So I took my chances and walked over to the cafeteria thinking that maybe they had food in there I could steal. As I got closer, I heard voices coming out from under the door. I stopped just outside the door and listened in before peeking through the window. It seemed like they were having this 'meeting' the guards mentioned."

Nora brushes off the notion. "Sounds more like a cooking class to me."

"No, trust me, it was a serious meeting," Caleb continues, "with what looked like the whole of the staff and people who run the Manor. I heard Ms. Withers addressing everyone, talking about certain peoples' jobs, what was going to happen the next day, some ball they are having soon—they even mentioned you, Stella. She read off a list of names of people who she said were in the lab, but at the time I didn't know what that meant."

"Oh my God, so they have like a camp counselor meeting in the middle of the night when all the kids are tucked into bed, sleeping soundly." Nora eyes Caleb with a glint in her eyes that makes him squirm a bit on my bed.

Charlie jumps into the conversation before Caleb can respond. He asks, "What did you do after?"

"I waited and listened to their muffled voices for about an hour. And then when I saw them getting ready to end the meeting, I ran like hell up to the dorm hall and got back in bed. A few minutes later the same guards came back, and that was that."

Charlie laughs in disbelief. "Holy shit. A whole hour of time when the Manor is dead asleep. With no guards manning the doors or cameras, no Ms. Withers stomping around in her heels…"

I feel like jumping with joy.

We look at each other like we've just picked the chocolate bar with the golden ticket, all stunned and staring with disbelief, but most importantly: excited.

"Are you guys thinking what I'm thinking?" Nora asks.

Charlie and Caleb nod.

I speak for them. "Caleb just discovered a time frame when we can leave. Slip out from under their noses."

"Exactly!" Nora claps her hands. "And I could kiss him for it."

Caleb blushes ten shades of red and pink, while my own heart flushes at the burst of love I feel for them all in this moment.

In a line, I tug them all toward me into a hug, which Nora unsuccessfully tries to escape. Charlie manages to duck out of it, and I look at him over Caleb's shoulders. The wink he gives me has the butterflies in my stomach racing laps around my heart.

After, Caleb asks, "So, back to what I interrupted, what was your dream about?"

I say nothing, unsure if I want to darken everyone's day.

I pretend to be fascinated with the embroidery on my uniform.

"Come on!" Nora throws her hands up. "It's better to tell us than hold it in."

I shake my head at her, not caring if they feel like they are missing out on gossip or something.

"I agree with Nora," Charlie says. "I think getting it off your chest will make you feel better."

Oh God. Not him now, too.

I roll my eyes and all he does is shrug.

"Fine," I growl at them. "You guys are insatiable."

"Whatever, you love us anyway," Nora retorts.

I roll my eyes again and begin recounting my dream.

Scratch that: *nightmare*.

I detail the wasteland I woke up in, and the sizzling air that suffocated my lungs. Everyone grimaces when I explain my bleeding leg and the dirty water I tried to clean my hands in. They all coil inwardly when I get to the part about the pieces of bronze head floating past me, and my realization that it was hundreds of chunks of the destroyed Statue of Liberty.

Caleb winces. Nora sucks in a heavy breath. Charlie shakes his head.

"That is insane!" Caleb is incredulous.

I nod in agreement and recall the figure I saw at the end. "Right before I woke up, someone was walking toward me. I couldn't see who it was, but thinking back on it now, I have the oddest sense that I knew them."

Nora likes to joke, but now she is dead serious. "Oooh, that's so scary. It could've just been someone caught up in that mess. I wonder what happened?

Her answer is a slight reprieve from wondering why I felt a familiarity in the figure walking toward me.

"We have to do something, tell someone!" Charlie interjects.

Nora looks at him as if he suggested we personally call the president. "Who do you suggest we tell? The guards? A nurse? Or how about Ms. Withers, who knew about Stella's dream before any of us did."

"I can't believe I'm about to say this, but maybe she will understand the severity of the situation and take it to people who can actually do something about it." Charlie's words are full of false hope and I'm pretty sure we can all tell.

I grab his hand. "I'm sorry, Charlie, but the only thing Ms. Withers will care about my dream is how she can use it to her advantage."

"Stella's right," Caleb says. "If she cared at all, none of us would be here under these circumstances."

Nora looks around the other people in the dorm hall, her face lined with sorrow as she gazes upon all the helpless people that decorate the room. "Caleb wouldn't be away from his little brother, I wouldn't be away from my sick sister, and Stella would be home making sure her mom is all right."

Charlie agrees, and the four of us sit facing each other, staring blankly at the blanket on my bed.

The dream replays in my mind like a bad song stuck on repeat.

Despite the situation, we hold our heads a little higher, walk with a bit more pep in our steps. Without fail, however, each of us continues to disappear into the lab for a day or two or gets put into a dreamy, hazy sleep in the dorm hall for hours on end. It has been another week, and since the day I went to the lab, I have only been back once. According to Charlie, the second time I spent exactly twenty-four hours seeing in the lab.

I remember the two dreams loosely.

The first was the hazier dream. A group of women huddled together, crying as they peered down at a hospital bed. Each woman wore surgical gloves and blue masks that covered the bottom half of their faces. For most of my dream, I studied the women. Some wept openly while others tried to compose themselves, console their companions. Toward the end, I glimpsed the person in the hospital bed. It was a man with stark white hair. He had crisscross scars on his forehead. His eyebrows were bushy and gray. Tubes emerged from his mouth and nose. His eyes were closed.

The second dream was of Charlie.

He was dressed in a three-piece suit with shiny patent leather shoes. He never stopped smiling, his eyes lit up as if he were watching fireworks. Our hands were connected as we danced in circles. Our surroundings were out of focus. Only Charlie remained in clear sight, and I have no idea where we were. A loud noise erupted, and our dancing dream ended, the two of us shaken from our clasp and pulled apart. I awoke to Ms. Withers standing at the foot of my bed, staring at me, scanning my face like she was trying to figure out a puzzle.

Nora and Caleb sleep in the dorm hall.

Nora usually has short dreams. She tells us the exciting ones, like the one she had yesterday about her favorite actor winning an Oscar. The not-so-nice ones are harder to get out of her—the one she had about her family huddled around her sister in the hospital, for instance. Those are like pulling teeth, and no one wants to be bitten by Nora, so instead we focus on the dreams that feel light, insignificant, silly.

While those dreams can seem meaningless, we've learned that even the smallest of happy moments that find their way through a crack in the floors or breeze in through an open window are worth holding fast to.

Caleb never wants to talk about his dreams, preferring instead to move on from them the minute he wakes up and only ever wanting to rejoin our conversation as if he never left, inserting himself into the subject matter seamlessly and leaving his dreams in the dust. Instead, Caleb recounts parts of his life that he feels safe sharing with me. One day, under the silence of the dorm hall, with only heavy breathing and machines humming to match his voice, he told me about how he and his brother would spend their days together.

"Despite school sucking, school days were the best because that meant we got to be away from home. Somewhere with reliable adults, rooms that felt fulfilling to be in, not suffocating. The cafeteria is always stocked with food, and the lights will always be on in the classroom. That wasn't something we could always rely on at home."

"You'll get back to your brother, don't worry," I reassured him.

"I bet he's at the old playground down the block from us. When we were much younger and figuring out how to avoid the volatile space that our home could turn into, we could walk to the park just a few minutes down the road from our house. We'd play, sometimes alone, sometimes I'd push him on the swings, or other kids would show up and ask us if we wanted to be in their game of freeze tag. But one winter day, when it was too windy to swing, and no parents were going to let their kids play outside in the cold temperature, we found a wood plank that was broken, that you could lift and crawl under. It led into an enclosed square space that supported the part of the playground you could climb up onto where the slide came down from, and where you could start the monkey bars. We squeezed through the open space, and found a little comfortable space, free of wind and slightly warmer from being enclosed within the wood structure of the jungle gym."

Caleb looked down at his hands that wrung together as he told me this story, a mix of emotions splashing like waves across his face.

"We spent a lot of time hidden away under the jungle gym. There was just enough light that peeked through the planks of wood, or on hotter days we'd leave the loose plank perched open to let in more air and light. We'd just sit under there, sometimes talk or listen to other kids play and go down the slide above us. But most of all, we just found peace in there. Not worried about what could be going on at home or if there'd be dinner when we eventually came in for the night. We only ever wondered if we were missed. Which I don't think we were, 'cause no one ever came looking for us. No one ever tried to come in through the open plank." Caleb looked up at me, "But I hope my brother knows I miss him. That one day I'll do my best to try and squeeze through the broken plank with him again."

"I don't doubt he does, Caleb." I smiled sweetly at him. "It reminds me of our willow tree."

Caleb smiled back.

Charlie is similar to Caleb, never so forthcoming with his dreams or painful memories of the past. But I don't give him much of a choice, so he'll indulge me when I beg. Our moments alone are never full of conversation, however. Sooner or later, he always leans toward me, untethering our feet from the manor floor.

Days after Caleb's revelation, we all lay under the weeping willow in the garden, our heads touching scalp to scalp and our bodies pointing outward like a four-pointed star. Charlie is on my right, his pinky finger brushing mine back and forth, igniting something in my stomach. We are past the point of butterflies in my stomach; it is now a Fourth of July firework display. I inch my hand closer to his, the blades of grass tickling my palm. He catches my movement and takes my hand in his, lacing our fingers together tightly.

"The key is still our biggest mystery," I murmur.

After our conversation in the dorm hall, Charlie and I retraced our steps to the door in the maze. When it comes time to finally use the door, we don't want to find ourselves lost in the Manor's twists and turns.

We take turns staying up at night to see if Ms. Withers continues to call her meeting. She does so without fail. Sometimes the meetings last an hour or longer, others only thirty minutes pass before the guards head back to their post outside the dorm hall.

"We only need a few minutes to successfully exit the Manor, make our way past the guard outside, and get to the garden door," Nora explains. "If we're running, we should be out of our beds and at the door in less than five minutes. That is, of course, if Caleb and Charlie can successfully knock the guard out." During our nights of investigating, we did discover that a single guard stands watch just outside the Manor's front door.

"How many times do I have to tell you I took boxing classes for a whole year, Nora?" Caleb declares exasperated.

"Don't worry, Caleb—she's just envious she won't get to be the one throwing punches," Charlie says, shadowboxing the air.

"I don't think it's a matter of who gets to punch the guard," I interject. "Just as long as the guard, in one way or another, fails at keeping us contained in the Manor for the night, and we successfully get to the door...with a key."

"Right," Charlie responds. "The key."

"Any clue as to where that's lying around?" Nora asks. "Probably the most important key we will ever use in our lives."

"If I were a key, where would I be?" Caleb sings.

I rack my brain for scenes of Ms. Withers' office. Her desk was impeccably clean, aside from a few papers and a closed laptop. She has bookshelves with some impressively huge books, one with a globe on top, a few plants scattered around, and a weirdly shaped crystal. Nowhere in my memory of her office is there a key, big or small. There is, of course, the possibility of a safe or drawers in her office that could have all the answers. From her neck only hangs the monstrous diamonds, no key in sight.

"Now that we have our escape route figured out, let's just keep an extra-sharp eye on the lookout for a key," Nora adds. "No matter its shape, size, color, or design."

"And then we'll grab it," Charlie says.

I hate to be the bearer of bad news, but I can't help but voice my concerns for the worst. "Guys, what if we don't find a key? Or what if we do but it isn't the right key, and we find ourselves all stranded in the garden with guards closing in on us? I feel like we need a backup plan."

No one speaks for a moment, my depressing words sinking into everyone's heads. Charlie turns toward me, and I look at him. The light sky-blue part of his eye that encircles his pupil glows in contrast to the shade of green that envelops us. His warm hand squeezes mine before he says, "Key or no key, we are getting out. Whether we hoist each other up and out of the garden onto the other side of the door or we do find the right key, the night we go into the garden will be our last night in the Manor." His voice gets quiet. In a whisper, to me and me alone, he says, "I promise."

"Thank you for your unwavering optimism, Charlie," Nora says sarcastically. "I, on the other hand, am not an optimist but a realist, and on special occasions a pessimist. Key or no key, thinking that we are just going to be able to jump over the garden wall and find ourselves falling into freedom seems pretty stupid." Nora's words are like someone stomping on a sandcastle. "I'm certainly not going to lounge around thinking we will just be able to walk right out of here undetected and untouched."

I let go of Charlie's hand and glare at Nora, who is still lying opposite me. "All you do is mope around, blaming everyone else and getting mad at people for trying to be even the slightest bit positive. At least we are thinking of ways to get out of here!" I don't hold back. "I was trying to make sure we have a plan if we can't find the key, and you threw cold water all over it! If you keep being negative about our plan, we'll never get out of here."

"I'm being realistic about the reality of our situation." Nora flies up, her face darkening. "If it was so easy to get out of here more people would have done it already."

"We aren't most people! We have each other, crucial information, and a solid plan."

Nora laughs. "You just think you're special, Stella. You get here and everything is about you. Hell, I bet you purposely tripped in the cafeteria on the first day to get everyone's attention and announce your arrival." She throws her hands up. "Here you go, you got it! You're Ms. Withers' prized possession, and you even found yourself a new boyfriend. In fact, I'm surprised you even want to leave the Manor—you're like the prom queen here!"

Caleb looks cowardly at the ground while Charlie clenches his jaw before opening his mouth to speak up, but I cut him off, my blood simmering too high not to yell back. "You know what, Nora? If you don't like our plan, then don't come at all." I get up, not wanting to be with her a minute longer. "You won't be missed."

I brush through the willow tree's leaves, a dramatic exit from the stage. Standing outside of the tree, I look right and then left and wonder where to go. If I were home, I would go to my room or text Callie to see where she was, where I could find her and vent about my troubles—neither option was available to me now.

With the maze on my mind, I go toward it, ready to get mindlessly lost in its many routes. The grass beneath my shoeless feet is soft, the dew collecting on my toes. I lose track of where I am and give up on counting the right and left turns I make, focusing instead on the little flowers that pepper the walls of the maze.

Orange, violet, and white.

Eventually the hedge walls of the maze come to a sharp V and I'm stopped in my tracks by a dead end. I walk toward one hedge and lean up against it, supported only by leaves and the sweet-smelling dainty pink flowers that tickle the side of my face. I close my eyes, taking in a deep breath and counting to five, and then let the breath out for another five seconds. I repeat this, my hands tangling with the branches and leaves by my side, becoming one. I grab on, anchoring myself in this moment and place, attempting to leave behind the sourness of Nora's opinions.

I feel a warmth breath by my face and before I can do anything a pair of lips touch my own. The familiar curves of Charlie's lips mold to mine. A floating sensation overtakes my body, an extravagant weightless feeling enveloping the parts of me that feel sad as Charlie's presence molds into me.

He ends the kiss and steps back and I follow with my face, not wanting to lose the comforting contact, but he is too far out of reach. He mirrors me and rests his body against the opposite hedge, the both of us entwined in the greenery. An electricity brims between the two of us and thickens the garden air, as if we need to separate before the static air shocks our lips numb.

"Are you okay?" he asks.

"Do you mean from your kiss or from Nora?"

He smirks. "I would hope you would be more than okay from my kiss…so Nora?"

I swallow. "It's hard enough trying to keep my head above water here. I guess I just hoped my friends could at least keep me from drowning." I can see the flicker of sadness that crosses his eyes at my words. "You make me feel like I'm wherever I want to be. The sun doesn't set, and we don't have to dream with you around…"

"But."

"But when I stop looking at you, I'm still here. We all are. And the last thing I need, any of us need, are Nora's negative comments."

"I don't disagree with you…"

"But."

"But I think we need to remember what we're all going through, respect each other's feelings and opinions about this crazy situation we're all in." He shrugs, disturbing the leaves around him. "I can't blame her for not wanting to get her hopes up."

"I get that, it's just…ugh!" I throw my hands in the air, my wrist catching on a twig by my ear. "I don't know what to say! I have all these negative thoughts running through my head while this other hopeful part of me fights through. Nora feeding the negativity makes the good parts of me feel weak, like when I get injected with the serum before I begin to dream."

We don't say anything for a little while, the charged air slowly settling into place.

"Listen, I won't pretend to have all of the answers. But the one thing I do know is that the four of us are all so different that naturally we are going to fight as those differences are aired out. But our differences are going to be our advantage here because the Manor wants us all to be passive teenage clones who lay back and dream. If Caleb hadn't been so anxious that he couldn't sleep, he wouldn't have figured out how we could leave unnoticed. Meanwhile, you found the door, and Nora's realistic impulses will keep us from any stupid decisions. We all need each other—despite our differences."

"What about you? What's your difference?"

"Me?" He smiles and pushes off the hedge, leaves falling to the ground behind him. He steps on a pink flower on his way over to me. "I'm important because I'm the best looking one here. Therefore, I boost morale."

Grabbing me by the waist, he hauls me into his chest, my laughter mumbled as he crushes me into a hug, my cheek plastered against his chest with his chin resting on the top of my head. "You're right. I don't like that you are, but you have a point."

"Damn right I'm correct about being the best looking!" He squeezes me harder into his chest. My cheek tingles as he laughs, the vibrations from his chest shaking my head.

"Wait, how did you find me back here? I don't even know where I am."

It takes a few seconds before he responds. "I dreamt about you walking in the maze the other night. I remembered the way you went, so I followed what I saw in my dream and found you here."

"You dreamt this? Did you dream the fight with Nora, too?"

He shakes his head, "No, my dream was only of you walking in the garden and around the maze mindlessly. When I woke up, something didn't sit right in my stomach, like I could sense your movements were fueled by anger, sadness. I put the two together when you left the willow tree."

"Wow, so this whole dreaming future events really is true."

"You doubted it?"

"In the back of my head I always hoped for it to be a lie." I downcast my eyes before looking back up at him. "It is a very small part of my head though. I'm not very good at lying to myself."

"I tried to tell myself this was all a dream, too, that none of this was real or that Ms. Withers and her minions were lying about our special abilities when it came to dreaming." His eyes grow serious, and I blink a few times against the intensity. "The moment I saw you, I realized all of it was real. I've dreamt too many times about you for Ms. Withers' words to be lies."

"I dreamt of you when I was in the lab," I blurt out.

Charlie can't hide his blushing at this. "What were we doing?"

"You assume you were with me?"

"Where else would I be?"

"We were dancing. It was weird because I could feel other bodies around us moving as well, but all I could see was you. You were all dressed up, and you were moving me around like a professional dancer, whisks of air brushing up against us as you pulled me around. It was thrilling, but also unnerving not being able to see what was around us. Everything was out of focus except for you and me."

"Hmm, I wonder what that was about?" His brows furrow. "It's weird you can't place the dream. One thing I've noticed in my dreams is that the setting is always super clear."

"In mine it's the opposite," I respond. "I never know where I am, or at least it's hard to figure out where I am. The people are always the most vivid parts of my dreams."

A cheeky grin spreads across his face. "Well, I guess that's lucky for you when you dream of me."

I can't help but laugh at his sorry attempt to be sexy. Before I can roll my eyes, he is pulling me against him again, bringing his lips down onto mine. Our kisses like a dance we have done for years.

I pull back, but only slightly. "I liked the dream."

He gives me a puzzled look.

"I liked it because now I know that, in the near or far future, we are together."

Charlie and I spend the better part of the day in the maze meandering through the loopy green corridors. We've tasked ourselves with finding the secret door in the maze, but our breaks along the way mean it takes longer than anticipated for us to find the fountain and the dark door behind it. Mid-step-down green corridors, Charlie will launch me backward toward his body, twisting me around until his lips find mine. I let him make me lose track of time and space a few times before getting us back on track.

We lean down to peer through the keyhole, but we are met only by light. There are no details that might give away what exactly awaits on the other side. Charlie knocks and pulls on certain parts of the door and surrounding wall and leaves, but nothing works.

He then prods at leaves and tugs at spiny branches. "Maybe the key is hidden somewhere in the bushes or something."

I giggle at this. "Yeah, or maybe it's at the bottom of this fountain and we have to swim in order to get the key."

I take a single breath and his body is on mine, pushing into me and pulling me down onto the grass below us. Laughter erupts from the both of us as we tumble around in the dew-covered grass that prickles our exposed skin. Charlie digs his hands into my sides, tickling me until tears form in the corners of my eyes. One minute I sit atop him and have his arms pinned above his head, his smile glaring back up at me, and then seconds later he flips us back over and continues his attack on my sides. My abs feel like I've done a hundred crunches.

"You think you're funny, don't you?" He tries to hold in his laugh.

"The funniest," I boast.

I lie down beside him and settle into his left shoulder, rest my head against his beating heart. His arm cushions my neck and our legs entangle below us, no longer able to decipher where I end and he begins.

The sky above us slowly shifts from a bright candescent blue to one speckled with dots of bright yellow and orange from the setting sun. The ground beneath us cools, growing mistier as the sun slips behind the high walls of the maze. The skin of Charlie's hand is a sherbert color as the sky above transitions from a clear ocean blue to a murky pink, mixed with stripes of blue and jagged strips of clouds. His upright palm darkens as deep reds meet the sky and mix with the light pink, turning them into a fiery orange, setting his tanned bicep on fire. The sunset erupts colors on Charlie's right arm in its final moments before surrendering to the moon.

I reach my arm over his torso to trace my fingers along his lit-up arm, trailing the veins on the inside of forearm. I continue my crawl of his arm and trail my fingers farther down to the palm of his hand, which is rough and slightly calloused. I draw circles around the center of his palm with my middle finger, slightly tickling him in return for earlier. My revenge only lasts for so long before his fingers reach down and clasp my own in his.

The liminal time that is dusk, where you are neither in day nor night but are instead transfixed in a wave of shifting colors, preparing for the next phase of the day, is my favorite.

Then a throat clears from behind us, the noise breaking through the colorful silence that held us, and I jump up from Charlie's chest, my fingers scraping against his.

Ms. Withers stares at me, a sly gleam in her eyes, her palms perched on her hips and one leg extended. Her long red fingernails tap the waist of her pristine white pencil skirt. "I knew I would find the two of you together. Ms. Grey and Mr. Foster canoodling in the garden." She gives us a pitiful look that makes me want to lunge at her. "The two of you do a less-than-good job at hiding your...affections. You reek of adolescent love." She shivers and rolls her eyes. "It nauseates me."

Charlie stands, and with his shoulders pushed back and chest puffed out, he towers over Ms. Withers. "Well, if it is so repulsive to you, then why don't you leave us alone."

"Oh, dear Charlie, do you really think that I trekked my way through this godforsaken maze in heels just to leave you two alone?"

"Sure." Charlie crosses his arms. "None of what you do ever makes sense to me."

Ms. Withers mirrors Charlie and crosses her arms. "Good thing I don't care what you think." She whips around, her dark hair flying through the air before settling perfectly on her back.

She takes a few steps forward, careful not to get her heels stuck in the soft grass.

Charlie stands like a statue, stoic and unmoving, and I sit on my knees, watching her walk away beneath the shadow of Charlie.

Ms. Withers stops dead in her tracks and without turning around bellows out an icy cold, "Follow me."

Not needing to be told again, I shoot up from the ground and Charlie jumps forward.

Reaching back, he grabs my hand, and the two of us follow.

It takes Ms. Withers less than a minute to wind her way out of the maze without getting lost. She doesn't look back once, reassured by our hurried footsteps behind her. When we exit, no one else is outside in the garden. Nora and Caleb are no longer under the willow's branches.

Usually the garden is packed during sunset.

A guard stands at the massive front door, as if waiting for us. *Do Ms. Withers and her guards know what we've found?*

Luckily, all the guard does is hold open the door for Ms. Withers and us before locking it for the night with a resounding thud.

The foyer is alive with movement, a sea of people swimming about. Guards and nurses move tables, candles, carpets, and chairs around the room while Lady A stands on the bottom step of the grand staircase, a clipboard in one hand, her other conducting traffic, pointing people this way and that.

Charlie gives me a puzzled look.

Ms. Withers stops quickly to talk with a nurse about something, and the only words I catch are "midnight" and "dress."

What in the world could they be talking about?

Charlie, still clasping my hand, makes a move toward the library, but we are only met by more commotion and people moving about.

"What is going on?" I'm utterly puzzled.

"Preparations for tonight's ball." Ms. Withers is closer to me than I thought. She has suddenly materialized right behind us like a ghost, making no sound at all.

"What ball?" Charlie asks.

"You wouldn't know about it, but Stella does." Ms. Withers looks at me. "That is, of course, if you remember your first day here."

"Unfortunately, I have worked hard at trying to forget my first day here," I say. "Especially meeting you."

"Dear Stella, you never fail to be so elegant and forthcoming with your words. It's one of the things I love most about you. You remind me of my younger self."

My stomach twists and turns at the thought of being compared to Ms. Withers.

"Speaking of the ball, I need you to come with me." Ms. Withers motions to me.

Charlie's grip grows tighter on my hand. "No."

"Yes," Ms. Withers counters.

"Why?" I interject in their stare down. "And where?"

"To my office. I have something to give you." Her words are less than reassuring. "Come on, there is nothing to fear...

for once." She smiles at herself and turns, once again walking away and expecting me to follow like an obedient dog.

I turn toward Charlie. "Go up to the dorm hall and I'll meet you up there once I'm done with Ms. Withers."

"Absolutely not, no." Charlie's words are unwavering and stubborn. "I'm not just going to let you walk into the lion's den alone. Ms. Withers proves herself to be more and more psychotic every day."

"Things will be a lot easier if you just let me go. Oddly enough, I actually believe her that there is nothing for me to fear right now." I give his hand one more squeeze. "Plus, I don't think she's going to hurt me after admitting that I remind her of herself."

"Yeah, about that…I think I'm going to have to rethink loving you now." He jokes. "Ms. Withers definitely doesn't fall into what I would describe as my type."

I'm about to laugh when what he's said finally hits me.

"What did you just say?" I begin.

"Stella!" Ms. Withers' voice cuts through the foyer like a sharp knife.

Reluctantly, I let go of Charlie, shelve this conversation for later, and follow Ms. Withers.

I catch up to Ms. Withers just before she opens the door to the long hall of offices. The noise of the door slamming behind us is dwarfed by the busy noise of people working in the office adjacent to Ms. Withers'. Through the door from the hallway, I can see three guards pushing around a heavy mahogany desk and placing expensive looking chairs around it. In the corner, another guard hammers nails to hang more paintings.

"A bit of a pest, I know," Ms. Withers comments.

I look at her quizzically.

"The noise," She responds. "I've had to live with the constant banging for the past few days. But it will all be over soon." Her gaze grows sharper at me. "In fact, by tonight."

"What is happening tonight?"

Before answering, Ms. Withers positions us in her office the way we always are. She sits in her throne behind her desk, while I sit uncomfortably in front of her, desperately hanging onto every word she says.

"Since you have so pleasantly blocked out our first conversations here, I will explain the ball again to you." Ms. Withers stands and walks over to an old photograph of a huge house.

Huge house doesn't do it justice.

It's a mansion, a palace. The Manor.

"The Manor has been around for quite a while, testing and observing Dreamers for longer than the two of us combined have been alive. Technology has sometimes advanced quickly and sometimes slowly, but most importantly it has prevailed since the very beginning. Tonight, when the clock strikes midnight, the chime will commemorate the Manor's one hundredth year."

Ms. Withers' words bring a sense of déjà vu, and I begin remembering our first conversation. Once again, I'm taken back by the length of time the Manor has successfully operated and "prevailed," to use her word. It is sickening to think about the past hundred years the Manor has lived and even more so to think about the possibility of one hundred more—people like myself, Charlie, Caleb, and Nora wasting away.

Ms. Withers continues, "What is even more exciting is that tonight we introduce our new leader to the Manor!"

"I thought you were in charge of the Manor?"

"I am." She doesn't skip a beat. "But the job is a hearty one and not meant to be done solo. In fact, the leader being introduced to everyone tonight will only be new to some faces."

"What do you mean?" Nothing she says ever makes sense to me.

"My business partner had to leave for quite some time to attend to some..." She looks me up and down, "...other business."

I can't help but shiver. "So now they're back?"

"Yes!" She claps. "And tonight's ball is all about the celebration of the Manor's one hundredth year, alongside the return of my magnificent partner."

"In crime," I mumble under my breath.

"Excuse me?"

I cough. "So, that is what the office renovation next door is for?" The picture grows a little clearer. "And the empty painting frame next to yours, that's where your partner's will go?"

"Clever girl." She walks over to the big chestnut dresser towering at the back corner of her office. "Now for the fun part."

Again, I shiver. Ms. Withers' definition of fun has never matched mine.

I notice that the dresser's handles are two shiny gold crescent moons. "I love you to the moon," echoes in my head.

Ms. Withers' hands cover the moons as she opens the dresser. I clench the arms of my chair, ready for some monster or creepy guard with a syringe to jump out at me as the thick wooden doors groan open. Nothing jumps out, however, aside from a sea of brilliant green. Gorgeous silk cascades downward like an emerald waterfall, fabric upon fabric flowing into itself.

I want to lie atop it, feel the glorious soft to the touch fabric beneath my fingers. Traveling up toward the bodice, the silk comes to an end where it curls under into itself, puffing out slightly and creating shape. Delicate, intricate lace begins where the silk ends and reminds me of tightly packed leaves and flowers with little room for anything other than the petals themselves. The lace climbs like vines to a high neckline and long half sleeves.

Ms. Withers swishes the dress around, the green swaying like tall strands of grass. "This will be your dress for the ball tonight."

"You want me to wear that?"

Ms. Withers giggles at my skepticism. "It is only a dress, not a straitjacket. Don't act so scared."

"I…I'm not scared. It's just that the dress—gown—looks like it should be on a red carpet and not just on anyone who can fit into it. Especially not me. Why do you even want me to wear it?"

For the first time since I've known Ms. Withers, her eyes grow kind, no longer having the intensity of a fighter in the ring. "Contrary to popular belief, certainly yours, you have become somewhat of a star pupil of mine. While your words have quite a bit of bite, your dreams never fail to please. Additionally, I want everyone to look their best tonight. What we are celebrating deserves decadence."

"Why? Why me?"

"Do you remember being a little girl and seeing the other girls get everything they wanted? Love from their parents, attention from their best friends, praise from their teachers, crushes from the boys they liked. Stella, you aren't the girl who gets picked last for kickball out of pity here. No, here you are the girl who is picked *first*, the one everyone looks at and envies." Ms. Withers clasps my hands tightly, her warm skin enveloping my own, "Because of your dreams, you have the world in your hands."

I have never felt less like the girl worthy of envy, praise, or a designer dress. Despite her grasp on my hands, her words feel loose and frail, further from the truth.

It is impossible to have the world in my palms if I'm stuck in the Manor.

"Why are my dreams so special? What makes my dreaming ability enviable?"

Her eyes refocus on the center of my forehead, as if seeing into my brain. "The girl who gets picked first never asks why, she simply enjoys it." Ms. Withers holds the dress high in her arms so the delicate silk at the bottom does not drag on the floor. "I would recommend you do the same."

She gingerly places the dress into my arms, and I hold it high, hoping not to ruin even a centimeter of this beautiful creation.

"Now go and get ready," she says. "The ball begins at ten p.m. sharp."

I leave Ms. Withers in her office, her keen avoidance of my questions only likely to haunt me more if I try to badger the truth from her. I'm nearly to the busy foyer when she calls after me.

"You, Stella, are that girl and more. Do not worry yourself about your dreams and why, everything eventually falls into place. And trust me, the night you are about to have will fill the dress's potential."

The dorm hall is empty aside from a rainbow of beds covered in colorful gowns and black tuxedos. Blue, pink, yellow, purple, and black passes in my periphery as I head to my bed and lay my dress down gingerly upon it so as to avoid wrinkles. A pair of silver strappy heals sit perched on the end of my bed, and I try them on for size. It takes a minute for me to get used to being a few inches taller, otherwise they fit my foot perfectly and how Ms. Withers knew my exact shoe and dress size is a mystery, albeit one I don't wonder about for too long.

Really, I don't think I want to know how.

I hear noises from the bathrooms at the end of the hall and I carefully take off the heels and head toward the excited voices carrying from the pink glow of the girls' bathroom, a sharp contrast to the groans and muttering voices from the blue glow of the boys' room.

Throughout the bathroom are rosy cheeked girls rushing from the showers to the sinks, where they dry and curl their hair and apply the new makeup that has suddenly appeared on a table closest to the entrance.

One girl named McKenna skips up to me, clapping her hands in excitement. "O-M-G, Stella! Did you hear about the ball?" She bounces from one foot to the other, hardly able to contain her excitement.

"Yes, I just heard about it."

"Come on, get ready!" She motions me toward the new makeup. "They gave us makeup and everything! I'm so excited!"

I don't want to hurt her feelings by voicing my true opinion. It is truly amazing how a party, pretty dresses, and some makeup can change people's perspectives. I wish I could let go like the other girls, and enjoy the moment of getting ready, but I can't seem to knock the suspicion growing in the pit of my stomach.

"What color is your dress?" she asks.

"Green."

"That will look so pretty on you!" She twists a strand of hair around her finger, practicing how she will curl it later.

"Thanks," I respond.

She looks at me like she is waiting for me to say something. I don't catch on.

"Mine is orange!" With that, she turns and skip-walks back over to the mirror where she chats with other excited girls and finishes towel drying her hair.

I search for a quiet space to calmly get ready. I spy Nora sitting on a bench at the back of the bathroom with a disgusted look painted across her face. The back of my neck heats and my pulse quickens, our unkind words rushing through my head. I'm not used to having fights with other girls, apart from my mom. Callie and I never fought about anything more serious than where to go get food or who is the best Taylor Swift ex.

My relationship with Nora feels higher stakes, and the thought of Nora never wanting to talk to me again is more nauseating than the time Callie wouldn't talk to me for a week.

Her eyes land on mine in the mirror.

Do I go to her? Apologize?

Pretend I don't see her and walk out of the bathroom?

I plant myself on the bench next to her. "Look I'm…"

"Stop." Nora turns and faces me. "I'm sorry. I shouldn't have jumped down your throat. Caleb yelled at me for blowing up over nothing before storming off, too, leaving me alone under the tree." She looks me in the eyes, a slight redness to her cheeks.

Her apology is not what surprises me.

Caleb, sweet timid Caleb, yelled at Nora.

She continues, "I sat there under the tree all alone, and it hit me. I wouldn't survive without you guys and your grossly annoying optimism. I don't like to admit this, so listen up, because I'm not going to repeat myself: You were right. We are going to get out of here."

I clasp Nora's hand, squeezing with all my strength, "And I'm so sorry for saying I wouldn't want you coming with us. It would break my heart to leave without you."

Nora's hand squeezes mine back. "Good, because I would find a way out of here just so I could find you guys and beat your asses up."

A sense of relief washes through me. "I can't believe Caleb yelled at you. Good for him!"

"I know." Nora bites her lip. "It was kind of hot."

I laugh so hard I almost choke, which causes Nora to start up so hard she begins snorting, which only makes us laugh harder. We are interrupted by a flash of yellow. A girl named Harper rushes by, her frilly muted yellow dress rubbing against our faces.

Nora looks unamused as she shoves yellow tulle out of her mouth. "Can you believe this bullshit?"

I chuckle. "I can't help but feel like we are being tricked. As we all walk out in our dresses the big bad wolf is going to jump out at us." Nora nods in agreement. "It is nice to see more smiles than frowns, though."

"Frowns, smiles, whatever. I just can't believe they expect me to put on heels and a dress!" You would think they were asking her to dance in front of everyone like a chicken. "I'm definitely not doing my makeup and curling my hair."

"Don't worry, Nora, I'll curl your hair and do your makeup for you," I say.

Nora nudges my shoulder with hers. "What did McKenna want earlier?"

"She mostly just wanted to tell me the color of her dress. Riveting stuff."

"Ha! This is her dream come true. All these girls thought they were missing prom, but here they go." Nora feigns a beauty queen's excitement when they find out they're the winner.

"Speaking of dresses, what color is yours?" I ask. Nora crosses her arm and fake zips her mouth shut. "Come on, I'm going to find out sooner or later."

"Not if I don't put it on."

"What are you going to do, wear your dirty clothes from today?"

Unfazed, Nora responds, "If I have to."

"Not if I have any say." I yank Nora up from the bench. "You are definitely missing your prom, so make the most of tonight and wear your dress."

She quirks an eyebrow up at me. "Don't piss me off, we only just made up."

"And don't piss me off, go get your dress." I playfully shove her away, prompting her to grab her dress.

"I like this new Stella." She shoots me a sly grin, "Sassy."

Through the chorus of girly giggles, I can hear a voice yelling at the boys through our shared wall.

Not long after, a sharp voice enters the bathroom: "Girls!" In unison we look toward Lady A, who snaps her fingers. "Get ready, time is of the essence.

I emerge from the shower thirty minutes later, my body scrubbed and smelling like pink grapefruit and mint. I comb my fingers through my damp hair before blow drying it. Blowing my hair out feels comical as I stand swathed in a pink towel only a few feet away from the room where I have been forced to sleep. The hot air rushing past my cheeks reminds me of my mom, and how it became a ritual of ours when I was in middle school for her to blow dry my hair every morning before school.

"You absolutely cannot go to school with wet hair." Her arms crisscrossed in an X over her chest.

"Ugh, mom, no one is going to care whether my hair is wet or dry."

"I care!"

She pushed me out of the doorframe and back into my room, over and into my bathroom, where towels and lotion bottles lay about. Opening a drawer, she pulled out my hardly used blow dryer, taking a minute to untangle the mess of cords.

"Come here." She beckoned me over to stand in front of her. "I care, because I don't want you catching a cold with freezing-cold hair sticking to your back. So I'll dry it for you."

Her eyes caught mine in the mirror as I settled in front of her. "But just this once."

I was too tired to argue. "Fine."

The hum of the dryer was surprisingly soothing in my tired early morning stupor, the presence of her hands raking gently through my hair comforting. I watched her dry my hair with surgeon-like precision, biting the side of her lip as if figuring out an exciting puzzle. I enjoyed watching my mom in the mirror, looking peaceful and unrushed, which contrasted her usually frantic self when she would rush from room to room in the house. I could sense the comfort and ease that this task gave her, something simple yet loving to begin her day with.

She caught my gaze looking at her, and formed a grin, winking at me as if saying, "I know, this is nice."

After a handful of minutes, she turned the blow dryer off, tucked it away in an organized manner in my drawer, and ran her hands down the length of my hair. "Look how nice this is, beautiful. Now you won't have a wet circle on your back every morning."

On the drive to school that day, instead of sitting pensively behind the wheel and not uttering a word, she hummed along to the radio, and I even told her about a presentation Callie and I were doing in third period. I got out of the car, and before the car door slammed shut behind me, I caught it mid-swing.

"Hey, mom, thanks for drying my hair. It's nice, feels good."

I bounced into school that day, my feet feeling slightly lighter, a hop in my step, an extra bounce to my perfectly blow-dried hair.

And it wasn't only just the once. My mom came into my room like clockwork fifteen minutes before we were meant to leave for school every morning for years, the two of us enjoying the time before our busy days began, where we were just mother and daughter, grinning sillily at each other in the mirror in between yawns. After my dad died, she started sleeping in, finding it hard to get out of bed, and I started to shower at night, wanting to scrub the day away under a scorching hot spray. I wish she was behind me now, the dryer in her hands not missing a spot, her kind eyes helping me prepare for the evening.

Luckily, it takes no time at all before my hair is hot between my fingers. Now comes the hard part: What do I do with it? I don't have time to figure that out, because Nora walks up to me in a matching towel, her hair so wet it drips onto the floor.

"I never even put this much effort into getting ready at home."

"You've only just showered?"

Her response is to groan. "I know. It was exhausting."

I laugh.

"And now we have to put on heavy puffy dresses." She grabs at my hand trying to drag me away from the mirror. "Ugh, come on, let's get this over with."

I don't let her pull me away. "Not so fast. First," I grab a makeup brush and yield it in front of Nora, "makeup and hair time."

She winces, as if I just grabbed a grenade and not a brush covered in blush.

The two of us get to it, proceeding to apply what little makeup is left, the girls having already ransacked the pile. I leave my hair as it is, slightly wavy from blow drying it. I apply a thick coat of mascara, loving how normal it seems to do something that was once a part of my daily routine.

A berry-colored lipstick is left in the pile of makeup, and I grab it, covering my lips in the raspberry-tasting tint. Nora lets me apply blush and a nude lipstick, then surprises me by perfectly applying a winged eyeliner.

I pick up my dress, undo the line of buttons that run down the back, and slip in feet first, pulling it up over my hips and waist. I slide my arms through the sleeves and pull it up over my chest but need it buttoned up.

Nora's blow dryer warmed hands tickle my back as she takes the time to perfectly clasp my dress up.

"Thank you," I say, the bodice fits snuggly around my chest.

"My turn. Now don't laugh or I'll take this off immediately." Nora emerges from behind me, and my jaw hits the floor.

She matches the bathroom.

"You look…"

"…like the loofahs in the shower." She plants her hands on the sink, staring blankly into the mirror.

"No," I say, catching her eye in the reflection. "That's not what I was going to say. I was going to say beautiful. Pink is unexpectedly your color."

Her plush pink dress matches her cheeks. Her dark hair appears even darker against the dress as it cascades over her bare shoulders, where her dress hangs on the sides of her upper arms, creating the perfect sweetheart neckline, the slight dip showing a bit of cleavage and giving Nora a more feminine look than usual. The delicate satin falls perfectly and the bottom sways back and forth as she stands, her gold heels peeking out when she steps. A crystal belt separates the top and bottom of her dress, resting at the point of her hips. Looking closer, I see that the crystals form a delicate rose pattern across the length of her dress. She is a sight for sore eyes.

Poor Caleb.

"Can I be your date tonight, Nora?" I ask.

"I would say yes, but Charlie would kill me if I stole you from him when you look like this." Her eyes rise from my toe to head "You look gorgeous."

I smile so hard it hurts the sides of my mouth. Nora's face echoes mine.

"Well," I say, holding out my elbow for her to grab onto. "Shall we go to the ball?"

Nora and I are the only ones left in the dorm hall. The room is no longer a rainbow of gowns and matching heels, and is back to its usual arrangement of empty beds. The sight is eerily nice. The faint hum of music comes from somewhere else in the Manor, the bass of the song softly vibrating the ground.

Two guards handle the portraits of Ms. Withers and the empty frame next to hers at the end of the hall. One polishes hers while the other undoes the glass shield of the other, readying it for artwork. We slip past the guards, Nora making faces behind their backs, and we make it to the grand staircase, the ball waiting below.

"Wow," Nora mutters from the top of the staircase.

I feel like I'm looking down at the stars. Star lights travel from the top of the bannisters and follow the stairs to the bottom, creating the illusion of a light wave. A candelabra sits on each step, as if guarding the pathway down. The breeze carries music up the stairs and sways the flames back and forth. The orchestra plays beautifully, the violins, harps, cellos, and piano all arranged next to the door. Each player wears a three-piece suit, even the women. Their music is hypnotic throughout the Manor.

The crystal chandelier shines especially bright from high above, bright specks bouncing off and creating shiny spots on the hard surfaces of the foyer. Rainbows cover the dark walls, and I look over at Nora, who has a tiny one on her cheek. We giggle to each other, astounded by the magical scene below us.

Girls in fabric of every color sway to the music. Some seem to hang back, take in the opulence of the scene, while others smile coyly at the boys scattered around them, who mostly look awkward and uncomfortable in their black suits, their ties practically choking them. A rare few handle the situation with ease, however, looking like princes out of fairy tales and born for formal wear.

"It's not a party if the wicked witch isn't in attendance," Nora says.

Ms. Withers does not bob up and down but floats effortlessly through the room, her dress bloody and red, matching her lips, nails, and heels, and hugging her like a second skin before pooling out around her feet. Behind her trails Lady A in the darkest black silk slip dress. Dancing couples quickly separate and allow them to pass.

Light and movement flashes from the library and different music floats through. McKenna rushes out carrying a couple of finger sandwiches, her orange-peach dress swishing around and her excitement effervescent in her aura. Her dress complements her tanned skin and light blonde hair perfectly, but another figure from the library stops me cold.

Charlie walks out of the library with Caleb, both dressed to the nines in sharp black suits. Caleb looks goofily handsome, his suit slightly wrinkled, while Charlie looks like he's auditioning to play James Bond. The suit makes him look taller and more angular, older and more professional, too.

Is he looking for me?

His eyes meet mine and he tries to keep the smile from the corners of his mouth. I can't help but blush, redness spreading from the tips of my ears and across my cheeks and nose. I break out in a wide smile, unashamed by how goofy I probably look, adoring puppy eyes and all.

Nora, meanwhile, has turned the color of her dress and tries not to stare down at Caleb.

Hearing the music, soaking in the glow of the party, standing next to Nora, gazing down at Charlie and Caleb, my heart feels full and happy.

The Manor slips away like the sun beneath the horizon.

Charlie walks up to me, his eyes scanning across the cascading green covering my body. "Is it bad if I say I'm kind of thankful for the Manor right now?"

"Just as long as you don't go drooling after Ms. Withers tonight."

He takes my hand, says, "I like green more than red."

I grab onto the lapels of his suit jacket and tug on them, bringing his body closer until we are flush against each other. "You've been holding back on me." He raises a questioning eyebrow and I place my hand on his tie, wiggle it a bit before centering it perfectly and tugging his head down, his breath dancing on my lips. "You look *really* hot in a tux."

Charlie can only get in one laugh before I crash my lips to his, completely overwhelmed by the moment's magic. The music lifts me, makes me feel like I'm no longer touching the ground as I wrap my arms around Charlie's neck.

Happiness hangs thick in the air, like a hot and humid summer day.

Caleb coughs.

"Get a room," Nora interrupts.

Breaking from my lips, Charlie looks at me, his eyes slightly glazed over before rolling them in Nora's direction. "Trust me, I would if I could."

"Caleb, you look so handsome!" I exclaim giving him a quick hug, trying to discharge the awkwardness of the situation.

Caleb stuffs his hands in his pockets.

In my mind, I urge him to grab Nora's hand, to put his arm around her pink waist.

People circle around us, dancing or simply moved by the energy in the foyer. Colors rush around us to the tune of the music, making me feel like I'm on a spinning rollercoaster. David, a boy I only ever see with permanent bed head, rushes up to us looking dapper in a navy suit. "Guys! There is a chocolate fountain! Chocolate fountain!" He shakes Charlie's shoulders before rushing off into another direction, almost tumbling into a girl in a purple dress.

"Ms. Withers probably poisoned it with the dream serum," Nora says.

I throw her a *"what the hell!"* look and she shoots one back that says *"What?"* like she has no idea what's up. Crossing my arms, I tap my foot and lift my eyebrow like an upset parent waiting for their child to realize what they have done wrong.

Doesn't she remember our conversation from earlier?

With a huff of reluctant air and another roll of her eyes she adds, "But I bet the chocolate is really good."

Nora starts to follow David to the fountain but stops, turns to Caleb, and grabs onto his hand before leading him away with her. Caleb stumbles over himself in surprise before turning back to us and quickly making his way. Charlie shrugs while I give Caleb a thumbs-up. The two of them disappear into the library and leave Charlie and I surrounded by people yet feeling alone.

"Why are they going into the library?" I ask.

"Our library has been temporarily transformed into the home of the famous chocolate fountain, amongst other things."

"Oh God, what will we do if our precious books get chocolate all over them?" I say with pretend concern.

"Read and…eat."

I catch myself laughing, and I realize it is my first time standing in the foyer feeling good. Usually I am full of dread about the lab or Ms. Withers' office.

I relish in this change of pace.

"You look lovely tonight, Stella."

Speak of the devil.

Ms. Withers gives me a once-over from my silver shoes to the top of my lacey neck, before slithering away to her next victim. Goose bumps pimple across my lace-covered skin.

"She's not wrong." Charlie pulls my attention to him. "You are the most beautiful girl here tonight."

"I'm more special than the chocolate fountain?"

He makes a show of contemplating his answer. "*Way* more than the chocolate fountain."

It hits me in this moment that he told me he loved me earlier.

With all the craziness, I had somehow forgotten—until now, as I catch myself wanting to say the same thing back. I am lost in his oasis eyes, peering back and forth trying to memorize each one of their tiny minute details and the exact feelings, sounds, smells, emotions of this moment.

No longer having to go on my tiptoes thanks to my heels, I tilt my head and kiss him gently on the cheek before asking, "Will you dance with me?"

A sweet grin breaks on his face. "I don't usually dance," he says, surveying the people swaying to the music. "But with you…I thought you'd never ask."

We find a pocket away from the bodies pushing up against each other, a space left just for us. The band by the door slows and the piano takes over, a singular honeyed sound. Charlie gently places his hands on my waist, and I wrap my arms around his shoulders, as if no one could take him away from me. His eyes outshine the grand chandelier. They are my favorite thing in the world, a lifeboat in a constant storm.

"What?" he asks.

I look at him quizzically. "What?"

"You have this look in your eyes, like you know something that's gonna win you millions."

"Oh, that type of look."

"Yes, this mischievous, sexy look you're doing right now! What does it mean?"

It's easy to drive the boy crazy.

"I'm just happy. Because of you." I look around at all the other smiling faces. "It feels wrong to be this happy in the Manor, surrounded by things that make me want to roll up into a ball and never wake up. To have Ms. Withers and Lady A standing over in the corner watching us intently without being bothered at all feels totally bizarre. The number of times I've cried, wanted to run away, shuddered in fear at the sound of Ms. Withers' heels approaching—none of that holds a candle to how I feel when I'm with you." I look him straight in the eyes, his gaze warm to the touch, "When I'm with the person I love."

His cheeks flush, and he crashes his lips to mine. Time slows, and I don't know how long we kiss. But when we break free, the violins have joined the piano and my lips feel bruised.

"You love me?" he asks, searching my eyes for any lingering doubt.

Biting my swollen lip, I nod, trying to show him just how much I do through the look in my eyes.

His eyes gleam with a sparkle, almost watering at the very bottom. A drop of water in his ocean eyes.

I already know the answer, but I want to hear the words.

"And do you love me?"

"I loved you before I even knew who you were. My dreams of you have been the most powerful force in my life, and to be honest, I can't blame the Manor for wanting mine when they're about you."

My heart explodes into a million little pieces before piecing itself back together.

I stop counting how many songs we've danced to. They all blend, one note, one melody, one piano key or violin string at a time. I've twirled around Charlie so many times, I feel drunk on the music and hum of the others dancing around us. The sparkle and flicker of the lights look like shooting stars and a bright full moon, granting all our wishes. The magnificent green of my gown flows all around, intermixing with the bottoms of other girls' bright dresses, creating a kaleidoscopic of fabric. The ground no longer feels too hard, the ceiling no longer like it's too short, but a gateway to all possibilities. I throw my head back as Charlie holds me tight to his body, spinning us around to the music. Looking up, I feel weightless, like I'm floating in water. My smile never once leaves my face as I get twirled around by Charlie, meeting other smiling faces.

I feel so comfortable, grounded, sedated in his embrace that for a moment I almost miss the back of Caleb's red hair and Nora's smiling face as their bodies move around ours. They are both rigid as poles, afraid to make too much contact with one another, potentially giving too much of their feelings away. They both smile at each other, every now and then glancing down to make sure neither of them is stepping on each other's toes.

Things are almost too good to be true.

Over the next few hours I dance with Charlie, jump around with Nora, and bounce in and out of the library to eat way too many chocolate-dipped strawberries. That is until Ms. Withers, like a red slithering snake, elbows and shoulders her way through the giddy crowd, making her way toward the staircase. She moves up the stairs, the candles flickering and swaying as she swishes past them, her movement nearly blowing them out. At the top, she snaps her body around and gives a slight nod. The music stops immediately, and the all-too-familiar tendrils of anxiety grip the pit of my stomach. A sea of murmurs and whispers fills the orchestra's void, and I turn to Nora, Caleb, and Charlie, who are all just as confused as I am.

Lady A's voice cuts like a knife through the foyer. "Attention, everyone, to Ms. Withers."

Ms. Withers clasps her hands. her distressing red smile cast down upon us. She takes a second to look at each and every one of us.

My palms begin to sweat.

"I am very pleased to see that everyone is having a wonderful time this evening." Her gaze zeroes in on me and stays. "However, the party is just now starting, and I would like to introduce you all to one of the reasons this ball is being held. As most of you know and have seen, after some time away, we are excited to welcome back one of the leaders of the Manor, and one of its great minds, no less. His presence has been greatly missed, and the Manor has felt the wake of his time away." Her smile grows more evil. "Please give a warm welcome to *your* new leader…"

A figure emerges from the door to her right, the door we were expressly forbidden from opening and entering. From it enters a tall, imposing man who walks confidently toward Ms. Withers and shakes her hand before standing at the top of the stairs like a king addressing his subjects below.

His eyes find mine.

A smile erupts on his face. A frown erupts on mine.

A familiar voice echoes throughout the extravagant space. "Hello, everyone."

My breathing slows, and my feet can no longer hold me up.

The room blurs, the colors that were once so clear and bright in my mind twisting and turning before they are nothing but a cloud of gray.

And then black.

I lie on the floor, my back cold from the marble floor beneath my lace. Pockets of light flash between the people surrounding me. Nobody moves. Charlie, Nora, and Caleb hover over me, yet each of their bodies is frozen in time. Charlie's hand outstretched for mine, Nora's face scrunched in confusion, and Caleb's hands wrung together.

What in the world?

I slowly get to my feet, careful not to disturb the frozen bodies around me. My dress brushes up against Nora's, the pink tulle around her feet swaying with mine, yet she remains still. Slightly wobbly on my feet, I grab onto Charlie's arm, which feels strangely warm and strong, each of his muscles distinct beneath my fingers despite his mannequin state.

I shove my face in front of his, attempting to coax movement from him.

Nothing.

I wave my hand in front of Caleb's face. When that fails, I shove his shoulder back, but he doesn't budge.

Just when things couldn't get any weirder here at the Manor...

Is this some new type of way to have us dream? Like horses standing up?

The band stands in the corner, mid-note and quiet. My dress swaying and heels clicking between everyone are the only movements and sounds in the room now. What freaks me out most is that even Ms. Withers and Lady A are unmoving. Ms. Withers' lips are puckered in a proud smile while Lady A's face is stone cold and serious. Their sudden lack of control suggesting that this is not a weird Manor science experiment but something else entirely.

I want to throw myself into my dorm hall bed, close my eyes, and wake up to everyone up and moving again.

And then—a noise.

The foyer door softly whines open, the sound magnified by the blanket of silence.

I turn, and the breath leaves my body as my father steps through the door and gently closes the massive door behind him.

"Dad?" I whisper, my voice like a shout in the room.

The kindest smile spreads across his face, dimples forming in his cheeks as he weaves in between frozen mid-motion bodies. His walk is the same as before, smooth with a slight tilt to the right from his busted knee. He's dressed in his usual work attire: dress pants and a white button-down shirt. As he gets closer, I smell his cologne, the familiar scent I once used to wake to each morning: apple, vanilla, cloves, and sandalwood.

My pulse tightens in the temples on either side of my face, and I can feel my cheeks flush red as my inner temperature spikes. A buzzing sound like a swarm of bees overhead starts in my ears, and I don't know whether to cry in joy or scream in fear at this sight. My dad is supposed to be dead, gone from my life for forever. Yet here he is, flesh and blood, approaching me.

"Stella Bella," he says, stopping a foot in front of me. "You look absolutely gorgeous."

"Dad?" I repeat. It can't be him, but everything about the man in front of me screams the opposite. "What, what are, what is…"

My thoughts race one hundred miles per hour while my body races on another track and before I know it, I've launched myself at him, my arms wrapping tightly around his head and shoulders, my nose wrinkling into the crook of his neck. A laugh shakes my body as he chuckles through my cobra like grip. He moves to loosen his arms from around my lace-covered back, but instead of budging I only tighten my arms.

"What are you doing here?" I croak the words into the side of his neck.

"Stella." He laughs some more. "You are going to have to detach yourself from me. I can't understand what you are saying."

Reluctantly, I let go, but not completely. I grab his hands, clenching them tightly in my own. "What are you doing here?"

He squeezes my hand with each word. "I'm here for you."

I can't help but smile as I stare into his mossy eyes. "To rescue me? How do you know about the Manor?" My words stumble out of my mouth, and my dad begins to answer, but I interrupt before the first word is finished. "Wait. I went to your funeral, but you're…" I look him up and down, my eyes tracking the perfection of his pleated dress pants and his pressed white shirt, not a smudge or torn piece of fabric. "You're okay," I land on. It's a question mixed with a statement.

His eyes change, grow serious. "I am okay, and you did go to my funeral."

"How, why?"

"Because I died."

I shake my head at this, an involuntary twitch. "No, you're here, holding my hands. Maybe you are still recovering from the crash, and this is all a bit confusing, but you're here at the Manor and you are going take me home. We can go home!"

"Yes, *you* can go home."

I try to tug him closer, my hands cramping already, and then it hits my ear, that misplaced word.

You.

"Stella Bella," he begins, looking down at the ground momentarily. "I can't go home with you. I *am* gone. From this life at least."

"I don't understand. I'm holding your hands, you can't be..." I don't want to say the word, risk making it real somehow.

"This is a dream, Stella. You are holding my hands because you needed me, so I came."

"A dream?" I wrack my brain, recounting the last few hours. I never consumed anything from the guards or nurses, and I certainly wasn't given the serum again.

If anything, in the last few hours I have never felt so awake.

"Yes, and I'm visiting you in it to help you. As I am the evidence in metaphorical flesh and blood, you seem to have the ability to manifest people into your dreams, as you have done with me right now. You have been for a while lately, actually. I've been in many of your recent dreams, but only on the periphery. It is the strongest pull in the pit of my stomach, as if you have a rope tied to me, and every time you dream your love and need for me begins to yank me to you. In this instance, I can feel your immense need for my help, so I came. Well, you brought me here."

I am still in my speechlessness.

My dad continues, "Of course, you don't need my help— you are so strong. You have proven your strength, your ability to push through anything, especially lately, and it is my biggest regret, my not being able to experience your strength firsthand."

Tears spill from my eyes. "But you can, you have to be here! How else. I don't understand being able to manifest you in my dreams? How?"

"But I am not—you must realize this. I can't explain the ins and outs of what is going on. I wish I could, but I'm not completely sure about how your abilities work." His squeeze on my hand tightens. "All I do know for sure is that the power and strength of your feelings span further than just your living consciousness. Far enough to bring me here to you for a little while. I suspect that if *you* love someone enough, want to see someone enough, *you* can conjure them into your dreams. Incredible."

I begin to cycle through the dreams I have had at the Manor, remembering each fine detail of the dreams. Certain details stick with me as I recall the dreams, and my dad's declarations begin to make sense.

The person I was sensing in my dreams but could never fully see, following me on the street, on the beach. The familiar scent of his cologne breaking through the smokey air. The presence

Ms. Withers was noting. It was my dad, has always been my dad.

He drops my hands and takes a few steps up the staircase before lifting a flaming candle from its holder. He places his outstretched hand into the center of the flame where it transitions from blue to orange and waves his hand back and forth through the flame. The flame sits still, as still as the moon at night. It is completely unaffected by his movements, and the scorching heat of the flame does not burn his hand.

After a few more moments he removes his hand from the flame and places the candle back in its place. He walks down and places it on my right cheek, and I flinch away anticipating a burning sensation, but nothing comes.

Cool skin on skin.

I take his hand and study his palm.

The truth sinks like an anchor to the bottom of my stomach.

"I feel so aware, so conscious of what is going on right now," I say. "I don't feel like I am dreaming."

My dad settles next to me on the first step of the grand staircase. "You are aware, that is what makes you so special. The capabilities you possess are amazing—beyond amazing—and I am so proud of you. As you now know, I have been lingering in your dreams for a little while now, and I have watched you handle some scary situations like they're a walk in the park. If I had to handle those dreamscapes alone like you, I would be a cowering mess. You are so strong, my Stella Bella."

I sit on the staircase, my knees relieved from having to hold up my confused body. "I want you to be alive here with me, not in a dream."

"We can't always get what we want."

I can't help but laugh at the irony of the situation.

"What?" he asks.

"I'm talking to you in a dream right now and here you are inserting a parental lesson into it. Will I remember any of this?"

"Of course you will." He playfully knocks on the side of my head, as if it were a door. "This head of yours is very impressive," he says, and I burrow into his shoulder, taking deep breaths as I scan over the people frozen in place before us.

Charlie, Caleb, and Nora still stand unmoving in the middle of the room, clueless to what is going on.

"I am here for a reason, the reason I have been feeling the pull from you to manifest in your dreams. Your need for me." he says, and my head bobs as he talks. "I have something to show you."

He rises and I follow his every movement, leaving no room for him to get ahead of me and disappear into a dreamy puff of air or stop mid-step and turn into a statue like everyone else. I match his steps up the staircase, the candles at our feet not flickering when he walks by, only when I do.

We reach the top of the stairs, and he grabs my hand, leading me toward the hallway of portraits.

"I don't know if you know this," I say, "but I've spent a lot of time here. I'm pretty sure there is nothing here you can show me that I haven't yet seen."

He grins at me, ever the knowing parent—even now. "Have a little faith, Stella."

He pushes open the door to the hallway and plants me in front of the two portraits: one of Ms. Withers and the other of her new partner. My dad removes the painting of her work partner before I can see it, the painted side pressed firmly to his chest, its wooden backing exposed to me.

"See anything interesting?" he asks.

I take a step closer, the lighting in the hallway dim from the night and unclear. It takes a second for my eyes to adjust, but I can make out four lines in the center of the frame. I look back at my dad. "A rectangle with a smaller rectangle on the back? I don't get it."

He rolls his eyes, a small motion that would have driven me nuts in a past life, but which only makes me ache to see him do it again now. He says, "Open it."

I work the nail of my right pointer finger into the crease between the bigger and smaller section of the frame. I wiggle the piece free, pull it away with my other hand, and it drops to the floor.

What sits nestled into the back of the frame leaves me speechless. Complete and utter shock grips me. I blink, scratch at my eyes, not believing what I see before me.

"Go ahead," he says. "Take it."

The flawless, golden brass shine reflects my shocked gaze.

"You came to show me where the key was," I say, holding it in front of my face, not yet ready to look away for fear it might vanish. When I finally do, I stare at my dad in disbelief.

He picks up the fallen piece from the ground and places it back onto the frame before hanging the portrait up again. It looks as if it was never moved. "Anywhere you are, anything you are going through: know you are not alone, and nothing is impossible. Not even finding a little key."

I don't know how to respond even as my body springs into action. For the second time tonight, I throw myself at him, this time nearly knocking him over with my bear hug.

"Thank you, thank you, thank you!" My right hand holds the key flush to his back. "I—*we*—would have never known it was back there."

Holding me out at arm's length to study my face, he answers: "That's what dads are for."

We walk hand in hand down the grand staircase and out to the willow tree, the moment reflective of so many we will not get to have in the future. The key is tucked within my free hand, kept warm and safe under the folds of my gown.

I lose track of time as we sit under the willow's curtain of leaves, my dad listening to me feverishly catch him up on everything that has happened since he left. Every now and then he adds his two cents, laughs at a joke or commenting on Callie's crazy behavior. At one point, his face turns serious and he asks about mom, wondering how she is handling things. At first my stomach turns, ashamed that I will have to admit to him that I had not been the nicest to her before ending up at the Manor.

But I give in, spilling my guts out to him about how I always felt irritable and unmotivated to feign excitement when she would talk to me.

"She is just trying to pick up the pieces of what happened after I left. Cut her some slack, Stella."

"I know," I lean against the trunk of the tree. "I try not to think about how mean I was, especially knowing how bad things were before the Manor."

"Well, it's even better that you have the key now so you can get home to her to apologize." He picks off a piece of bark, rolling it between the pads of his fingers. "Tell her you love her, and that I do, too."

I smile over at him, "I will."

He jumps up from his seated position, dusting off the grass from his pants. "Speaking of, it's time I let you go so you can get back to her."

I grab at his arm, my blood pressure spiking. "No, please, let's stay for a little while longer."

With his hand that is wrapped around my own, he uses his body weight to haul me up to a standing position. "This is your dream, so technically you are in charge," as he talks, he leads us out from beneath the willow, the long branches and leaves brushing against the tops of our heads. "But I'm going to take this opportunity to be a dad for one last time and tell you what to do." We stop just before the front door. "Wake up, go inside, get your friends, and leave. You have the key now. Nothing is stopping you. Leave the Manor behind and only take with you the knowledge of what your dreams are capable of and do good in this world. Make a difference. Despite how Ms. Withers and the Manor have treated you and your ability, it is remarkable and you should be proud of it. Be excited about where your dreams will lead you."

"I can do all those things. I can go home and be with mom, tell her I'm sorry, that I love her, but you won't be there." I plead with him.

If I can manifest people into my dreams, then why can't I have to power manifest them back into my *life*?

"But *they* will be." He points into the Manor, into the window to the left of the door, where we can see the side profiles of Nora, Caleb, and Charlie. "They are the best friends I could have ever hoped you would find. And him," I can tell he is focusing solely on Charlie's side profile now. "I do wish I could have one of those 'I'll kill you if you hurt her' conversations with him, but I know he never would. He loves you with all his heart." My dad smiles back at me. "He has my approval."

I break away from focusing on Charlie's side profile, his lips, nose, and defined jawline shaping his handsome face from the side. The look my dad gives me is one I have never seen before, but it is one I had imagined receiving in moments such as walking across the stage to receive my diploma or when he would have eventually walked me down the aisle. His eyes speak a thousand words.

"Callie on the other hand, the jury is out on what she'll think of him. She might be too jealous to approve." He laughs.

I laugh, too, the mundane nature of talking about a friend from home and something unrelated to the Manor is refreshing.

"So, there it is, the last chore I want to give you." He places his hands on my shoulders. "Will you do that for me, or will I have to threaten you with something like, 'if you don't do it, I won't let you hang out with Callie this Friday night'?"

I smile up at him and in a teary voice I answer him, "I wish you could give me a million more chores."

We meet in the middle, his arms squeezing my mid-section as I hang onto his neck like a little kid swimming for the first time with their parent. I take in one last breath of his familiar scent, memorizing the notes I was smelling all this time: apple, vanilla, cloves, and sandalwood.

Our hug ends too many hours too soon. He pulls back and we look at each other for one last time.

"I love you to the moon," he says.

"And back."

I come to on the floor, my dress spread out around my chilled body. The noise echoing in the foyer startles me in the aftermath of all that quiet.

"Stella!" Charlie falls to his knees beside me, pulling me up into a seated position.

"Oh my God, Stella, what happened?" Nora appears behind Charlie, Caleb right beside her.

I swallow down the hard lump in my throat, choke back the tears I can already feel forming. Each of my dad's words still rolls around in my head, echoing from my dream. I reel in the realization that I can manifest people into my dreams, people that I need to see, people that I love, people that I thought I would never get to see, hear, smell, or touch ever again.

"Can you hear us?" Charlie grabs my arm, flinging it out from under the side of my dress. "Are you okay?"

I hear the clink of metal against the marble floor as my hand opens.

I'm confused until I catch the glimmer of gold.

The key.

I snatch it up, fold it into my dress before anyone can notice it.

Looking up into Charlie's eyes, I tell him I'm fine and lean on him to help me up, pretending to fan myself with my hand. "Must have just been all the dancing and excitement from the night."

"Excitement?" Nora is dubious and her voice makes no effort toward hiding it. "Ms. Withers was just introducing us to the new guy. I wouldn't call that *excitement*."

I roll my eyes at her and flatten my dress out, feeling for the key. The cool metal calming my nerves and bringing my heart rate back to a steady pace, or so it seems to me. Around us, I hear some people get shoved around as the sound of heels clicking feverishly over to us becomes increasingly louder and louder.

"Ms. Grey!" Lady A stops a breath away from me. "What are you doing?"

"Give her some space, she just fainted," Charlie tells her, placing a protective arm between us.

Lady A's eyes are now the same color as her dress in anger. But I try to play it cool, not give anything away. I step up to Charlie's arm, signaling to him that I am okay, that for the time being I don't need protecting.

"I'm sorry, Lady A—I didn't mean to cause a scene."

I can feel Nora's eyes flash on me with disbelief, which has seemingly become her new default, though I can't fault her for wondering why I'm suddenly so agreeable to Lady A's bitchy attitude.

If only Nora knew what I knew.

Beyond Lady A comes a swath of red in our direction, Ms. Withers. "Perfect timing, Stella. I was just going to come over here and introduce our new leader, Mr. Clarke."

Hearing his name causes the glow of the chandelier to vanish and the candles to all flicker out. A hush sweeps across the room as the band slinks away. My eyes focus on the approaching man, and one by one the dark suits and rainbow of gowns that surround me fizzle out of my sight as I stand face to face with him.

Mr. Clarke, my calculus teacher.

Mr. Clarke stops in front of us, Lady A and Ms. Withers on each side of him. "Ms. Grey, it is wonderful to see you again."

Caleb speaks up, his voice squeaky. "See her again?"

Mr. Clarke's attention never leaves me. "Yes, Stella and I have known each other for a little while."

"He's my...he *was* my teacher in high school. Calculus."

Ms. Withers can't help but let out a mischievous chuckle, the red of her dress bouncing as her body hiccups.

Nora steps to my side. "Well, they don't teach us math here, so you're not needed."

I cross my arms over my chest. "Come to check up on my ability to solve for X?"

"Not quite." A grin forms on his face, the right side of his mouth upturning slightly. "Leading the Manor is my profession, teaching calculus to a group of uninterested high schoolers is simply a momentary assignment."

"Mr. Clarke takes jobs at high schools around the country to monitor the behaviors of high schoolers in order to find Dreamers." Ms. Withers and Mr. Clarke look like an evil match made in heaven.

"I was at your high school teaching only until I identified a Dreamer, and…"

"It was me."

"You didn't exactly hide your knack for dreaming, at least not very well. In almost every class I would find you dozing off, looking out the window. It was clear to me that you were a Dreamer by the way you entered an unbreakable state when you daydreamed. That little friend of yours would always try to get your attention but only truly gained mine—and it focused in on your behavior. I itched to find out what you were dreaming of, desperate for the Manor's monitoring equipment."

Charlie, no longer distracted by my safety, steps up closer to him. "So, you're the reason why she's here, why we are all here?" His voice is a mix of stern accusation and threat.

"You give me too much credit, kid. I'm only responsible for a few of you—we have others assigned to multiple other schools, all of us out there to discover Dreamers."

"Stella's been here for a few months," Caleb remarks. "Have you been hiding around the Manor since then?"

"Unfortunately, no." Mr. Clarke motions to Ms. Withers. "I was assured that Ms. Withers and Lady A could handle running the Manor while I finished my teaching job. You see, I couldn't just leave once Stella went missing or it would look like I was the one responsible for her disappearance."

"But you are!" Nora and I both yell at the same time.

He laughs, our anger clearly the most comedic thing he has ever witnessed. "Yes, but they cannot and will not know that. It would be terribly difficult to get another teaching job."

My narrowed focus on Mr. Clarke loosens, and I notice now that everyone else around us is listening to our conversation on the tips of their toes, desperate to understand more. Even the men and women of the orchestra band seem to be enthralled in what is going on.

"Why are you back then?" Charlie asks. "I'm sure you guys aren't done kidnapping and imprisoning people."

Mr. Clarke is unfazed by Charlie's tone. "Ms. Withers will be leaving shortly to go on assignment at another high school."

Nora shakes her head. "Oh God, those poor kids."

She's right. Dodging hot dogs in the school cafeteria somehow seems preferable to having Ms. Withers as a teacher.

The she-devil steps forward and takes a moment to look from one set of eyes to the next. "Don't worry, I won't be gone for long."

And we won't be here for much longer.

Mr. Clarke claps his hands in front of his protruding belly. "It was lovely to see you again, Ms. Grey. And the rest of you," he scans Nora, Charlie, and Caleb, "well, I look forward to getting to know you all better."

He turns on the heels of his dress shoes, the sound worse than fingers on a chalkboard, and starts to leave. Ms. Withers and Lady A smirk at us before following him through the parting crowd, as if he were royalty visiting his people. Mr. Clarke wanders through the throng of boys and girls, introducing himself and exchanging one-sided pleasantries before arriving at the door leading to their offices.

"Nothing like a good ole' reunion," Nora mutters.

"Geez, never in my wildest dreams did I think my creepy calculus teacher was anything more than just a boring high school teacher."

"I wonder which teacher at my school discovered me," Caleb murmurs.

"Same," Charlie echoes, staring at the ground and seemingly lost deep in thought. Collecting himself, he looks to me and says, "You sure you're okay? You fainted, and then Mr. Clarke—all of that was pretty intense, I mean."

His question brings me back to my dream, back to my last conversation with my dad. Reflexively, I smile at all of the wonderful things we talked about, especially at his approval of Charlie.

"One hundred percent okay," I say. "My calculus teacher showing up out of the blue is the last thing that is going to faze me here." I reach out and grab Charlie's hand in my left and Nora and Caleb's in my right. "Plus, I don't care about him—I have something to show you guys."

I pull them all to the library, where the only movement is the melted chocolate cascading down the decorative fountain. I lead us all into the back-left corner of the room, a corner I know cannot be seen from out in the foyer, something I learned while trying to figure out spots where I could kiss Charlie in private.

I shove my hand into my makeshift pocket and pull out the key. Its sharp edges feeling glorious in my hand.

Caleb is the first one to speak. "What is that?"

All their gazes are fixed on what I am still clenching in my hand. I loosen my grip on it and let it dangle from my hand.

"This…" I hold it out for them all to see clearly, "I got it, well, it's—"

"—a key!" Charlie interrupts me.

"*The* key." Nora whispers.

I give them an edited version of the truth, unsure or unwilling to explain it all to them otherwise, some part of me wanting to keep the secret for myself. "I discovered where the key was hidden in a dream. It has to be the key that opens the hidden door at the end of the maze," I say, everyone's mouths falling open as one, the shock reverberating between us all. I look at each of them in turn, steady myself. "This is the key that is going to unlock our escape. And if I'm right, we're leaving—*tonight.*"

A million different thoughts fly through my mind, a mix of anxiety and anticipation crossing in my eyes as I stare at myself in the mirror. I'm the only one left in the bathroom, and I wipe the makeup from the night off my face, black smears appearing under my eyes as I scrub the mascara away. My eyes water, and before I even notice I've broken out into a full-on cry and leftover black specks of mascara bleed into the pink porcelain sink. With my makeup wipe, I clean up my face and scrub at the sink until my knuckles hurt.

I want no remnants of myself left here at the Manor.

Everyone is in bed by the time I leave the bathroom. Some people are already asleep, others lean across, talking to bed neighbors or sit up looking at the guarded doors, anxiously waiting for the nurses to plug us in for the night's dreams.

Caleb's bed is the first I pass, and he sits up straight, watching me walk to my own, and I can't help but give him a slight smile.

I pull back my own itchy covers and tuck myself in.

Nora is lying down on her back, her eyes wide open and moving back and forth as she counts the beams on the ceiling.

I find Charlie across the room. Our eyes meet, silently assuring each other that we are ok. He runs his hand raggedly through his hair before rubbing his eyes with the other. When he's done, his hair sticks up, defying gravity in the most ridiculous way, and I chuckle at his new appearance.

He smiles, and I follow his lips as they shape the words, "I love you."

"I love you," I mouth back.

I am pulled from Charlie at the sound of Nora's soft voice next to me. "Stella."

I turn to find her laying down facing me, her hands tucked under her cheek. I mimic her position and lay my head atop my pillow. The night is not yet over, but it feels heavenly to rest and breathe evenly just the same.

"Are you nervous?" she asks.

I dig the edge of the key into my palm before loosening my grip slightly. "No," I tell her, and maybe she believes me, because she has no answer. "I'm not going to let myself be nervous. I have this dark feeling in the bottom of my stomach, but I'm not going to let it grow like I have so many times in my life. We've been through too much to allow fear to take over." I watch Nora's eyes as they grow big like a kid's do when they are confronted with something scary. "We deserve to be strong, need to be strong. We have no option but to get through this."

Nora nods slightly, her cheek rubbing against the back of her hands.

"You and me, remember? We're going to leave together." When I say together, a single tear slips down and slides over Nora's nose, dropping onto her bed.

I want nothing more than to comfort her, wish away all the bad things that have happened to her, to all of us, but the unlocking of the metal doors freezes me. In a flash, I am on my back, staring into the ceiling, holding my breath. I can hear the doors swing open, followed by clicks.

Click, click, click.

Ms. Withers' voice forms icicles in my ears. "Bedtime…"

She proceeds down the long hallway, checking that every bed has a body. Her mere presence sends everyone who'd been sitting up and talking to friends under their covers like little kids afraid of the monster in the closet.

I feel her laser stare as she passes by my bed, her heel clicks growing louder and then dimming as she passes. Once she is satisfied that everyone is tucked in like good children, she stops in front of the metal doors and turns to address us all one last time for the evening.

"In the spirit of this festive night, we want you to have a pleasant night's rest. There will be no monitoring this evening. Sleep tight…" I watch as she walks through the doors flanked by guards. She turns back just once, her head just over her shoulder and know she's looking directly at me as she adds softly, "…and don't let the bed bugs bite."

Heavy breathing and soft snores filter through the space, signaling that everyone is asleep.

Well, almost everyone.

The anxious electricity coursing through my body has kept me from drifting off to sleep.

The soft patter of feet alerts me that Charlie and Caleb are coming toward Nora's bed and my own. We sit up, careful to not make too much noise from the ruffling of our comforters and creaky bed posts. None of us has to say anything to one another, our exchanged knowing glances say it all. Nora and I carefully climb from our beds, and we reach the end of the dorm hall together having woken no one. A few stirred as we tip-toed past, but we looked at each other with concerned gazes before wordlessly agreeing that no one had awakened. A guilty twinge pinches at my chest, but I remind myself that, once I find a phone, I'll call the police and alert them to the other kidnapped people in the Manor.

Then it can be Ms. Withers' turn to feel like a prisoner.

Charlie rests the side of his face against the metal door, listening for guards on the other side. I peer out one of the only windows in the dorm hall and scan for the moon full and high in the sky, and I know we are hours into the night.

Charlie waves his hand to get our attention before giving us a double thumbs-up, and I hope I'm the only one who catches the slight tremor in his hands as he lets us know the path is clear.

Aside from a few creaky wooden planks, we make our way silently into the portrait hallway. Charlie was right, the only faces we're met with are the dead ones in the hanging pictures. Hand in hand with Charlie, I follow behind Caleb and Nora toward the end of the hallway.

Ms. Withers' portrait is no longer alone. Mr. Clarke's stares back at me with the same face he would glare at me with from the front of the classroom. He looks bored, a wickedness deep in his eyes.

My compliments to the artist. He really captured it with this one.

Charlie tugs my hand, beckons me through the open door to the staircase.

A harsh whisper from Nora—"Stella, let's go!"—as she holds open the door.

My feet move despite the part of me that feels oddly glued to this portrait, and before I fully pass through the doorway, I look once more as their eyes follow me out of the hall.

The grand foyer is eerily quiet. Moonlight filters through the windows below the staircase and a dim aura of light peeks through the window of the cafeteria door. I motion for everyone to stop moving and we all listen as voices seep through the cracks.

"I am delighted to see the Manor full of healthy young Dreamers." Mr. Clarke's voice is unmissable. "But I do think they seem *too* at ease. I propose we have them dream more. Ms. Withers, let's schedule all of the Dreamers into the lab in the upcoming days and increase the production of the serum to be used in the dormitory hall."

The four of us exchange disgusted looks.

Ms. Withers responds, "That is a wonderful idea Mr. Clarke. One *I* was actually going to propose myself, as we have our quarterly dream summit meeting soon. We wouldn't want to show up empty-handed, and it would certainly be nice to stand out as having an exuberant number of useful dreams this time around. It will certainly attract more clientele."

"Most certainly."

Mr. Clarke and Ms. Withers' discussion feels like a cat and mouse game of who can be the most in charge at this meeting. But hearing their conversation is good. It is good news because this means the nightly meeting is being held, and we have successfully met our window of opportunity.

Our window for escape.

Mr. Clarke continues, "And I hear you have some promising content from Ms. Grey's dreams."

"The most promising. Her dreams will serve to be fruitful at the summit. Enviable even…"

Charlie tugs my hand, beckoning me forward. "Come on, we should keep going."

"No time like the present but to get the hell out of here, it seems," Nora says in response to what we can hear from their meeting.

The candles from earlier have all been blown out, though they remain on the staircase. One by one, we make our way down the grand staircase for the last time, each footfall feeling heavy and loud despite the silence. We crouch, curving our spines as we run-walk to the final door.

Touching the golden handle of the door that will lead us outside into the garden feels like the first breath you take after submerging deep in water. We find it unlocked and creak it open, more heavy breaths rush through me. The tightness that had planted itself in my chest and grown and grown from the moment I arrived at the Manor begins to break into little pieces and drift away like individual dandelion petals in the wind. Sneaking through the sliver of space the opened door gives us, we break out into the night and I can breathe easy again.

Caleb quietly shuts the door behind us, erasing all evidence we ever left.

Just as the four of us tumble out from the Manor, a guard, towering tall above us all, charges our way. His muscled arms pump back and forth, the grass beneath his feet crunching.

Nora launches herself off the cement step and onto the grass, her right-hand reared back, the points of her knuckles white as snow.

Nora's fist hits the guard's nose and there's a cracking sound, sharp and wet, like lightning miles off the beach shore. A burst of red forms beneath the guard's nose as he falls to the ground, the grass blanketing his passed-out figure.

"Holy shit," Charlie's voice is in utter shock with surprise oozing off his words.

Caleb can't look anywhere but at the monstrous man passed out on the ground. "You, you...knocked him out cold."

"Yeah, and it really hurt." Nora's hand is already turning a deep purple, her knuckles slightly cracked and bleeding. "Kind of wish I stuck to the plan and let Charlie take care of him."

"You did amazing," I say, my hand out to inspect Nora's.

"Don't," she says. "It's fine. Let's just get out of here."

We take off running, the air whipping between us as we float feverishly across the lawn, the grass crisp beneath of our feet, until we come to the weeping willow tree, the long leaves that protect its center swaying back and forth, opening before us as if welcoming us back into its embrace. We pass the weeping willow, and farther into the garden we come upon the maze.

Everyone slows. We have one chance at this, and we need to follow the correct route to the door. Nora and Caleb's gazes all fall to me and Charlie.

We found the hidden door the first time, and it's time for us to find it again.

The night is dark and the golden key in my palm absorbs the full moonlight, making it appear brighter and bigger. I try to meet Charlie's eyes, but his gaze is stuck on the key. One step, and then two, and I am in reach of him. With my other hand, I grab for Charlie's arm and pull his hand out to my extended one, forcing him to lace his fingers through mine, trapping the key in the warmth of our palms.

The deep luminescence of his blue eyes is all I can see as stagnant black surrounds us. Their electric glow guides me and I know I've walked these steps before. I navigate the maze in a mindless daze, led by his rich blue eyes, following them this way and that, walking long corridors shrouded by high dark leaves, making our way to its heart. In the distance, a noise breaks me from the azure spell. At first, it's a trickling of water, and then as we take more steps it turns into a full-fledged flow of rushing water.

I dreamed this moment.

The blue eyes beckoning, guiding me through the void, the noise of water interrupting the spell…

Laugh, cry, scream—the impulses all strike at once, but Nora's voice stops me from any of them. "The fountain!"

Charlie's eyes are no longer the only source of light as the moon returns, swathing the bronze of the fountain, glistening light as the water cascades down and rushes around in a circle, moving hypnotically clockwise around, sloshing over the edge at different intervals and wetting the surrounding grass.

"Oh my God! I can't believe we found it!" Nora yelps with excitement. She rushes to us, throws her arms over both of our shoulders, giving us her strongest squeeze.

Nora's hug lifts my hand from Charlie's and the key falls to the wet grass below us. Caleb crouches down, picks up the key, and then hands it back to me. "Here. I say we get this over with."

"Hey! Stop!" The guard that Nora punched runs up the maze pathway, breathless and leaking blood from his nose.

As I yell "No!" feeling like our escape plan is tragically slipping away, Nora nervously exclaims, "Shit, I don't think I can punch him again."

"Uh, guys…" Caleb's voice is shaky, and he makes a move to go toward the guard, but Charlie jumps in front of us.

"Go!"

The guard is nearly to the fountain, but Charlie stands tall and solid between us, the fountain, and the door.

"Charlie, what are you doing? Let's go!"

Charlie whips his head around to look at me. "Someone has to stop the guard, or our plan is definitely ruined."

Charlie turns back as the guard reaches for his shoulders. The two engage in a back-and-forth struggle, one second Charlie has the advantage over the guard, the next the guard dominates over Charlie, pulling his clothes, hitting weak spots on his body, scratching his face. Watching their fight is like seeing a car crash on the side of the highway. I can't help but look, can't help needing to see what is happening. His grunts in defense against the guard are agonizing, and I can't peel my eyes away, needing to make sure he triumphs against him, and we can leave together.

Charlie notices me feverishly watching their movements, "Stella, go! I will…fight…him…off." His words are muttered out in-between jerky movements.

Nora grasps the back of my shirt, trying to pull me toward the door, but I don't let her.

"No, Charlie, I'm not leaving without you!"

Charlie catches my eyes quickly as he whips around to shove the guard toward the wall of the maze, the leaves and branches cutting up his arm.

"Make sure the key works, unlock the door, get yourself, Caleb, and Nora out safely." I hold onto the blue of his eyes before he tells me one last thing. "I'll be right behind you."

I hear my dad's voice again, telling me to leave the Manor behind, find my mom, love her, and do good in the world. My head and heart battle it out, echoing the physical fight playing out in front of me. Do I stay or do I go? My dad's voice in my head grows louder than Charlie and the guard's physical struggle, my head overpowering my heart, and I finally succumb to Charlie's instructions.

I nod and turn my body toward where I once found the door. My own breathing crescendoing in my head, replacing the soft rush of the fountain behind me. The rustling of leaves, feet on grass, and the chirping bugs around us fades beneath the nervous and painful beating of my heart. It takes me only five long strides before the hedge is close enough to tickle my face as I lean into the leaves. I lead with my hands, the tiny thorns and twigs of the hedge slicing away ribbons of skin. I push harder, until my knuckles scrape across wood and I know I've found the door.

In sync, Nora and Caleb take one final anticipating breath behind me, holding in the air.

"What if—" the words hardly make it out of my mouth, tears burning the back of my throat, "—what if this key doesn't work?"

In a voice I can't quite make out, I hear, "it has to."

In another, "it will."

I point the key toward the lock I've left my other hand on, too afraid to lose it.

My breathing stops.

I push the final lingering leaves out of the way.

I position the key in the keyhole.

A loud clink fills the dead of night silence as the key strikes the keyhole.

My wrist turns, and against all odds, so does the key.

The key turns until it clicks with something inside the door, and the cracked wooden frame of the door opens away from me.

Lifting my foot, I take a giant step through the hedge, my clothes catching slightly on branches.

Nothing can stop me.

Feathery grass sways and spreads out as I step forward, and I look up on the other side.

I am met by an open field beneath an inky black sky.

One by one, we break through the hedge and step across the wooden door frame and into the open field. There are no gates, walls, hedges, or constraints ahead of us, only open space.

Only freedom.

Nora rushes past me, her body flying through the tall grass with a whooshing sound. She swings her torso around, her arms floating atop the cattails, her smile bigger than any I've ever seen before.

"Caleb, come here!" She giggles out her command.

He races toward her, the grass only reaching his knees. She grasps his hand and flings him around in carefree circles, like she's dancing with a doll here in our newfound oasis, enjoying the vast open land around them.

The missing heat of Charlie's body behind me sends chills up and down my arms. "Charlie?" I ask, barely a whisper above the drowning silence of the night.

I reach back, hoping to grab his hand so I can turn him toward me and look into his eyes, relieved by their blueness. But I feel nothing but the chill-tipped air. A deep panic unrolls throughout my body, beginning at the tips of my feet and settling as an anxious hotness in my cheeks. They flair at the realization that he did not come through the door. That he did not escape with the three of us. That he is stuck on the other side of the wall. That the guard won. That he is still in the Manor.

I turn around and stare into the empty air that stands between me and the locked shut door. On this side, more long and spindly vines of heart-shaped leaves cover the door, camouflaging its chestnut wood presence. Moving toward it, I listen for noise of Charlie on the other side, hoping that maybe he simply got stuck and is trying to open the door on his own, the guard he was fighting bested and laying on the ground. But I hear nothing, not even heavy breathing over the slow movement of the midnight wind in the air. I hold my ear to the chilled wood for a handful of seconds. My hand rests unmoving on the door handle as no one on the other side attempts to break free.

The sweet smell of fresh-cut grass blows past me, the cool air moving strands of hair in and out of my face. The movement breaks me from my concentrated trance at the door, and I look to my right as Nora squeals with joy.

Caleb holds Nora by the hands and swings her around so fast her feet almost lift off the ground.

I begin to walk to them, leaving the hidden door to remain hidden, silent, and a secret behind me. Over Nora's squeals I can hear the heavy thud of my heartbeat in my eardrums as they keep in time with the crickets. Each step farther away from the door becomes louder and more painful. My feet leave stomped imprints in the tall grass, a trail of fallen cattails behind me, like a trail of snowy footprints.

Nora is now picking apart a flower, with each petal chanting, "I leave the Manor, I don't leave the Manor." The final petal she plucks from the stem lands on "I leave the Manor," and she smiles bright at Caleb, who is grinning down at her like a puppy in love. Nora throws up the petals. They float for a moment before landing in her hair, peppering her chocolatey hair white. They both have not noticed Charlie's absence amidst their own giddiness.

I stop in front of Nora and pluck a few petals out of her curly hair. "Charlie…"

Nora's eyes light up as she takes me in, yanking my hand down so I stumble onto the tall grass that blankets the edges of our bodies. Cattail flowers crunch under us, softening my body's fall to the ground.

"Stellaaaa," she sings, "We just escaped the…" Her voice grows louder with each word until it stops dead in its tracks.

She perches up on her forearm to peak above the towering grass, looking for something, someone. Caleb follows her gaze, looking left and right frantically.

"Charlie!" Nora begins to yell out for him.

"Nora!" I whisper-yell at her as I plant my hand over her mouth.

Caleb moves to rise above the grass to go in search of Charlie, but I grab his hand and keep him close. With or without Charlie, if the two of them keep making a loud spectacle, we will all find ourselves back inside the walls of the maze sooner than we'd like.

Under my hand, her muffled voice tickles my palm. "Where is he?"

I let my hand fall from her face, and flop down to her left atop my own bed of grass. I watch the top of the tall grass sway and mix with the stars of the inky night sky before muttering the words I had been avoiding speaking into existence, "He didn't make it through."

I reach out, skimming the damp compacted grass, and grab onto Nora and Caleb's hands next to me. I link us together, needing to ground my body in this field so I don't float off into a deep despair, or worse, ruin our escape from the Manor.

"He's still there." I swallow the cold air and it burns. "In the Manor."

No one says a word. We lie cocooned in the tall grass as individual strands of hulking green stretch and shadow our bodies.

We lie like this for I don't know how long, an emptiness in my head disallowing me to think of plans, worry about being caught, or how to help Charlie.

"Stella," I can hear Nora's hair scrunch against the grass beneath her. "What...are you...should..."

Caleb finishes for her. "What do we do now?"

I sit up onto my elbows so I can see the two of them sprawled out next to me in the grass, their bodies burrowed around strands that ebb and flow and sing with the symphony of crickets we lie amongst. Both of their eyes reflect the moonlight, searching deeply into my own, but I have nothing to give back, nothing to say. I am a river run dry, a desert without years of rain, a heart with a piece left behind.

I don't answer them. I can't answer them. So instead, I look upward toward the sky, hoping to my find answers hidden amongst the stars. I count the stars directly overhead, losing my place when I finally blink. When I do, I spot a satellite effortlessly gliding in the sky, appearing to my eyes as if it is navigating its way in-between every single star and planet. It is unblinking, smooth, and steady in its path.

I wonder where it is going.

I wonder how to save Charlie.

I wonder where we will go.

The answers are unclear, everything still muddled from the Manor. Whether I like it or not, I am changed. The Manor unleashed a knowledge within me, something I will never be able to forget. I have seen and experienced things I once would have overlooked or forgotten about the minute I left my bed. Now, however, I feel a tug in the deepest part of my being telling me that, no matter the circumstances, the Manor has instilled in me a responsibility I cannot let go of. A responsibility I must confront each time I open my eyes from a dream.

Lying amongst my friends, between the strands of towering grass and cattail flowers, I believe in the certainty of my dreams the same way I believe in the petals clenched in my fist. I believe in what my dad said to me, that my dreams are an ability I have that marks my strength in this world. And I believe in the certainty of my feelings for Charlie, and that I cannot proceed in my life without him.

And then I find myself slipping from that certainty, much like slipping into a dream at the Manor. It pulls me deep into the ground, where I no longer feel the chill of the midnight air, but the warm solid blanket of earth. I am uncertain and confused, and I wonder—I wonder where my dreams will take me, the trajectory of them unknown like where the satellite in the sky is headed.

EPILOGUE

The dormitory hall pulses with the steady rhythm of heavy breaths, in and out, as the Dreamers sleep, dreaming in blissful ignorance. The vibrant music, sweeping gowns, and the tuxedos of the evening have all been forgotten. Each body in each bed is in a different world, dreaming of different people, seeing vast landscapes, hearing different languages, experiencing unique and bizarre scenes to which their dreams expose them. One girl could be in a country she's never heard of, watching two nation states battle each other for power. Another in their hometown observing a darker culture they never knew existed right under their nose. The Manor prefers the ones that shock the Dreamers, the dreams that take them miles outside of their comfort zones and perceived awareness, uncovering a bigger world, realities that they could have never imagined.

A clicking noise disrupts the pattern of breaths, the hall no longer peaceful with warm breaths, but filled with the icy anger of Ms. Withers. In the sheer darkness of the early hours of the morning that bleed through the windows, Ms. Withers' red heels glow against the stone floor. Her steps are feverish as

270 Ryan Elizabeth Penske

she walks the length of the hall, her eyes falling hard on each sleeping body before stopping and glaring at the four empty beds. The empty beds feel like empty shelves in a trophy case, the lost potential blatant.

She snaps her head back at the metal doors, a wicked glare piercing through the guards, "I want every damn inch of the Manor searched."

Her voice is feverish, almost too fast for human ears to understand. The guards blink in silence at her, frozen in their place at the panic that leeks through Ms. Withers' words, an emotion they never thought could penetrate her serious, calm, and collected exterior.

"Do I have to do it myself?" Her words slither past the beds like a snake, laced with a venom that makes the guards run off at her command.

Ms. Withers turns around, her eyes burning with an anger and tiredness that is beginning to create a pounding migraine in her right temple. Left alone in the dark hall, usually a space she finds peaceful and calming when all of her Dreamers are dreaming, her mind wanders down a dark path, negative thoughts acting as magnets to the dark hall. The dormitory hall now makes her nerve endings feel itchy, her heart beat uneven, and her breaths short.

As if she is a prisoner walking to her unfortunate fate, she ambles over to the empty beds, picking one to sit on and rest her tired feet. The frigid sheets beneath her legs taunt her, maliciously reminding her of her failures tonight. Her hands glide across the soft material of her dress, moving the red fabric as she reaches for the sheets and crumpled blanket beneath her body. She squeezes, the tops of her knuckles bulging and growing whiter with each increase of her strength. The material becomes taught and crumples in the palm of her hand, forcing the ends of the bed to become undone and inch toward her body.

Ms. Withers releases a heavy breath she did not know she was holding, while she loosens her grip. She lets herself take a few calming breaths, counting down from ten as she stares at the crumpled sheets around her. By the end of her count, her breath is in sync and just as calm as the breaths of sleep that surround her.

She lifts her gaze, reluctantly looking at the two empty beds across from her. Both appear hardly slept in, only a small indent on the pillows and folded-back sheets. They must have left early in the night then.

The dreaming computer equipment next to their beds taunts her as the screens blink an "error" sign. The screen blinks like an eye, one second black, the next white with "error" written in red across the middle of the screen. The white sheets of the empty bed for that mere second become a red hue as if the screen itself is searching for the culprit that prompted this error.

If only it were that easy and the machine could do her job for her, Ms. Wither thinks. She knows that she will not sleep until Stella, her annoyingly smitten boyfriend, and two snarky friends are found and returned to the Manor.

A mix of defeat and utter rage courses through her body as she gazes at the bed and screen that should be monitoring Stella as she dreams. The information gathered from Stella's dreams since she first arrived at the Manor have been priceless, literally. Stella has been an invaluable addition to the Dreamers at the Manor, her ability to dream multiple dreams that are vivid, crisp with color and detail that seem more real than reality, has astounded Ms. Withers. Stella's dreams have befuddled even her, as Ms. Withers has noted an unidentifiable presence within them, one that even Stella seemed unaware of. Who is this person, how are they ending up in Stella's dreams, and does Stella know something that Ms. Withers does not? In the profession of monitoring brain activity and dreams, it is almost impossible for Dreamers to keep secrets from her.

Almost.

But in all her years of working at the Manor and monitoring the deepest cognitive visuals of teenagers' dreams, she has never come across someone quite like Stella. Her vivacious and curious nature while awake is echoed in her dreams, something that is addicting to Ms. Withers.

That is why, as Ms. Withers sits in Caleb's empty bed, her heart slows in sadness, confusion, and anger as she glares at the empty spaces before her. The "error" on the blinking screen only reminding her of the errors that this celebratory evening has brought about.

The strong metal doors slam open at the far end of the dormitory hall, making Ms. Withers jump an inch from the bed. Mr. Clarke storms in past the guards who hold back the doors, their eyes cast down, too afraid to meet his eyes. Still dressed in his attire from the ball, his black pants shift aggressively across his legs as he marches toward Ms. Withers, his coat jacket moving side to side around his waist. His tie, however, sits eerily still on the center of his chest.

"Withers!"

She is surprised Mr. Clarke does not wake any of the other Dreamers when he yells at her, as she is sure that Lady A in her office downstairs can hear him roaring in fury.

Ms. Withers looks him dead in the eyes as he approaches, not cowering at his intimidating presence. She rises slowly from her seated position so that when he gets to her, he does not look down at her. She adjusts her dress, flattening the disturbed fabric.

"What the hell have you been doing while I've been gone?" Mr. Clarke barks at her as he arrives at the bed adjacent to Caleb's empty one, the boy sleeping within it undisturbed. "Clearly not your job!"

Ms. Withers does not bother responding, but instead lifts an eyebrow as if to say, "Go on then, tell me what is so important that you had to storm in here."

"The garden key," the pupils of Mr. Clarke's eyes enlarge, overtaking the dark gray of his pupils, "is missing."

Like a punch to the chest, the answers of this night's debauchery fall into place. Stella and her friends stole the key from behind Mr. Clarke's portrait and left through the door in the maze. How they discovered the door and key eludes her, but those questions do not matter at the moment. All that matters is that Ms. Withers knows how they escaped the Manor, which direction they must be going, and how to find them. According to the night's time frame, they could only have left within the last two hours, not enough time to make it out of her grasp.

This realization unfurls like a freshly bloomed flower in her chest, sparks of excitement and anticipation moving throughout her once tense muscles.

Ms. Withers looks past Mr. Clarke toward the open doors, light from the hallway bleeding into the dark hall. Her red lips curl up in a smile, the corners of her lipstick cracking revealing pale skin beneath. Stella's empty bed sits in the corner of Ms. Withers' vision, but it no longer taunts her. Instead, she feels lighter, her feet no longer like lead blocks filling her heels.

"Withers, what are you..." Mr. Clarke is dissatisfied with her silence, but before he can further bark at her, a guard stumbles in through the metal doors holding a hunched over body.

Mr. Clarke directs his attention to the guard. "What is this about now."

His words are stern, the end of each like a bite of something sour. But Ms. Withers' earlier headache begins to fade as she allows the guard to limp in past her. The guard's scratched up and bloodied hands hold up an unconscious body, the head of the body falling forward and its feet dragging along the floor.

Ms. Withers trails behind the guard, stopping only when the guard throws the unconscious body of the Dreamer onto an empty bed. Ms. Withers' travesty of a night seems somewhat redeemed when the guard finishes dumping Charlie onto his bed, his disheveled brown hair swishing over his forehead. Cuts and scrapes scatter across his pale face, marring his boyishly handsome allure.

The corners of Ms. Withers' red lips turn upward as she pats the guard on his shoulder. She notices he has similar bruised and bloodied marks on his face, and she has never been so happy to see blood in her life.

"Thank you. You did an outstanding job tonight; your efforts are greatly appreciated." The guard nods in appreciation. "Go down to the lab, the nurses will have aid for your troubles."

The guard limps away toward the metal doors before disappearing into the night. Mr. Clarke glares back at Ms. Withers in the darkness of the dorm hall, his eyes alight with anger. She does not allow his anger to dampen the positive revelations that are growing within her.

"Withers, while it is reassuring that *some* people are doing their job right around here, we still have the problem of the three missing Dreamers."

"Hush!" Ms. Withers snaps her attention away from Charlie's troubled face. "You will wake the Dreamers."

Ms. Withers no longer feels the bowling ball-sized pit of dread in her stomach, and no longer views Stella, Nora, and Caleb being missing as a problem. No, not with Charlie here, left behind and hurt. Mr. Clarke is wrong. She knows that Stella would never have left Charlie intentionally, and that wherever she is now, her dread for him and his future at the Manor would not let her get far.

"Don't you dare hush me." Mr. Clarke grasps Ms. Withers' wrists and squeezes too hard for her liking. "What is your plan of action? We need to discuss how their escape was even possible. But more importantly, how are we supposed to present our collected dream information at the summit when our most prized Dreamer has just escaped right from under our noses. *Your* nose!"

Ms. Withers, ignoring Mr. Clarke, yanks her hand free of his clenched fingers and struts down the dormitory hall, her steps confident and cool again. She would enjoy the rest of her evening, get some rest before the sun eventually rose over the garden maze. Stella and her friends will be back at the Manor in no time.

Stella can try to disappear, but like her dreams, the Manor will always be there.

And the best part: Ms. Withers will be the hero for getting them back.

ACKNOWLEDGMENTS

I would not be where I am today, with this book in your hands, if it were not for the love and support of my parents. I thank you both for letting me embark on this incredible journey to chase my dreams of becoming an author, a journey that at times seemed unlikely and scary. When you told me I needed to get a summer job, and I answered that I was writing a book, you allowed me to write and dream of where this book could go, and I will be forever grateful for that. You both have taught me that working hard and doing what you love and dream for is the most important thing in life. I cannot wait to write more books and make you both proud.

This book would also certainly not be where it is today if not for Marianne Moloney, who I stumbled upon in the luckiest of coincidences. I thank you immensely for being a part of this process with me, being an early reader and editing eye, telling me that you can see this on the big screen, and for connecting me with the right people who love the story and characters just as much as we do. I am so thrilled that together we get to see these real dreams come true, and I look forward to many more to come.

Thank you to Tyson Cornell for being open to receiving The Dreamers, reading it, and taking a chance on me and my story. I will never forget receiving your email and the first call we had, where the beginning of all these pinch-me-moments began. You have been a wonderful person to work with and have opened my eyes to the wonderful world of publishing, and I am so fortunate to work with you and the Rare Bird team.

Many wonderful acknowledgments to Guy Intoci and Hailie Johnson who read, edited, and worked through the dredge of my terrible grammar and confusing moments. I was very nervous to go through the editing process, the red pen on paper image terrifying in my head, but working with Guy made editing enjoyable, and I appreciated his collaborative and not red-pen-like editorial hand in making The Dreamers the book it is today.

A million thanks to everyone on the Rare Bird team who participated in making my dreams come true. And to Lisa Marie Pompilio who made the cover of my dreams. As a reader and book nerd, who doesn't love a beautiful cover? To have my own that captures my vision of the story is, again, another pinch-me moment.

Finally, I would like to thank my friends and family who shared in my excitement along the way and said they could not wait to read The Dreamers. Your genuine excitement and congratulations have meant the world to me. Tia, thank you for being a second mom to me and always telling me to dream big. Isabella and Sophie, for being like sisters, and Stella for letting me steal your name! And in memory of Andre Ribeiro, who in part inspired the love and care I wrote for Stella's father. Of course, thank you to my grandfather, Mr. Fun, for instilling a value of hard work in me. Effort equals results.

And I thank you, the readers, for picking up my book and reading alongside my dreams.

P.S. Thank you to my brother, Roger, who claims to have held out on reading a book until he could read mine.